ETERNAL
VIGILANCE

ETERNAL VIGILANCE

Gabrielle S. Faust

IMMANION
PRESS
Stafford England

For all of those I love who have fought the darkness within them and emerged victorious.

And for all of those who have fought bravely and lost, may your souls finally find peace.

You are still loved.

PRAISE FOR ETERNAL VIGILANCE

"Gabrielle Faust's new book, Eternal Vigilance, is Haiku pumped to the max! You can smell the roses, but first, you feel the prick of the thorns, and you drink the slow, seeping blood. Lock the door, turn off the telephone, pour a glass of fine Cabernet, get the dog next to your chair, and immerse yourself into Faust's world...a 'world that fears silence, a culture that never breathes'. In her world, vampires are romantic, street smart, and, yes, dangerously sexy. Trust me, you will enjoy the trip." –

Gary Kent, Director of *L.A. Bad* & Producer of *The House Seven Corpses*

"Like if Anne Rice had gone cyberpunk. Gabrielle Faust is an author of immense talent, and Eternal Vigilance keeps the reader enthralled from the first page to the last." –

Sire Cédric, Author of *Angemort* & *Dreamworld*

Acknowledgments

It has been said that it is easier to give birth to a child, than to a book. In many respects, from my experience, I feel that is true. There is a certain excruciating agony that transcends the mere physical that an author reaps from the creation of a novel. It can drive one to the brink of insanity. Yet, somehow, we persevere and trudge forward with our swords raised high, despite our wounds, old and new. Why? Because it is the reason we live and without it, existence would cease to hold meaning for us. Life would become merely one more paycheck from one more job in a florescent-lit cubicle. If we are lucky enough, we find those individuals along the way that see our maddening creative struggle and lend their support and love to our cause, despite whether or not they always completely understand us. Our angels, our fierce tribe of warriors watching our back against the siege: from the initial conception, through the pain and anguish and final jubilation of bringing forth one's dream into the world, there have always been those who have cheered us on, in some capacity, through the years. I am very blessed to have had just such a tribe surrounding me during the creation of *Eternal Vigilance* and it is to those I would like to raise my glass to toast. My personal road as an author has been long and hard, filled with devastating struggles and trying tragedies, which might have shattered a less willful person. Without these souls around me, I might not be the author I am today...

First and foremost, I would like to thank Storm Constantine and Immanion Press for taking me under their wing and giving me the gift of becoming a published novelist. Storm, your kind and wise words completely changed my life and the road that I was on as an author from the moment we first corresponded. I cannot thank you enough for all that you have done and can only hope I to never let you down as one of Immanion's authors. Fiona McGavin, my editor...what can I say? You completely changed my perception of editors! I am forever blessed by your insight and skillful critique, which has, no doubt, made *Eternal Vigilance* what it is today! My gratitude is overwhelming. Michael Marano, my mentor and friend. Your presence in my life has been an immense blessing, guiding me through the brutal world of publishing and lending me the strength to preserver when times were at their darkest. Gary Kent, your love and zest for life truly changed me, from the moment we first met. Like a father, you have always believed in me, and my work, and I cannot imagine my life without you in it.

Thank you to the brilliant photographer, Wojciech Zwoliński, for allowing the usage of his self-portrait for the cover of *Eternal Vigilance*, and to Keith Nanyes for his exceptional promotional shots. I wish you both the utmost success in all that you do! Anne Gibson, my best friend, you are an angel in disguise! You have stuck by my side, cheering me on and renewing my confidence when I had, at times, lost it completely. Friends like you, are far and few between. Kerry Whitbread for her constant promotion of my work in the land down under, E. L. McKaigh for her assistance in the United States, as well as all of the other souls around the world who have selflessly worked on my behalf without even my asking, you are amazing. To Sire Cedric, Andrea Dean Van Scoyoc and Eric Enck for their continued encouragement. Thank you to the International Order of Horror Professionals for their support and promotion. My mother for passing on her stubborn tenacity and love for words; my father for passing on the insanity of the Faust name and his creativity...

And to all of the other friends whom have stood beside me since the beginning, laughing with me, consoling me, drinking with me, and being brutally honest with me, for as long as memory allows, thank you! There are so very many people who deserve consideration and I hope you will not judge me too harshly if I have not listed you all individually here. Know that you have touched my heart and my life in a way that is permanent and irreplaceable...

With Eternal Gratitude,
Gabrielle S. Faust

INTRODUCTION

By Michael Marano

The first time I spoke to Gabrielle Faust, my mouth was full of blood.

The phone was pressed against my face, which was swollen tight as a drunk's liver after my dentist had performed a procedure on me that I found out later she'd only previously performed on a cadaver.

On a bet.

We were talking about vampires, in case you couldn't guess.

So, let's decode this moment, shall we? A *Marano*, descended from a long line of alchemists, was talking about vampires to a *Faust*, descended from a long line of alchemists (or, at least one in particular), using a device the receiver of which looked like it had been used by Colonel Mustard in the dining room for a hasty bit of bludgeoning, thanks to the scab-spittle dribbling from my pie-hole. If that moment had been included in a novel, any self-respecting editor would have whipped out a blue pencil like Mace Windu whipping out a lightsaber and cut it for being too obvious.

It was all very Goth.

But not in the way most people would think.

Fulcanelli, the coolest alchemist of the 20th century--a guy who's so cool, people still argue over whether or not he really existed or if, like Elvis or Joe Hill, he isn't still floating around out there someplace--put forward in his book *The Mystery of the Cathedrals* the idea that the great Gothic cathedrals of Europe aren't just big temples of Christendom, but coded stone texts holding the secrets of the alchemists going back millennia. He suggests that the word "Gothic" is really a form of the word "argot", meaning a "coded slang". "Gothic art", or "*arts gothiques*", is really a form of "*argotiques*", a secret language used to confound those uninitiated. You Dario Argento fans out there might know a nasty iteration of Fulcanelli from the climax of *Inferno*, in which he appears as a horrible old man alchemist/architect in a wheelchair. The ideas of *The Mystery of the Cathedrals* are the backbone of Michele Soavi and Argento's *La Chiesa*.

In more ways than one, Gabrielle Faust, whose name is an argot of "the fist of God's strong mistress", is a Gothic writer. Yeah, she's a cool Goth chick (and I gotta say, if she were a character in a novel, any self-respecting editor would ask the author to change her name, as "The Fist of God's Strong Mistress" is subtle as a brick to the thalamus). The book you're about to transmute with the tracks of your eyes is coded and multi-layered, dealing as it does with a vampire apocalypse. "Apocalypse" comes from the Greek, meaning a "lifting of the veil". And what does a lifted funereal veil mean for somebody who's already dead? Or is it a funereal veil? You tell me. In any case, the book is a stone text, a cathedral to be walked into. Maybe because of the emotional layers of the book, it's not just Gothic, but Baroque.

What veils it lifts for you is up to you.

Michael Marano is a Bram Stoker and International Horror Guild Award–winning horror writer, fiction editor of the online horror publication Chiaroscuro (www.chizine.com), and a nationally syndicated commentator on genre film for the Public Radio Satellite System show, Movie Magazine International.

Eternal Vigilance
Book One
From Deep Within the Earth

Darkness within darkness.
The gateway to all understanding.
–"Tao Te Ching"

1

A deep rumbling like the chaos of a storm rising from far within the earth's interior clawed its way to the surface. From near the center where it was always warm, it bridged time and space, traveling through the fluxing structure of existence, caring little for the restraints of our defiant physical laws. I could feel it reverberating through the thin blades of grass beneath my arms and legs. I dug my fingernails into the rich black soil beneath my palms and stared up at the gray dome above me. It churned and writhed with the wind, spinning in upon itself like a massive silver serpent squeezing the life out of the atmosphere.

The dragons of the land were awakening. Wrapped in mist and fire, slate scales of blood and jet, they rose in a warning of chaos and inevitable change. Their cry was a call to the very core of the universe to return to the forgotten altar where they were once worshiped, where blood was spilt to sate their demand for balance, and hymns were sung in their name on moonlit eves. My reason refused to accept such a possibility: that beasts that had once incited both fervor and fear in the eyes of my grandfather could truly return. Every nerve within me screamed with a primal fear that I could not deny. Paralyzed, I lay still and watched and waited.

The winged serpents roared again and reality quaked. The vibrations traveled from the packed soil and sediment to a place that seemed lodged deep within my bones. The sky began to melt, the contours of the gray clouds shifted away from one another to recede in the wake of an engulfing darkness. I gasped as a piercing cold crashed into me as if the sea reached out to consume my soul. Like quicksand it drew me down into its womb, pushing the air from my lungs in a hollow soundless scream.

The sky became a distant sliver before my eyes. The

ghost of a damning unearthly wind howled aggressively in my ears, the distant sunlight becoming icy and fractured. For a moment I drifted, my will leaving, entranced by the fading beauty of the world I had once known. Suddenly, the dragons shrieked again sending wave after wave of shearing vibrations through the very marrow of my bones. I struggled against the invisible pressure that held me captive. My heart careened against my ribs until I thought they would shatter. The palms of my hands slammed down against something hard and smooth as I momentarily regained the control of my arms. I gasped. Instinct, bred of war, moved my hand to reach for my sword, but it was no longer there. Panic! Desolation! I gasped for air as the universe collapsed into my chest...

My eyes fluttered open.

Darkness. Dense, formless shadows pressed down on me with the weight of a corpse. All sense of dimension was lost to me in the pitch dark. My stomach twisted in a nauseous delirium, my teeth chattered uncontrollably as if from a severe hypothermia. Blind in my instinct to fight, I began to flail, searching for a way out of the smothering nothingness. My fists collided with a hard flat surface—thick marble—to my left and then to my right. In a fleeting moment of clarity, I paused, the silence a high-pitched wail deep within my skull. I pressed my palms against the cold flat surfaces to either side of me. A heartbeat passed through my fingertips and into the stone. Confused rage engulfed my soul as the second of hesitation snapped like a matchstick. I slammed my body against the smothering walls containing me, fighting furiously against my prison. Whatever sanity might have remained vanished in a hellish unearthly shriek as I punched upwards with all of my strength.

Something exploded above me. The air rang with the sudden impact as a thick cloud of dust and hard tiny shards of stone rained down upon my face and arms. Coughing and sputtering blindly, I pulled myself from the coffin, falling to the floor with an unceremonious thud. For a long while, I lay curled up on the icy stone floor shivering, my arms wrapped tightly around my bent legs. My lungs ached from the dust and grit that filled the air around me, that settled like a thin veil of ancient holy gauze upon my skin and hair. My body convulsed uncontrollably with pain, my mind whimpering as it raced without rhyme or reason, clawing for the fragments of dreams that now spiraled away from my grasp like shreds of white silk in a cyclone wind. It was cold. It was silent.

Gradually, my heart began to ease and with it my mind. My muscles began to loosen making me weak and queasy as the adrenaline rushed through my veins and into my stomach. Slowly, I opened my eyes again. I lay at the base of a massive stone sarcophagus. The tiny tomb was windowless and drenched in shadow. Angles and planes were one and the same, shadows converging in the same ephemeral fashion as if swept to a dusty corner to be forgotten. It was a strange archaic beauty of a time long past. I marveled at my surroundings; it was as if I was seeing the features of the room by moonlight. Time had not dulled my preternatural vision and I found myself lost within the cold alien beauty. A shudder breezed through me. Icy recognition gripped my heart as I began to separate the remaining tendrils of dreams, wrapped like whispers of cobwebs, from reality.

Chunks of what had been the lid of the sarcophagus lay scattered around me in dusty irreparable ruins. With trembling fingers, I reached up and grasped the sides, using their solid strength for support to pull myself unsteadily to my feet. A dull ache invaded my legs as I attempted to use them, the muscles hurriedly repairing and rejuvenating themselves even as I rose. It made me wonder just how much time had passed since I had crawled into that box. It was a strange and distant sensation, that of my own tissue knitting together in fibrous strands, becoming stronger and stronger with each second. I listened to the blood rushing through my ears, simply learning to breathe again.

With great care, I turned from the coffin, my gaze drifting along the unadorned, stone walls to finally rest upon the small chamber door. Gradually, like sand sifting through the cracks in an Egyptian temple, my memories began to fall about me. The truth was sickeningly sharp, twisting my innards, the images like swarming hornets. The spell I had cast upon myself was supposed to have been permanent; I was not to have awoken to the world ever again.

A nauseating anger ripped through my bones. I staggered towards the door and, with trembling fingers, traced the outline of the crucifix chiseled on the stone. I watched my fingers as they danced delicately across the intricate and ancient curves. How skeletal the digits appeared: animated bones bathed in false blue light. My eyes traveled over my wrist to my arm. So thin, the flesh, an albino white almost transparent, marred by ropes of blue veins that wrapped around my arm like earthworms. In much the same way that a starving prisoner forgets the pleasures of food, an aching numbness had replaced the unquenchable Thirst that had bound me to my madness. I could barely even remember the smell of blood or the taste of the flesh that held it. My parched swollen tongue danced over my sharp fangs testing the tips in search of my past.

I felt the remnants of my former paranoia return, stalking the edges of my mind; savage little beasts. How long had I slept and what remained of the world above? The human race was a hive of industrious destructive insects. I had seen revolutions spawned of revolutions, bloody wars quickened from the ashes of their predecessors. The centuries, flying past me as quickly as mortal decades, had elevated and leveled empires, cultures, and technologies, all the while dictating a silent directive of slow planetary death. The fabric of the world I had left behind had been riddled with a heavy stifling fear. Layers upon layers of devious demons crept up behind the sleeping denizens of civilization whispering their black intentions in riddles even a child could discern. No one listened, though, to the ever-pervasive moan of global societal collapse. No one dared to breathe the truth. Scream and the glass might shatter; sigh and the house might blow down. They were too enamored of watching the dirty whirlpool spiraling down deeper and deeper to a place of no return.

I had tried to watch it all from the detached place that all Immortals watch life. At least, it should have been a detached place. I was too young to have had my heart grow numb and, possessed with the idealism and naivety of innocence, embraced my new path with every ounce of my soul. I tried to change the world. I tried and failed, and after a mere two hundred and seventy years of Immortality, had found myself driven to the brink of madness by my own powers and an embittered disillusionment.

I had always longed for the aloof arrogance that seemed to come so naturally to most vampires. Where the hearts of others of my kind seemed to turn to stone as the centuries passed, mine only became tender, my antipathy for all that was vicious and cruel about the world nearly crushing my spirit. As my powers progressed and my unique ability to absorb the memories of my prey evolved, the atrocities inflicted, whether with malice or ignorance, and the sadness of humanity became a mantle of broken glass I donned each time I fed. I could not understand how my kindred could swim in excess and gluttony, when everywhere I looked there was chaos and pain. At times I hated them; at times I envied them. They saw the world as a tediously simple game in which they partook only for mild amusement: a world that they ruled with ease and without conscience or remorse. Mortals were random senseless creatures, their lack of unity was their undoing. I had never been able to see it that way, always too swept up in the philosophical debate of man versus vampire, predator versus prey and the great evolution of the universe's preordained plan. The others had said I retained too much of my own ancient sense of humanity. They had said it would be my eventual downfall.

My pulse pounded in my ears as I considered the possible fate of my own race in the cruel fist of Time. From my prison deep within the earth, there was simply no way of knowing what had become of them.

I sank to the floor, barely able to draw breath as my mind raced over the infinite scrolls of confusion: a madman debating truth with his own reflection. The world I had turned my back on had been polluted and tortured, the ranks of humanity seeming to have lost complete control of their own governments. Societal voices had been buried beneath the screech of propaganda and loyalist contributions, technology evolving around them at such an infinite speed that the line between fact and fiction had nearly faded completely. What if time had not taught the lessons all empires must learn in one dawning era or another? Was it conceivable that the world still grew outside, more gluttonous and numb and silent than the patronizingly pacified generations before? My heart slowed and plummeted, a stone ricocheting off the rotten gullet of a dead tree. Red tears of anguished rage streamed down my gaunt white cheeks as I pounded the walls like a child denied. NO! No. *Nooo.*

It was useless.

I was awake.

* * * *

Venting the last of my blind rage and frustration upon the crypt door, I made my way up the maze of the catacombs. I followed my instincts without question, traveling the ruined stone pathway that would lead me to an uncertain destiny. There was obvious destruction to the narrow corridor. Here and there the ceiling or wall had given way, as if a catastrophic explosion had shaken the earth years before. Tree roots arched from the holes in the walls, warped and snaking tentacles of some petrified sea anomaly. Small iconic statues and cremation urns that had once adorned the alcoves of the walls lay shattered at my feet. The soft crunching of the fragments made beneath my weathered black boots was enough to quiet my internal fretting for a while. I focused on the sound and clawed through the debris.

Time seemed to have been my enemy. I had grown incredibly weak and feeble, so *human.* A breath of fresh air seemed as impossibly mythical as ambrosia as I clambered over a gnarled mass of tree roots that bridged the walls of the dank gritty passageway in their search for nutrients in rotting bones. As I neared the entrance to the hall, a raucous symphony of crickets and the deliberate scurrying of beetles replaced the dull munching of earthworms. Insects. How strange that they meant freedom.

I burst through the last of the doors and stumbled, gasping, into the thick night air. After being deprived of light or sound for so long, my senses were set ablaze, burning and crackling as the material world in all its crystalline chaos exploded into my body. The moon's brilliance burned into my eyes like a prison yard floodlight, the gentle hum of tree frogs reverberating like the aftershock of gunfire. I squinted into the night, hands clutching the sides of my head until, slowly, the night began to retreat. The cemetery into which I had emerged was in ruins. Had an earthquake shaken the blessed earth where I had lain? I was shocked.

Headstones lay shattered upon a butchered field of mud and upturned grass. The ancient oaks that had once stood guard over the quietude of the cemetery were badly scarred and beaten. The largest one had been split in two, its limbs rotting upon the ground in front of me. I staggered forward and dropped to my knees, my chest rising and falling as I fought to bring the sweet and cold night air into my lungs, rich with uprooted earth and cleansing rain.

Suddenly, I felt a presence in close range. It was human, male and very young. I blinked, slowly surveying the space around me. A childish anger filled me at the thought of being disturbed so soon. Mixed with a violent outrage at the bleakness surrounding me, my body became rigid and tense. In my weakened state, I hesitated to trust my senses. Even though my instincts told me this boy was indeed mortal, I could not be sure. I lowered my breathing, tucking my thoughts deep inside me just in case something *else* might be listening.

The mortal was getting closer. I thought of retreating back inside the mausoleum, but a heavy and foreboding pressure stayed me with a predatory will of its own. I could smell his scent; the rich, salty perfume of sweat intermingled with the pungent copper of young blood. My chest constricted, pain arcing out through my abdomen and throat. I fell forward, barely able to stifle the scream that struggled to free itself from my soul.

"Hey, mister? You alright?" A quavering adolescent voice accosted my shaking form.

I hesitated for a moment, my fingers digging into the dirt in front of me. His voice was full of fear and jaded anticipation. His mind was an open and unguarded book. The youth's primal urge to flee conflicted with his instinct that told him I might have something worth stealing and, if nothing else, it was a tale to tell to the disarray of fractured friends he would return to later that evening. Without actually looking at him, my face lowered towards the earth from which I had come, I could see him within my mind: a battered youth, painfully thin with starvation. His clothes were ragged and heavily mended with crude hand stitching in raw hemp thread. His hair hung across his smudged tan features in jagged bleached locks. His body was rigid with tension, his gaze unwavering as he pointed the long cylindrical barrel of a scarred AK-47 at me. He was a fierce and proud spirit trapped within the battered decaying flesh of a human being, scared and beaten but too proud to buckle and be warmed by charity.

Curiosity finally overwhelmed him. The youth jumped from the large chunk of stone where he was perched and approached me cautiously. His worn army boots made soft sucking sounds in the mud with each step. He stopped an arm's length away, sure that I was too weak to be a threat. I lifted my eyes, turning my head towards him only enough to catch him in my line of vision.

His gasp punctured the steady moan of the wind, sharp and short. The shallow slate pools of his eyes widened in confused fear. From his mind burst forth the horrifying image of me as I knelt in the mud and stones. I had become a monstrous construction of white waxen angles and hollow sunken caverns that stretched as purple bruises beneath my dark hazel and gold eyes. What once served as hair stuck to my scalp in dust-matted locks of dark yellow streaked with brown bits of rope and twine. It hung over my eyes as a disheveled curtain. My skeletal frame was a craven thing all but naked draped in the remnants of my ragged clothing. The torn fabric of my paper-thin shirt lifted in the wind with a life of its own.

A pounding rhythm echoed from deep within the youth's chest, resonating within my sensitive ears. I began to rise. Slowly, dreamlike, a mummified creature of creaking joints and sinew. The young man's feet seemed cemented to the mud and stone. Even as I approached him, the sleek black outline of his weapon still saluted me, though it trembled in his grip. A cold predatory intensity locked his gaze to mine as my hand reached towards the gun. Though he was no innocent soul, his confusion was heartbreaking in its honesty. Such silent appeal was lost upon me as the numbness that had replaced my starvation retreated. Empathy for humanity had no righteous place before the primal demand of the Thirst and my conscience was quickly crushed to dust by its power as the mad current of the young mortal's pulse drowned out my newfound reality.

I felt myself reaching out to him with my mind, threading tendrils of my will through his mind to coax him into submission. For him, I sculpted a new image of myself, one that I plucked from my own memory, when I was flawless and beautiful in my eternal youth. His eyes widened, his lips parting in an unspoken question and I knew that what he now saw before him was unexplainable and holy, a vision of a god resurrected. I reached slowly towards him, a living statue of contorted wax, and removed the gun from his shaking digits, letting it slip heavily to the ground. It struck the weathered stone with a crack that reminded me of splintering bone. We stood mere inches apart, our scents blended: stale earth and salty sweat. The smell caused my heart to contract painfully. My fingers brushed the sides of his arms. Even clothed in the thick, decades-old army jacket, I could feel the electrifying tension buried beneath the subtle warmth of his skin. Every ounce of his being screamed out, but as his thin pale lips parted, slack and dazed, the only sound that escaped was his shallow breath.

I wrapped him in the archaic cold of my embrace. His will was mine to mold, though his pulse still made his skin burn and vibrate with a futile fierceness. My right hand traveled slowly up to lodge firmly on the back of his neck as I lowered my mouth to the soft flesh of his throat. The agony of my starvation exploded to the surface of my own essence, devouring what little reason still clung weakly to my mind. My fangs plunged deep into his flesh, through skin and muscle and tendon to rape the tough vessel of life force that ran through him. Blood, hot and coppery, erupted in my mouth spilling over my tongue: molten shards so sinfully wicked and delicious and taboo. I lost myself in the sound of his heart caught in the draft of my kiss. I let the beast consume me.

Serpentine, I coiled my arms around him tighter and tighter, my body shaking in the orgasmic pleasure that I had long since forgotten; an aching, spiraling ascension that rendered me merciless as it surged through the fibers of my body. Sugary electric impulses, an arcing lightning, thrilled me as his heart began to slow. His memories flooded through me in a tidal wave of unfettered emotion: his orphaned childhood amongst the ruins of the city, terrified scavenging for food between derelict buildings, a brutal indoctrination of beatings into the only family he ever knew, pain, anger, hatred, confusion. I fought to dismiss them, to keep them from invading the deeper parts of my soul. As my body filled and replenished its barren reserves, his clung tenaciously to life, but now it was slipping away, strangely saddening me. I suppose it was the realization that nothing had changed; I hadn't slept away the evil dreams as I had so longed to. The demon had not been exorcised. I still took life and gave nothing in return. I was still a vampire.

I pulled back from the gaping wound torn in my stranger's throat. Nothing neat and clean as I might have done in the past. Starved and frenzied, I had ravaged his body. I could see the last threads of existence leaving his eyes, a small white receipt swept away upon wispy currents of wind. What he might have seen in those last few moments would forever remain a mystery to me. I only hoped that it had not been a vision of me.

"Thank you," I whispered in a voice inaudible to mortal ears and I graced the soft dirt-streaked skin of his cheek with a simple kiss.

I let him slip from my alabaster arms, which were already healing with the power of the new living blood that coursed just beneath my flesh. He crumpled at my feet, an existence soon to be forgotten. It began to rain. For a long while, head bowed as if in prayer, I stood vigil over the broken body until the soft cries of his friends reached me over the storm. I knelt beside the youthful form of my one-time lover and gently ran my fingertips over his eyes, lowering the lids that were now a pale gray to match his stare.

I began to walk quickly towards the city.

2

I entered the dark, wet city from the east. Except for the swirling wind and rain, there was little movement, the night air strangely vacant of what I knew of the modern world. Several blocks from what I remembered as an interstate highway that cut through the center of the city, a strange and eerie sensation began to creep in just below my skin. The once raging river of commerce, concrete and gasoline that flowed from Canada to Mexico was quiet. I could no longer hear the caustic tide of traffic that had once droned the siren's call of progress. The buzzing flickering streetlamps, the wreaking odors of carbon monoxide and ozone were absent. I could not even hear a distant television accidentally left on all night by a dozing denizen. A thick silence emanated from the city before me, the rank breath of a dormant beast. It coiled about my body, tight and demanding. At one time I had hated the noise of the city. Now I ached for it.

A few of the rickety shacks that once crammed themselves beside one another on tiny barren lots still stood. Most, though, had been swept away, as if by a tornado so that barely even the foundations were left to peak up through the scarred ground. The earth was reclaiming itself; neighborhoods were now overgrown with thick rambling vines, dandelions, and shadows. The scattered beaten hovels that remained reminded me of the ancient pioneer ruins I had often seen throughout the rolling Texas hillsides, leaning top-heavy against an unseen shoulder. Gutted and black from within, the city's hovels cowered before the presence of the savage night. Through the overgrown tree line, I could make out one or two buildings that glowed dimly. For whoever lived there, it could only be their last resort. My mind wandered dreamily through their moldy halls of splintered wood and peeling yellowed wallpaper. Midnight and amber rooms recklessly decorated with rusted relics surrounded souls that cringed with every movement. Their lives ached with a void of interminable darkness quickened in the brutality only war can evoke.

Hostility, like a fine dank mist, seeped into the pores of my skin. It was a feeling of always being followed by malevolent intentions. I gazed up at the swollen harvest moon that watched me suspiciously; I knew I was unwelcome in this new world.

Everything is unwelcome, I thought with fear as my feet sped over the broken concrete towards an uncertain fate.

The city lay wrapped within a web of mottled light and shadow; it beckoned to me, taunting me with secrets. The crumbling homes gave way to mountains of grungy gray concrete, riddled with spidering cracks made by coarse branches of weed. Banks of shattered architecture sloped upwards like a tidal wave frozen in its ascent to meet the long stretch of broken blacktop that graced their shared summit.

I had left behind a world that feared silence. It had been a world immersed in a culture that never stood still, never breathed and never closed its eyes. A culture that I had hated with such raw abandon that I had turned my back on it. I had fled the incessant drone of a society of neurotic, impulsive, and insanely intelligent youth and their older obsessive counterparts. Their chorus riddled my waking hours with high-pitched meaningless chatter ricocheting about the walls of my skull. It had been a sound whose purpose I suddenly understood was to fill the empty space the world had created with all of its concrete and steel. I stood alone beneath the highway's overpass. It arched over me, the skeletal remains of some long extinct leviathan. I paused, listening to the rush of my own blood through my ears as it fused with that of the boy I had killed.

That sound of the screaming city had made us believe we were not alone. My mind searched for a glint of reason through the thick frost of shock that surrounded it. Now, all of the strength, all of the courage I had once sensed in the stone and mortar of the city had crumbled and blown away. It had been a mirage.

I was such a fool to believe the world would improve in my absence.

I moved past the hollow echo of the highway and along a darkened stretch of city high-rises. The same destructive pattern that had plagued the eastern neighborhoods continued to the outer edges of the central business district.

Stores leaned harshly against one another, glass shattered from towering display windows. What was left of the rubber soles of my boots crunched the scattered shards as my weight shifted uneasily from foot to foot. Debris filled doorways where patrons had once loitered aimlessly on their exploited lunch hours of cappuccinos and bagels. With the exception of a few banks, law firms, and the Salvation Army, the eastern section of the business district had not been heavily populated. However, very few of these stoic "modern" feats of architecture still stood. Some fooled the eye with a flawless glimmering surface only to reveal a gutted skeleton. Others were simply sharp-edged memories. It was now painfully evident that whatever had once struggled within those gritty lots had been exterminated; the void left by their forced departure stung my soul. A gnawing curiosity mixed with souring fear curdled in my stomach: how could the world I had known as so impermeable have become so utterly obliterated? Again, I wondered just how much time had passed?

The subtle amber glow of distant light caught my eye as I reached the top of a steep incline. At one time, I would have considered such warmth an intriguing blessing. Now, I approached it with caution. I knew too little of this new world to be blundering about as if I were its predator and master. My position in life was still uncertain. I was nearing what I remembered to be Congress Avenue, the main thoroughfare that cut through the middle of the city. It had been a marred silver carpet of struggling businesses and trendy restaurants that stretched from the regal pink granite capital to the muddy gray-green of Town Lake. At least, that was the way I remembered it.

A sound tweaked my ears. I froze in mid-stride, tensing and turning slowly on the balls of my feet to face the direction of the noise. Like the distant invasion of a horde of ravenous locusts, the shrill metallic whine was not quite organic, not quite mechanical. It wound its way through the maze of alleys and avenues towards me. It came closer and closer at an alarming speed; I could detect the slight soft whirring of a small motor, the distinct pungency of steel. I dared not even breathe. I pulled my thoughts deep inside me, locking them away from prying minds, and knowing that I was not fully restored to my previous flawlessness, gathered a more complete mirage of *humanity* about my lanky pale form to fool the eye, heart, and mind of any onlooker. Rivulets of rainwater trickled over my skin, clinging to my eyelashes, making the world disappear from time to time.

I waited.

It rounded the corner of a derelict building a block away. My eyes widened in disbelief. My mouth fell slack. A construct of glimmering cobalt-infused titanium and black rubber wires hovered a few feet off the ground, motionless. The sharp acidity of ozone emanated from it, the only odor I could perceive beneath the soot and grime of the city's slow breath. I stood my ground, more curious than fearful. I wanted it to see me.

The machine sped towards me with a sound halfway between a contented cat and a furious cricket, then abruptly stopped to float directly in front of me. A brief shiver riddled my flesh uncontrollably. My instinct wanted to pull me away from a surreal abstraction it could not completely comprehend. It appeared to be a modified hovercraft the size of an adult trike, streamlined and flawlessly sealed with a smooth shark-like skin. Soulless, yet beautiful, a technological dream I had only seen in violent films. I let my eyes travel over the gleaming midnight blue surface of the machine's base, then to its small cockpit that suddenly hissed up and back to reveal a stern humanoid figure seated within.

My heart careened against my ribs as my mind fought to absorb the minute details of this synthetic construction. Had my senses deceived me? I had detected no trace of human in the machine. The pilot of the craft was alien in and of himself, seeming more an extension of the vehicle than a separate entity. I searched for an expression behind the mirrored visor

27

of his helmet, but all that gazed back at me were the beads of water that clung to its surface like symbiant life forms.

"State your purpose here." The voice was emotionless and flat; a synthetic tone programmed for authority without conscience. Combined with the incessant whir of the craft's operational propulsion system, the intonation of his question was oddly hypnotizing. I concluded that the figure must be a police officer, of sorts, though something instinctively told me his authority was of a military nature, rather than that of a mere neighborhood watchdog.

I hesitated nervously, wanting to study the creature that interrogated me for as long as possible. I explored *it* with my senses, gauging my opponent on all levels. A strange scent lingered about the patrol unit, part organic, part ozone and silicone. It confused me. I noticed that the flesh of his forearms had been replaced by interlocking plates of the same midnight-colored metal of the hovercraft.

That explains the scent. He was a hybrid of man and machine. I frowned in contemplation. Humanity had finally realized its nightmares of a cyber-organism.

"State your purpose here. Now!" The voice boomed down at me again.

I did not like being interrogated. I stared up at the hovering patrol. I knew I did not have long before it would take action against my insubordination, but I had to know exactly what the limitations of this creature were. If I were only on the fringes of what my city had become, the gods only knew what lay ahead of me. Opening the secret valves of my mind, I reached out with my consciousness carefully towards the thing before me.

I slipped into his mind with a shock as brilliant and fleeting as static electricity. I inhaled sharply; his "mind" was more terrifyingly different than anything human or vampire I had ever touched. It was a fluid maze of preprogrammed emotions and responses that wove an intricate web of electrical currents and blood through the still living tissue that encased it. If computers dreamed of human anatomy the way we dream of circuit boards, it would have been the embodiment of their wildest fantasies. I searched for the tiny hidden whorl of needy approval lodged deep within all minds; that coveted portion of our humanity that we grudgingly share, divvying it out to those most worthy. If I could find and alter that part of his mind, I would know that he was still at least partly human and thus, defeatable.

Seconds ticked by in uneasy defiance, neither of our gazes wavering. The rain persistently intensified as if urging us to end the charade. I watched as opalescent drops clung to the slick surface of his helmet and forearms. The patrol unit began to move its hand, reaching for something discreetly hidden from my line of view. It was too late though, I had already found all that I needed.

Before my mind's eye the acceptance trigger I had probed for seemed to flicker, simultaneously appearing as a swirl of electrical impulses surging through human tissue, and a tiny piece of computer chip, green-pearlescent shot through with a fine gold linear maze. I wrapped my mental fingers around the tiny area coaxing it into submission. It opened to my suggestions with an unnerving ease and allowed me to plant my impressions deep within its labyrinth...*harmless*...*lost*. Though I had experimented deeply with certain technologies as they evolved over the centuries, I had never attempted to use my powers on them; the most complex architectures had always posed little challenge for an intellect such as mine that processed information at a light-speed beyond any mortal programmer. The *mind* of the officer before me contained none of the dysfunctional human peculiarities or dispositions. Its technical resistance was almost intangible as I overrode its minor security programs, and I could tell that its biomechanical *personality* was accustomed to others altering its patterns.

Quickly, I withdrew from his mind. "I'm sorry. I must have taken a wrong turn somewhere."

There was a long pause as my voice died away beneath the torrent of wind and rain. I could make out the faint glow of a string of digital text as it flickered in tiny obscure lines across the inside of his visor. Perhaps he was searching a remote database for records of my identification? If so, he would find nothing. I was beginning to fear that I had underestimated the complexity of his mind when he finally spoke.

"Sufficient." He lifted his arm and pointed a long metallic finger towards the way I had been heading. "This sector is off limits. Trespassing is forbidden." The tone was cool and definitive, leaving no room for explanations or arguments.

"Of course...officer," I whispered under my breath as he sped away into the ruined cityscape.

* * *

I was a child once again.

How else to describe the pure, innocent awe I felt for the world. No matter how battered or bruised, each nook and fold carried within it a perfect crystalline mystery so sweet that I longed to take it in my teeth and taste it: taste it and know it as I had done when I was but a very small child. Perhaps that was what I had begun to lose in those long years before my Sleep, the feeling of seeing things with fresh eyes, of seeing things that were new and foreign. I felt alive again, as I had in the first few decades of my Immortality, when reality was still sharp and surreal. This alien landscape; I wanted to absorb it, to understand it.

Perhaps, I had not given the world long enough to find my true place in it? The Dark blood had only served to amplify the voice of the starry-eyed philosopher I had been in my mortal youth. Too quickly, I built a *religion* to lift my newfound brethren beyond the shackles of the curse that they believed doomed them to be supposed minions of the Christian Satan. My religion gave them purpose and hope and pride. However, just as I had seen the flaws in every other religion or philosophy I had studied, so too did my own begin to fracture from doubt and fear and anger.

My physical and mental vampiric powers had progressed far beyond others my own age, cursing me with the ability to take into myself the pasts, the memories, of my victims. I was not yet strong enough to control the power and eventually madness and pain began to gnaw viciously at the edges of my sanity. Knowing I could not go on feeding empty promises to the fledglings who followed at my heels, I turned my back on them and fled. Hundreds had died by their own hands in the nights that followed my resignation, the hopelessness too much for them to handle in a world they already had trouble accepting. One particular coven of Elders, led by an eight hundred year old Scottish vampire by the name of Adian, plotted my murder after their own fledglings gave themselves up to the sun. However, they had underestimated my powers and in a bloody battle just before dawn I killed Adian and his warriors. Their deaths only further alienated me from my Dark brethren as many believed my murder would have been justified.

What they did not realize was the tremendous toll the fight had taken on me, mentally and physically. In the final moments before Adian's death, I had drunk deeply from him, draining him completely of both blood and spirit as I savagely tore his throat open. Adian's blood had poisoned me, his memories nearly eradicating my own until I could barely distinguish imagination from truth. Soon I believed that it was I who had once been the eldest son of a great Chieftain and not merely a philosopher and the son of a shipmaker. There was no reasoning with me. No one could tell me otherwise. Since they could not publicly sentence me to death, the Council of Elders ruled to disown me permanently for my crimes, both in my abandonment of my disciples and the slaying of my own kind. No vampire upon any continent would henceforth acknowledge my existence. At first, I thought I had been given a lenient sentence, as I did not desire to speak to my brethren as it was. However, I soon realized that it was far worse than any other punishment they could have bestowed upon me, a social exile that left me completely and utterly alone in a world I already despised. I retreated further into my madness and isolation. I wrapped my indignation around me as if lying down to sleep in a field of broken glass, daring those on the outside to reach for me. When not even the closest of my kindred, or even my very Maker, reached out to offer me solace, some out of fear of the Elders' verdict and some of their own festering loathing of me, I realized I had truly lost everything.

Now, I felt the scars of my own treacherous slumber. The confusion of the new world around me evoked stinging tears that hovered near the corners of my eyes before relenting and spilling down the sides of my face, already slick with rain. They were not tears of pain, or frustration, but of a sudden need to understand and be comforted.

The avenue I had once strode along so many restless nights before had been transformed. Etched within my memory was a wide four-lane street lined sparsely with fledgling trees and peopled with business clientele, musicians, and colorful nomadic homeless. To the artistic melodies that had drifted from dark, eclectic side street bars, it had spoken hazily of history newly paved over by ignorance; at night it had whispered of hard times and new wealth.

Now, it was as if the skyscrapers had all but vanished. Some destroyed, some barely standing, but all gently receding into the rank exhale of darkness. Beneath these hollow towering structures, that spoke more as looming ghosts than solid physical entities, had erupted a chaotic maze of tents, booths and tiny makeshift hovels. They clustered together like driven sheep. The sleek and sophisticated modern society I had witnessed emerging in the years before my long sleep was now dust, replaced by the harsh cry of survival that echoed eerily off the ghosts of 21st century progress.

Voices swarmed about me like hungry spirits eager to visit the flesh again. A million caustic sounds burned a twisted path to where I stood at the edge of the mayhem, just beyond the reach of the light. People shouted at one another over the cacophony of haggling, trading, and bartering their lives away in one way or another. Voices filled with strife and hunger pleaded in angry incessant terms for another vague opportunity. If the light had not been so harsh and pervasive, if the rain had not chilled my face, I might have expected the abrasive kiss of desert sand on my skin. Again, I questioned the sanity of all of this, the solidity of this hallucination of mine. I could have still been sleeping, my mind tormenting me with the fretful anxieties of the past. But even if it were a dream, I could not deny it held my attention completely.

I plunged into the crowd. Instantly, the sensation of drowning overwhelmed me as I was pulled deep within the steady downstream of flesh. Heavy, spicy human scents forced their way into my nose and mouth. I sneezed violently, nearly falling backwards over my own feet. Jasmine, spice, patchouli, curry, mixed with the underlying odor of unwashed limbs and street rubbish. Too many hot bodies filled with blood crushed up against me, tempting my still starved body. I blinked and tried to fight the urge to devour them all.

I swam to the edge of the crowd where the current was not so intense. A long set of rough, undyed canvas awnings had been strung along the walkway to protect loiterers from whatever peculiar weather might occur. I leaned against the rough wood of a small food vendor's stall. Rich aromas of roasted foods drifted out of the window and into the street. The world pressed in on me, smothering me. I struggled to breathe, to quell the rising nausea in my stomach. I had been foolish to think I could reintroduce myself to society so quickly after waking. I closed my eyes and quieted my thoughts, retreating deep inside until I stood alone and silent. To the outside world that flowed unyielding around me, it would have seemed as if I had simply vanished.

I let several moments pass in meditation. When I opened my eyes, the world seemed a much quieter place. For the first time since the cold marble of the tomb, I truly felt the ground beneath my feet. I did not feel alone, however, I did not feel separated and above my surroundings. There was someone else there, someone who saw through my shields, who knew what I was and watched me very carefully. Slowly, I scanned the crowd. I spied her a few feet away. She was a tall girl, and young. No more than sixteen. Her clothes—a pale yellow-white tunic, bound at the waist with a thick brown leather belt, and close fitting pants of a darker brownish-blue—were made of thick, rough linen. They hung loosely over her painfully thin frame: her girlish chest and willowy limbs. Her long black hair fell in even straight pleats over her narrow shoulders, fanning out delicately at the ends.

She stood so still that any other might have mistaken her for a statue. Only I could see the quick and shallow rise and fall of her chest and the subtle tremors that passed through her clenched fists where they hung at her sides. I met her eyes and knew her instantly for what she was: *a telepath.*

She knew what I was as well. Somehow, I felt she even knew *who* I was. I could read the fiery fear and wonder within her, though her mind was shut up tight and virgin behind steel walls of paranoia: a secret fortress like none I had ever sensed in a mortal. For this alone, she instantly held my respect, though I still wondered about the fear that emanated from her very pores. Even on my worst days, I had never evoked such dread. Perhaps I had not fed enough yet to reverse the waxen monster that had emerged from my slumber?

I turned towards her, wanting to approach her. The sudden movement startled her. Like a frightened deer, she bolted from her post. I found myself following her even before I could consciously decide otherwise. Through the landslide of human flesh and grit, we flowed in a twisting turning dance of predator and prey. She was fast and her aura so heavily cloaked that even my vampiric senses could not track her by mere mental prowess alone. At times it seemed that she lingered just beyond my fingertips, a blur of sylphish black and yellow. At others, she simply disappeared into the muddy shapes and shadows of the market, a fierce taboo I would never live to embrace.

She stopped. Rather, I *sensed* her stop. The furious surge of panicked energy rushing through the masses simply ceased. I froze, finding myself tripping humanly over the steps I had planned to take. I scanned the crowd slowly.

Perhaps my mind is playing tricks on me.

Perhaps she wasn't real. The idea was not so absurd. After a prolonged Sleep, my mind might not have been functioning with its old reliable speed and I had not been of the soundest mind in my last years before the Sleep. Sensory overload was assaulting my every pore with a vengeance, trying to reclaim my memories and me. But, then again, perhaps I had not imagined her.

I spied her through the forest of ragged dark limbs, a flash of raven's wing dirtied by the honey of muddy, flickering street lamps and smoke. I edged closer, cautiously trying to blend as a chameleon might against the coarse alien skin of a new branch. Her back was towards me as she spoke to a gentleman in coarse black clothing of unusual height and thinness, a willowy reed of cool masculine majesty whose waist-length white hair fell in glossy curtains from his gently nodding head. The sheets of milky threads, shot through with strands of yellow and palest brown, obscured his features as he listened to the whispered concerns of the little telepath before him. The world flowed around him as if he were part of something far removed from earthly sins and common reality.

I knew this man.

He raised his eyes and I found myself staring deep into the hollow corridor of my past. One eye, a fractured amethyst of astounding shimmering light, the other a swirling mist of aqua sea foam. Set wide and almond shaped within long, delicate features, pale as the face of the moon, his gaze held me painfully as I silently stared at him, shocked and terrified. Even as I watched him uproot himself and begin to move slowly through the crowd towards me, I felt my lips parting, searching for words to explain the confusion, elation, and horror that flooded the whorls of my brain. All sensation left my limbs; even the caustic music of the market seemed muffled and timid as all other senses became secondary to sight.

I felt fingers brush my cheek, feathery and silken. I knew he stood inches away from me, and yet the world forever receded from my grasp as if I were being pulled eternally backward into a void.

"Seafra?" I found my voice as my fingers covered his. "Sea?"

He said nothing as he held his palms against either side of my face. His eyes locked with mine, unblinking and cold, his expression distant and impassable. The river of noise and flesh that was the marketplace flowed around the two of us. Sea's lips parted as if he wanted to speak, but simple words were not enough to capture the confused chaos of emotions I could feel radiating from his soul. A cold dread wrapped itself about my spine. There was judgment in his gaze, heavy questions that stayed his heart from the friendship we had once known. I suddenly feared he might turn his back and walk away from me.

His eyes dropped to the ground as he shook his head

Gabrielle Faust

slowly, his long white-blond hair waving softly with the motion. He wrapped his arms about my shoulders and pulled me tight against him with a heavy sigh. "Damn you, Tynan. Damn you..."

I said nothing, but buried my face in the rough linen of his shirt. Though the past tainted our reunion with a bitter and restless tension, I was thankful nonetheless. I knew how slim a chance it was that Sea had crossed my path so soon after my reawakening. Any other Immortal would have crucified me on the spot or simply refused to acknowledge my presence at all. Indeed, I could not believe that he spoke to me now. He had punished me with decades of silence after my fall from grace. Consciousness suddenly felt too heavy a burden to bear and my limbs filled with a leaden weariness that made my bones ache.

Sea pulled away, gently disentangling himself from my emaciated form as if he were afraid he might break me. Silently, one arm still wrapped securely about my shoulders, he led me slowly through the swarm of human survival. His soul was shut to me in a way I had never experienced before in our history as Dark brothers, though I could sense that he communicated freely with the young telepath as she followed close behind. Perhaps he tried to comfort her, to ease her fear of me? I had no way of knowing, nor did I truly care enough to find out. My senses had become overloaded till they hummed deafeningly on the brink of white noise. I needed more blood to repair the damage of my long slumber. I needed a place to rest my mind.

Sea led us to a narrow side alley off the main thoroughfare. As we turned into the dank, rotten shadows it was as if a dense curtain fell down behind us. The undulating cries and smothering perfumes of the throng receded quickly, replaced by the melodic trickle of water through drainpipes to the slick broken pavement below. Halfway down the alley, Sea stopped before an old metal door recessed into the ground floor of the high-rise to our left, its dark green paint heavily marred by the elements and peeling away in thick long panels. As Sea fished a small gold key out of his pocket, I looked up. The door appeared once to have been the side entrance to the lofts on the upper floors of the office building beside us, but was now forgotten and rarely used. Above the door hovered a heavily rusted fire escape that looked as if it could no longer bear the weight of a human. The lower segment of ladder swung freely in the light wind, its broken, ancient hinges moaning quietly. I couldn't imagine anyone living in the derelict building. Anyone, except a creature such as Sea.

"Tynan?" Sea's soft low voice shook me out of my contemplation.

I looked away from the black windows inset into the gray stone building. Sea stood holding the door open, his pale skin and hair making him appear like an apparition swimming amongst the layers of gritty shadows.

I nodded and stepped past him through the low entrance. He quickly passed me, letting the heavy door fall shut behind us with a deep echo of metal upon metal that spiraled down the short hallway and up the battered stairwell. This time, he did not wait for me to follow but began his quick ascension up the stairs, taking them three at a time, his feet barely creating a whisper on the scarred metal. Feeling I had little choice, I followed him up two flights to another metal door leading out from the landing into a narrow black hallway. The smell of aging mildewed wood and soiled wall paint engulfed me as I walked through the open doorway. I could feel the girl's eyes locked on my back as she followed silently at a distance.

The ghosts of the building lamented a time when it had been elegant and chic, its residents young and beautiful and wealthy beyond reason. It had been a powerful, reckless age when the architecture had been conceived, but that history was now all but dead and forgotten. I wrapped my arms about me as I felt the hungry spirits crowding close, inquisitively probing for answers to their demise. As I neared the entrance to the loft, the sound of a match striking a tinderbox hissed across the air; flickering amber light bloomed into existence, spilling out into the hallway where I lingered.

Hesitantly I entered, the door closing softly behind us. I sighed, rubbing my face with my hands. The telepath slipped past me like an eel in the dark. Someone touched my upper arm and I looked up. Sea stood in front of me, his eyes glowing like jewels in the faint light of the candles. The telepath stood silently beside him, her expression still wide with fear and uncertainty.

"I'm so sorry, but we have some business we need to finish tonight." Sea's tone was strained and secretive. "Please make yourself as at home as you can. There are clean clothes in the bedroom closet. Take what you will. We will return as quickly as possible."

I held his unblinking gaze for a long moment, my soul silently imploring him for answers I knew he would not give me. I closed my eyes and nodded my understanding.

He gently squeezed my upper arm. "We will speak when I return."

"I know." My voice was barely more than a graveled whisper, "I know..."

3

"Tynan?" A soft sigh of an angel, a chime of silver tones that surely no mortal ears could hear. The prickly fibers of the universe congealed beneath my back. They reached me through the thin layer of my shirt making my skin itch in places I couldn't reach. After rinsing the last of the grave stench from my body and dressing in a loose tunic-styled shirt and linen pants scavenged from his wardrobe, I had found my way to the living room of Sea's tiny apartment and collapsed on the horribly worn couch. Hesitantly, I opened my eyes for the second time.

I blinked, allowing my eyes to adjust to the dim, ethereal light that permeated the surfaces I struggled to distinguish. As my eyes relaxed into a comfortable aching focus, I stared up at the pebbly surface of a thickly painted ceiling. Doused in the gold and gray of a subtle ambient light, it appeared warm and somehow familiar, as if I were waking to a room that had once held the crowd of calm celebration. I inhaled a deep breath of air to anchor myself. The room smelt of old incense and dusty yellowed pages with a cool synthetic undertone. I couldn't help but remember my mortal friends in their dark little hideaways of tie-dyed curtains and tattered clothes, innocent souls who were now little more than white bones. The thought sent a sharp current of pain through my chest and into my stomach.

The adrenaline rush of elation I had experienced upon first stumbling into the new city had subsided, succumbing to reality's heavy hand. For the first time, I wanted to truly cry, to open my soul to the wind and rain and offer my sins up to whoever would listen. To pound the earth and shriek at the sky until the blood tears that stained my skin dried into a bitter acceptance, an acceptance that I had yet to find. I knew the torment was evident in my face; my brow throbbed from the deep furrow planted there by thought. I raised my hands to rub away the last condemning evidence of my torture. I was ashamed suddenly; I had no right to mourn what was lost.

I was the one who had run away.

I could feel Sea's presence very close to me, lingering on the edge of my sight, beside me, in the shadows. He was a paradox of emotions that fluttered chaotically, an ocean of lost moths. Concern, fear, anger, hope, denial. Sadness. He made no effort to contain the extremities of what he felt, letting them wash over me in raw untidy waves of heat and ice. Perhaps it was his way of accepting my return. Perhaps it was his way of getting even.

"Welcome back." His statement did not seem meant for my ears and I pretended not to hear. This was not how I had envisioned a reunion with my best friend.

"Where am I?" My voice was hoarse sandpaper sliding against the thick silence of the room. I made to lift myself from my vulnerable position in order to feel equal in the presence of my dark brother. The motion made my vision swim as if gravity threatened to enslave me forever to the sofa.

"Safe and *alive?*" The words slipped from his lips drenched in quiet, bitter wonderment. A statement. A question. An accusation, like a soldier confronting the one who had abandoned him on the battlefield.

I winced. "Sounds like you've heard better news before," I kept my voice flat and full of blue-black shadows. I could not meet his eyes. I knew he studied me as a sphinx might consider a lost traveler. Instead, I let my eyes interrogate my new surroundings.

Walls draped in darkly batiked sheets of material combined with the cloyingly burnt perfume of long extinguished incense to swath the chamber in a rich Bedouin decor. A small lamp sat to my right, on a sagging bookcase of dusty plywood and scarred cement blocks, but it was not turned on. Rather, a warm sensuous light wavered from a pair of thick white candles near it. The room was cramped, filled with much-loved furniture that whispered softly of a distant time past, coupled with the harsh reminders of a new era. In contrast, removed and alone in a far corner, sat what appeared to be two laptop computers on a rusted metal writing desk.

They were different from the ones I had remembered: very small, no bigger than a paperback book, no thicker than a stenographer's notepad. No cords or wires anchored them though they burned brightly in the dimness of the room. Sitting side by side, they were conspiring twins humming their high-pitched lament of ice, leeching the warmth from their corner of the room.

"I'll leave, if you wish." I spoke softly, sadly, already attached to this strange new place. But I could feel a wrenching tightness in my gut: I was unwelcome here.

Sea shook his head in disbelief. "You *abandoned* us." It was a whisper, nothing more.

Fire speared my soul. Sharp, hot blades of indignation shot through my heart. *How dare he judge me!* My fists clenched, sharp ivory nails piercing the soft flesh of my palms as I struggled not to strike him. My head snapped towards him. I couldn't speak. I wouldn't.

I met his eyes. His beauty was still as icy and piercing as the summer sun off an iceberg: alien, dazzling, and inhospitable. For a fleeting moment beneath the study of those peculiar eyes, I thought I might crumble and fall at his feet, begging his forgiveness. Stubborn pride would not let me. There was nothing to gain from it except weakness.

"I know what you're thinking, Tynan, I can see it in your eyes. You think that my accusations are selfish. Are they?" He let the question hover between us for a long, suffocating moment. "You were a leader, a mentor to lost fledglings cast out by a cruel and unforgiving society. You told them they were strong. You told them not to give into sorrow and the temptation of death. But it was just a lie, wasn't it? You turned your back on them and vanished!"

"*Vanished?* Just 'vanished' you say?" My body trembled as the memories of my resentment and anguish burst to the surface from the vault where I had imprisoned them. "The Elders had disowned me, or have you already forgotten? Do you forget so soon my battle with Adian and the other Elders who tried to murder me? Yes, I did a grave injustice to my followers by losing faith in my own philosophy, but it was only when my own teachers turned their backs on me that I decided to take a hiatus from this wretched world!"

I wanted to spit in his face, at his selective memory. I glared at him from beneath the matted curtain of my hair. "And you! You were nowhere to be found. The moment the fallout began it was you who *vanished*!"

Sea stared at me, his expression sad and distant. "No, Tynan, that is not at all how it happened. You gave up. You allowed them to push you away, but there was no Council verdict that declared your guilt. You decided that all on your own."

He shook his head wearily, a thin curtain of luminous white hair falling across his face. "We searched for you for so many years. I watched them make a holy migration to the shores of Scotland where you were born. Immortals of origins I never knew existed drawn together over the centuries. Complete strangers, some even enemies, and yet, all knew of you, all respected your teachings, your struggles. They had heard of your pain and thought you had given yourself up to the sun."

He sighed, folding his hands as if in prayer, pressing the tips of his long willowy fingers against his lips. I started to speak, but he continued unheeded, "They thought your death honorable and came to pay their respects to a kindred soul now freed. I can still see them, clinging to one another for solace, searching for some lingering element of hope that would convince them not to walk the same path. Your 'death' was a tragedy. It was legend."

"You lie..." I whispered, my jaw clenched till I thought my teeth would shatter. "Why would they mourn me, the one they hated so much?"

"Lie? Damn you, Tynan! I watched through my tears as they burnt your belongings and cast the ashes into the sea." Slowly, he turned to face me. His expression brimmed with an anger barely contained. "And now you simply show up, *alive*, from some *hiatus*, as you put it, and expect me not to question you? You expect me *not* to judge, but embrace you as I always have? Now you sit here and mock me like you're some fucking holy *messiah* resurrected. You mock me and the hundred years of mourning I have paid you!" He was shaking, an angel bitterly uncomposed.

I couldn't breathe; I felt numb and disoriented. A hundred years? My mouth fell open. I could find no breath for words. I had no idea of the events that had followed my "death." I thought my disappearance a blessing. The paranoia that had ravaged my mind began to creep back in whispering to me that I should not trust him and the words he hissed. Perhaps it was my own guilt that made me angrily deny the tale he wove.

For the first time, I noticed that the strange telepath from the marketplace sat curled within the embrace of a frayed velveteen armchair, deep amongst the shadows behind Sea. She cradled her legs protectively, pulling them up tight against her chest, beneath tense, thin arms. She looked more like a scared child than a young woman. I sought out her eyes, pleading for some sort of human understanding. Her eyes did nothing but widen with fear and silent accusations. There was no doubt she had been fed strange epic tales about me. I placed my face in my hands and sighed heavily.

Sea leaned in close until I could feel his breath on the side of my face. "What of those who loved you? Do you even care? Mortal and Immortal alike—they *loved* you." Sea was merciless. "Look at me, damn it!" He grabbed my upper arm and shook me hard.

I recoiled from his touch as if it were poison. "I am truly sorry if I caused such grief with my departure, but it was what they asked for. Yes, I admit that, I deserved to have my life taken from me for all of the pain and misery I wrought on my followers. I should not have fought Adian." Memories of the gruesome fight flashed before my mind's eye. "I should have let him kill me."

I could hear my own voice shaking with a weary anger. "Do you not think that my heart broke when I knew that the philosophy, the religion I built for our race was just another bunch of empty fairytales? Hundreds took their own lives because I turned a hypocrite!"

I paused shaking my head, my eyes squeezed shut. "But I did not want this. I did not want to be a martyr. I was not supposed to wake up…"

There was a long pause as my voice died away. Sea sighed, relenting for a moment. The anger that had boiled up was proving too exhausting to maintain. There was a strange tense moment in which I didn't know whether he would strike me or embrace me; his vice-like grip on my arm blocked out the world until it was only he and I. I held my breath and tried to fade into the sofa cushions. I was not strong enough yet to face such confrontation.

His grip began to loosen. I sensed the energy draining from his attack. "I am sorry...I just...I have been angry for so long. What happened, Tynan?" He touched my shoulder lightly, warily as if I were a caged animal. "I've been waiting a century for an explanation."

I pulled away slightly. My head reeled from the adrenalin coursing through my system. A stifling claustrophobia descended upon me, clawing at the walls of my mind. I hated the very fact that I had to explain myself so soon after awakening. Then again, what had I been expecting, a joyous celebration of my return?

"Why do I owe you anything? You did not testify to the Elders in my defense. You did not help me reconcile my shattered sanity. I was the one who wanted to die! I was the one they all turned their backs on and denied my existence. And now I must explain myself like a common thief? Now you sit and judge me with some pathetic scorned pride?" I sighed, very little venom left in my words.

Sea said nothing.

"You want an explanation? An explanation as to why I became disillusioned with my own philosophies, with the very religion I built to save our damned souls? How I could build such a religion that thousands could surrender themselves to, only to wake one night and realize that it was all a lie? How can I explain that to you?" I was shaking as I relived those years when the mists had begun to burn away from my ideals.

"What can I say? I loathed the human race for its cruelty and the idea of feeding off its vile essence sickened me. I loathed our race for its barbaric, selfish pride. I wanted to escape the monotonous violence I had witnessed for so many centuries, that I felt so painfully each and every time I fed. At the end, I was a sad, pitiful, desperate creature. I was very good at hiding it from the ones I loved, though, for I knew it would only appear as weakness, or worse, selfish madness to them. My teachings, my philosophies...I suppose they meant something at one time, something profound and built with pure intentions, but in the end they were hollow, meaningless...like me." I edged even further away from Sea till I hugged the far end of the couch. I stared blankly ahead at the darkened hallway. "I have a feeling that your memories of the past are much more glamorous than mine."

I cast an uneasy glance at Sea. He was watching me closely, his expression still vague and unreadable. And then the words began to pour from my lips. Sea sat unmoving as I retold the tale of that fateful night. I looked away, but I could still feel his gaze boring into the side of my skull. "The night I felt the last of my will fade, I had seen the world through a veil of red tears. I had been beyond reason when I returned in search of Phelan and burst through the doors of his mansion, drenched to bone from the raging storm outside..."

Phelan's image was forever seared into my mind's eye; his languid, perfect form, his emerald eyes and fierce red hair spilling over the shoulders of his royal purple garments like molten lava. Two thin braids separated from the rest of the mane fell regally to each side of his pale face like an ancient tribal king. He seemed an icon to be worshiped, something too pristine and exotic for this world. He seemed my last hope.

Before the hungry orange flames of the towering hearth of the Great Hall, I fell to my knees. My starved fingers tight around his wrists, I begged him to help me take my own life. I pleaded with him to kill me. I suppose, in my angry twisted heart, I figured he owed me that much.

He refused. Outraged beyond words, he shoved me away. "You know I cannot! You are my Darkling, of my own blood!" He hissed, and then as if regretting his violent tone, he whispered more gently, "Do not think that I do not sympathize. I would be an ignorant fool to preach otherwise. You must trust me, though, that this too shall pass. Go back to your meditations. The world will call on you when the time is right."

I would not listen. To me it was as if he stood upon a pedestal mocking me. My Maker *mocked* me! As he made to embrace me, reaching out with fingers, pale and cold as marble, I howled and struck out at him. Frustrated red tears streamed down my cheeks. The look on his face told me I had made a grave mistake. He turned away from me to stare into the fire. It was over, done, the last shred of respect and honor between us crushed unrecognizably into the earth.

I fled the ominous pressure of his austere wisdom, thinking to defeat my own cowardice once and for all. There were passages that ran far beneath the foundations of his modern castle. Phelan Daray and his followers built sacred tombs and corridors long ago when they first came to the New World, when the lands were still recklessly wild. There, I found the room in which Phelan continued mentoring fledglings in the magical arts and where he still kept his Book of Shadows: a volume of spells bridging the one thousand years of his existence. Deep within that man-made womb, lined with rows of forgotten crystal bottles, sanguine with black liquid and thick with the musty stench of mildew, I realized that there was no turning back.

From that moment on, the night was a frantic blur of fragmented sequence. I held his Book in my shaking hands, I cursed his name, and then I stood in the midst of a cemetery. Terrified and shaking, I could not remember how I had gotten there. My mind was no longer my own; my trembling limbs felt attached to invisible wires, pulled along by a will far stronger than my own. I had lost all grasp on my shredded sanity. Forcing myself within the protective structure of a neglected sepulture, I ran deep into the earth until I found a forgotten tomb that surely no mortal would ever dare to disturb. There, I cast the spell of Ageless Sleep upon myself.

"I suppose I never thought it would actually work...." My voice trailed off and I noticed for the first time that I had crumpled onto the couch like a small child. I felt lighter, as if the heavy hand that had held my heart had let go. Sea had moved to sit beside me. He stroked my hair softly as he listened. As the silence received the fragmented end of my tale, he sighed.

"I am not sure what to say...or whether to even believe all of those flowery words." He looked down at me. "You have much to amend for, but I suppose we have all made a few mistakes over the years." He held his words to my chest like a gun.

"Really?" Sarcasm seethed, razor sharp on the edge of my words. The tightness in my chest returned. "Amend, eh? How big of you to forgive me that easily." I sat up and ran my fingers through my hair. "You've waited a long time for this, haven't you? Agonized over what you would say to me?"

"Don't flatter yourself." He chuckled. My exasperation appeared to amuse him somehow. His smile, though warm, was strained; I knew his forgiveness was insincere. He was still struggling silently with some road-worn demon. "I'm going to ignore that in light of your weakened state. You can't possibly understand the full repercussions of your actions yet." He reached out and placed his hand lightly on my forearm as if instructing a child.

I slapped it away. "Don't." I suddenly felt alone in the world again and wanted to remain that way.

"Tynan...I...I was angry with you when you left. You took the easy way out and left me to pick up the pieces. I was furious when I saw you tonight." He paused. "But I can't deny the fact that I did miss you. And it is good to see you again, no matter how wrong I think your actions were. I don't know. It's just that, well, everything's changed...so very much has changed." He shook his head sadly.

"I can sense it." Invading fingers of chill molested my skin causing the fine hairs on the back of my neck to stand on end. I got up and moved to the open window to my left. I breathed deeply of the night air, crisp with the scent of rain. It was useless to argue with Sea about the legitimacy of my actions; I didn't know this person who sat accusing me, patronizing me. I didn't want to. The market lay like a gently humming stream of dirty gold below. The skeletal shell of the city stretched out and away from me, silent and foreboding. "It's almost as if something crude and violent has stripped away the soul of the city. It's mute, captive." I turned my back against the cool night air and leaned against the peeling paint of the windowsill.

"There is more truth in what you say than you may ever know." Sea stared blankly at a space somewhere between heaven and hell. "We need all the allies we can get these days." Statement or plea? It was hard to tell.

"Isn't that right, Alessandra?" Without looking at her, he asked the girl in the chair.

She did not answer.

The telepath still sat on her perch, a wan and watchful owl. I suddenly resented her presence; her attempts at invisibility intruded upon the intimacy of our painful reunion. I found myself wondering what their relationship was based upon. The air between them was tense and brooding on a deep and refined level I could not yet define. For a long while, the three of us sat in awkward silence, the telepath and I exchanging uneasy glares while Sea remained lost in the maze of his own private thoughts.

"You've picked a fine time to come back, I'll give you that much." The tone of his voice had changed. It was stronger, business-like.

Apprehension tightened within me. "What do you mean?"

"Well, I suppose I should bring you up to speed on the last one hundred years." He uttered a short, stifled laugh.

"Hundred years…" I repeated numbly.

"You were gone for quite a while," Sea snorted. He stared down at the floor, his features obscured by long sheets of white-blond hair.

"Ah, where to begin? It was the end of 2011. 'Everything's under control,' the government had cooed as if it were just another territorial war over oil rights or American hostages." He turned to look at me with a sad sort of fatigue in his eyes. "It never ceases to amaze me just how good politicians can be at making millions believe a barefaced lie."

I sat on the windowsill, leaning back against the chipped white frame. I watched him carefully. "What happened?"

He sighed loudly through his nose and looked away. "The world's foundations were crumbling at an ever-increasing speed. Man's greatest downfall was, and still is, its selfishness...that is, aside from its inherent ignorance. You know how it was before you left. The world was a political chessboard; its inhabitants mere collateral damage. Well, it only got worse.

"They called it 'Apocalypse 12.' I call it stupidity. I call it pain and suffering that could have been avoided if only the few in charge had listened to the wind, but, then again, perhaps not. Perhaps Fate had simply grown weary of making excuses for us? Who knows, but within a year things had gotten so out of hand that it was only a matter of a few lines of code before someone decided to take advantage of the situation.

"At first it appeared that nothing out of the ordinary had occurred; it took nearly twenty-four hours for the world's leaders to realize exactly what had happened. As they went to test their toys, their warheads, their bank accounts, they found them inaccessible. Databanks, satellite systems, you name it. Someone had cleverly rewritten the military codes for every nation in the world; someone had siphoned every drop of the world's monetary reserves into private pockets. Someone had slipped in and lifted the king's purse while he was sleeping. Everything, locked down tight and secure. That someone was an underground cyber-movement that dubbed themselves the Tyst."

"Tyst?" I rubbed my eyes as I thought. "What does that mean?"

He paused, watching me intently. "As far as I know, it is an old Swedish word for 'silent'." He leaned back into the sofa cushions. "From what I have heard, the group originated in the Netherlands and consisted of one or two primary units on each of the main continents. They have existed since the early 1950's, working in complete anonymity to establish a global network of various scientific and political geniuses with one universal goal in mind: worldwide restructuring of societal and governmental hierarchies. Ex-CIA and KGB intelligence, renegade scientists and informants from a wide array of fields allied with the Tyst Project seeing it as the only way to save humanity from annihilating itself. As technology evolved, integrated systems engineers, symbiotic biotechnologists, and nanotechnology experts were naturally introduced into the fold. The most brilliant and devious minds of the 20th and 21st centuries secretly united for a single cause. There are many theories as to how they completed their work. History is written by the ones in power and is rarely an exact account. Written and rewritten; you know how it works."

"And no one rose up? No one challenged this movement?" It seemed a little unrealistic that the world would just roll over and show its belly without a fight.

"Oh, no, no, no. There were wars. Brutal, bloodthirsty wars. There still are. It was by no means the smooth transition they had planned for. In fact, it ruptured the entire societal structure and, when the first wave of dust settled, the Tyst were the ones in control. They held the keys to the world's main sources of weapons and fuel, and enough money to buy whatever still remained." He shook his head as if in resignation.

"The Tyst were already deeply entrenched within every major country like a terminal cancer. Nations panicked, shutting their borders unsuccessfully. Civil wars erupted as people pointed the finger at each other in their desperate search for a neck to hang. The demons in our beds are the ones we always forget to watch, but this time the demons had no faces. That was the horrible beauty of the Tyst's plan; the isolation that resulted from the mass panic weakened everyone. The only problem with their plan was that, as with all utopian dreams of erecting the perfect societal system, they did not take into account just how bitterly humanity would retaliate. Soon enough, it was as if their original intentions had vanished, yet they were not about to surrender and retreat for it would have meant certain death for the entire Tyst Project and its followers."

"The next twenty years were hellish anarchy." Sea paused for a moment to gauge my reaction. I had none. It seemed my predictions had come true after all. "The Tyst were in control. They moved in, confiscating the remaining power and food sources while cleaning up the loose ends of any vein of technology that might have given the rebel forces an edge. They outlawed the most basic computer systems to the common masses. Again, isolation techniques to break the will of the people. However, behind the walls of their fortresses, they implemented the beginnings of what is now known as the Chronous matrix, an intelligent, organic computer program capable of instantaneous and random evolution. It is what lies at the core of the Tyst regime, what gives them their true power and it controls absolutely every aspect of their world."

Something shifted uncomfortably within my soul. I turned away from my study of the market below, my eyes settling on the two computers glowing in the corner of the room. Sea's story sounded too rehearsed, too perfect in its timing. I wanted to question him on his acquisition of the machines, but held my tongue.

Sea was lost in his diatribe and continued his tale oblivious to my mounting suspicion. "With the Chronous securely in place, the world began to change in an even more drastic way. The Tyst's numbers were growing steadily, day by day, as people swore their allegiance out of fear. They had seen the very foundation of their existence shattered and realized that they were, for the most part, completely incapable of fending for themselves. If you wanted to stay alive and feed your family, you kept quiet and did as you were told. Starvation quickly wore down the resistance of many, especially those trapped in the suburban sprawl. A chasm formed in the fabric of society, a deep rift between those who sought a path back to their old way of life and those who had forsaken all links to the past. Those who rebelled retreated from the city in search of older, more powerful ways of seeking their revenge. They are called the Phuree."

"The Phuree, where are they now?" I kept my eyes on the crowds of the market far below my window perch. I had the sudden strange feeling of being watched very closely. I shifted uncomfortably. The aged springs of the couch whined pitifully as Sea lifted himself up. He stretched his arms up and over his head, arching his back.

"Nowhere near here, if they are wise," he chuckled. I didn't like the laugh. It was the laugh of a conspirator.

"And why is that?"

"Because they will be shot on sight, or worse, if discovered. You see, there is no First Amendment, no Bill of Rights, and no Constitution, in this country or any other for that matter. Only the Declaration of Global Restructuring as enacted by the Tyst Empire. The Phuree do not recognize the DGR and the punishment for that is death." He paused for a moment, folding his arms over his chest. Reaching up with his right hand he rubbed his chin in thought, his gaze far away in reflection.

With a small sigh he looked up at me. "They could have blended in, gotten inside the system and probably, with time, broken it. But they chose to be loud and brash and violent in the early years. They have modified their approach since then, but today's generation still pays dearly for the actions of those early leaders."

"If not in the cities, then where do they live? It seems the Tyst could ferret them out if they really wanted to. That is, if the Tyst are as powerful as you say they are." I raised a skeptical eyebrow.

"The Phuree are nomadic and tend to roam the more remote areas of the earth, places where it becomes treacherous and laborious for the Tyst forces to track them. However, I have heard rumors lately that, as their powers grow, and their abilities to cloak their locations from the omnipresent eye of the Chronous intensify, they are becoming bolder, moving closer to more hospitable environments. They have become a formidable force, feared and hated for what they represent." Sea stared out the window at a point far beyond the city that lay outside.

"And what would that be?" I asked.

Sea's gaze snapped back to meet mine. "The annihilation of the last shred of modern life. The Phuree mean an end to everything the Industrial Revolution created, or at least, that was the main objective of the original uprising. They are a symbol for the complete destruction of the last remnants of the old civilization, a leveling of society and a return to a much more ancient mystical culture. You see, as people began to try to rebuild their lives after the initial strike by the Tyst, they found new walls within which to build them. Those who still craved the luxuries technology offered clustered around the fortifications the Tyst built within the capital cities of the world. They were like June bugs competing for a light that they thought held warmth and life. That is where we are now." He gestured to the small apartment in which we sat, "What you see here is a luxury even within the *amagins*, the capital cities."

"Ah...I see. People would consider this a luxury now? How sad." I cringed at the idea of how far removed the world was from the one I had left. To me, it did not seem that the Phuree's alternative was so terrible, but I was not part of the mortal realm. It was not my place to judge humanity's desperate coveting of the past.

"And outside the amagins?" I inquired, returning my attention to scrutinize the bustling tent-lined street. My body ached as I watched the river of mortals below. I felt myself leaning too far out the open window and caught the edge of the windowpane above my head.

"Beyond the amagins is a world the likes of which you and I have not seen in centuries." Sea's voice was full of wonder tinged with a far more dark and treacherous element.

His tone snared my attention again, forcing me to focus. Slowly, I tore my gaze away from the street and turned back to face him.

"Over the past hundred years or so the Phuree have entrenched themselves deep within roots of a power so ancient that neither you nor I can remember its origins. Technology, as they see it, brought all of this upon us. Though their tribes must still utilize certain aspects in order to combat the advanced weapons developed over the years by the Tyst, the Phuree leaders, for the most part, have turned their backs upon it, forsaking such means in exchange for an elemental power strong enough to bring down their enemies once and for all. As I mentioned, they are extremely adept at obscuring their locations with powerful spells. Even the most sophisticated scanning system will, more often than not, overlook a group of Phuree. That is what makes them a true threat."

Sea could see my skepticism and reprimanded me softly

53

with a wave of a long willowy finger. "The Phuree might as well be up against gods, but, trust me, never underestimate them. They have their ways... *powerful ways.*" He did not elaborate.

His words left me tense with curiosity. I shook my head. "No, I do not doubt that. For some reason, I always knew that a war like this would come to pass one day. Yet, I am still stunned it has waged on for so long."

He shrugged slightly. "As with most wars, it is not so simple as one side versus the other." His brow knitted as the weight of thought slowly pushed him to lean against the arm of the telepath's chair. "Besides, some wars have festered for millennia. Many of those ancient wars are still very much alive despite this new regime."

I watched him for a long, silent moment. I could not gauge him, not as I used to. His emotion, his conviction, seemed to ebb and flow as the tide. "And where do you stand, Sea?"

There was a long moment of silence. His eyes met mine; they were cloudy, mysterious. He looked away and sighed. "Somewhere in between, as I always have been." He waved his reply away in a blur of sinewy white.

My head buzzed with a thousand questions I knew could only be answered with time. I stared out of the open window once again, my ragged fingernails digging deep into the chipped white paint of the rotten wooden windowsill.

Something wasn't right but I couldn't put my finger on it. "And those?" I gestured towards the computers humming their hollow melody in time with one another. "I thought you said the Tyst outlawed technology to the common masses?"

"True." Sea never wavered, "It is illegal except to a choice few who receive papers signed by the Tyst Dictator, Lord Cardone III, himself."

"And you have such papers?" My head snapped back towards him.

"Have we vampires ever asked for anything from a mortal?" Sea smirked. It was a game to him, just as life had always been.

I frowned, disconcerted, and looked away. "What is the

year now?" I wondered aloud, not entirely sure I wanted an answer.

"2111." His voice suddenly seemed a little more clever, a little more cautious, as if the wheels that creaked inside caused his words to reverberate ever so subtly. "Like I said, you picked a fine time to come back. A fine, *fine* time."

There was something simply too sweet in his words, something too melodic to be sincere and I found myself wondering what Byzantine plans lurked just beneath his smile.

He crossed the room and placed a cool, amiable arm around my shoulders. There was an uncertain tension there, tugging him up and away and beyond my peculiar situation. What beautiful, deadly vine had wrapped itself about me, icy fingers like devious roots sending tendrils of bitter confusion through my shaky senses? I wasn't sure if I should struggle. I wanted to trust what he said. It was all that I had to go by in this new world I had been thrust into.

Sea was my oldest friend. Even though, at the end, he had turned his back on me with the rest, he had still been with me since the very early years of my Immortal life. I tried to convince myself that I should be grateful that he had not simply walked away from me, leaving me to fend for myself. Fear silenced my tongue, fear and suspicion. However, it was not the kind of fear that ravages us when we are convinced we shall fade to nothing if left alone, or the treacherous belief in the *inherent* goodness of the soul. It was more an overwhelming aversion to drowning in the putrid air of this insidious new era that forced me to trust him. Whether I liked it or not, I needed his experiences as my roadmap.

A hollow knock at the front door severed the silence.

The telepath, whom I had all but forgotten about, suddenly jumped from her chair. "Jasmine." She breathed, as if relieved, and ran down the dark hallway.

Sea moved away from me, taking a step into the room, as the sound of the door opening and closing and then soft voices drifted through the shadows. I remained perched warily on the windowsill, a strangled voice within me begging me to leave. The cool night air slipped in beneath the ill-fitting clothes I had borrowed from Sea's closets, causing the fine hairs upon my neck and arms to bristle. I watched, warily, as the telepath emerged once again, holding the hand of another woman. She appeared slightly older than the telepath with long strawberry blond hair shot through with deep brown and gold that reminded me of falling autumn leaves. Dressed in a long sleeved tunic of soft brown, belted at the waist with a length of colorful braided hemp cord over a long skirt of patchwork silk, her supple strong body seemed to whisper as she walked with the movement of the fabric. She paused as she entered the room, her deep brown eyes widening with curiosity as they rested on me.

Sea held out his hand towards the woman. "Tynan, I would like you to meet Jasmine. She is a dear friend of the Immortals and someone you may always trust."

I said nothing, but held Jasmine's gaze. The deep musk of her scent, salt, amber and clay, caused my chest to tighten terribly and my jaw to ache as I found myself wondering how she might feel in my arms as I drank from her. The Thirst was becoming harder to control.

As if sensing my need, Sea moved to stand beside Jasmine almost protectively, eyes narrowing as he watched me. "Alessandra and I have asked her to help you."

"Help me?" My breathing became shallow as I tried to pry my eyes away from Jasmine's.

"She knows of a place you may stay tonight, a vacant loft unit that is secure until you are able to find other accommodations. She is also wise of the places safe for our kind to feed."

I tore my gaze away suddenly, fixing my stare upon Sea. I frowned, suddenly angry at his attempt to dispose of me. I felt as if I were being treated like a leper. "Why are you asking this of her?"

"I am sorry Tynan. The night is nearly over and there are still pressing matters which I must tend to before sunrise. It is too dangerous for you to roam alone when you are so new to the city and, I'm afraid, you simply can't stay here." His jaw tensed as his words hovered in the air between us.

I shook my head, laughing bitterly beneath my breath. "Some things never change." I whispered, more to myself than to my audience.

"I'm sorry old friend." Sea said coldly.

"Yes. So am I." I said.

4

One year later...

I felt the dust gathering on my features as the east-born wind made its twilight entrance upon the city. Tiny particles of daily lives ground into the residue of history. I felt empty and undefined, strutting a perilously thin line between heaven and hell. The smell, the acidity of progress and the sweetness of decay filled my nose: elements of existence I had somehow escaped. Thick rich clouds of gray had begun to roll in all but obliterating the night sky. The soft distant rumble of thunder curdled space and time. It was all I could do to breathe.

Sometimes you want to be taken down, down deep and dragged to the bottom to have all the breath shaken out of you. You close your eyes and wait for the pressure of unfamiliar hands that never comes, and imagine the silence that must be what heaven is conceived in. The scars fade away in a sad haze like a gentle breeze while you try to sigh your life away. The musty incense of ancient altars, the musk of lost virginity, the ache of long forgotten wounds; these impressions flood your senses, overwhelming your soul and further engraving the truth that you will never know who you are, for you are everything. You sink further into the place where you exist, a place where no one can reach you. Or, so I had hoped.

I waited for that final gust of smoky wind that would carry me home to infinity, a nameless, faceless flagstone of human facade and immortal bones, huddled and numb beneath the yellow-orange glow of the street lamp.

It never came.

Instead, she found me on a street corner. The sweet chime of small silver bells snatched me back, anchored me down, with a fresh cool reality above a night grown stale and sticky with too many attempts at fame. It brought tears to my eyes. Crashing back into myself from wherever it was that I drifted, the sights and sounds of the city began to tumble down upon me again, circling me like hungry wolves.

I remained perched upon the curb for a long while, knees drawn up to my chest with my arms wrapped about them, marveling at just how invisible you can become. When you simply stop vying for other people's attention you become little more than a molecule; a floating, invisible element embedded within the infinite structure of the universe. You drift forever on end till something painful brings you back to the conscious collective insecurities of the individual. It sounds pompous and predictable, but it's true. We are nothing without our insecurities.

I scanned the crowded street for my would-be angel. Sifting through sweat-streaked limbs, thick as the undergrowth of some dense dark rain forest, I searched with opened senses for evidence that the bells were real. I began to doubt myself after a while, and to begin my retreat back into the effortless dark place of dreams I had been awakened from, when I heard the chiming again. Before my thoughts could solidify into reason, I felt my breath shorten, my heart beginning to race within my chest as I stood and searched for the sound.

Her image was distant and distorted. I felt she could be no more than a block away, for the sound of the bells wrapped around the conversations of the people who crowded the short strip of street. I closed my eyes, feeling the brush of arms and thighs against my back as I stood on the edge of the sidewalk. She emerged from the smoky confines of a small bar and stood leaning against the elaborately painted wall of the establishment's exterior. The deep rhythm of some dark and decadent melody followed her, seeming to trail lazily about her, reluctant to let her leave. Behind my eyelids her image sparkled, her essence purifying the stale auras of the vendors and buildings and jaded amagin dwellers.

Mesmerized, I closed the distance between us in a matter of seconds. Only the most perceptive would have noticed the wind I disturbed with my movements.

Five. Four. Three. Two. One. *Contact.*

I brushed the side of her face with the back of my fingers. Time stopped as the arc of electricity flew between Immortal and mortal flesh. She gasped as she felt the intense power of an unexplainably ancient presence. My hand dropped to my side as her eyes found mine, my body mere inches away from hers. She was archaic in her beauty; a new-aged Egyptian goddess in thrift-store rags. Long black-brown hair woven in places with beads and trinkets and colorful thread, lips lush and dark and eyes a brilliant hazel lined in black that held a frightened wonderment as they widened and watched me.

When mortality encounters its opposite the reaction is often as sudden and violent as a flash of lightning. The souls sense the intense chasm separating them and long to jump towards each other. It is whole and animalistic and irresistible; a drug to experience, to be the other. Immortality desires the oblivion that death can bring; mortality craves eternity.

We always want what we can't have.

There was a resistance within her that made me want to pull her against me. A stubborn soul, a fierce spirit; it made me smile. I found myself leaning in even closer till my lips brushed hers. Her flesh was so warm, blood racing through thin young layers of tissue in the frantic effort to stay alive. She recoiled slightly, teasingly, stepping back lightly. And I heard again, the soft metallic chiming. I glanced down at her ankle where tiny silver bells lay strung around the slender limb. I thought I would unravel at her feet. Her scent was rich and musky like that of freshly turned earth, the sweet perfume of the youthful decay, the living world where sunlight and bittersweet dreams remained.

It overwhelmed me and I found myself reaching for her hand. Slipping my long snowy fingers into her warm salty palm. She flinched slightly at the unexpected cool of my flesh upon hers. She was an open book to me, the pages, smudged and smeared by time's tyrannical forces, speaking to me silently with the broken tongue of her purer essence. The realization that I was made from a different mold and blood filled her with excitement and confusion. I felt her tense beneath my light touch, but made no move to leave; the unspoken pact between us had been sealed.

The white noise of the street surrounded us with a strong brutal embrace: the pungent sting of cigarette smoke and spilt drink, the raucous cawing of the intoxicated swirled about us mixing with the angst-riddled wail of music. I held on to her and moved through the crowds. Dodging flailing arms and sweat-stained gestures of immediacy, I led her down a darkly lit side street and collapsed against the cool dank stone of a building, pulling her against me like an insecure lover.

"Where are you going?" In the shadows, far away from the orange glow of the street lamp her voice was barely more than a strangled whisper.

"Have you ever seen the river at night?" I stroked her hair as if consoling a small child.

"Only from far away." She fell silent once again.

We passed the bones of abandoned warehouses and bomb shelters, the skeletal remains of docks and gates desecrated with fresh hieroglyphic stripes of red and black paint. Broken glass and derelicts were all that remained of history, of vulcanized urban America. Decadently rusted iron rails that once bore the weight of old freight trains now sunk into the smooth gray concrete that threatened to consume them. We stepped delicately over them.

All great civilizations fall. Not all are committed to memory.

The temperament of the city began to change again. Newly constructed dwellings rose amidst the ruins, monoliths reaching for the inky heavens with concrete spires and mute iron against a backdrop of rotten wood and rusted wire. The night had become almost silent. Thick as Tennessee molasses, shadows dripped from every bend and crevice. An oily sticky substance, the darkness drowned out the voices of the masses. I could feel them, hidden away within their uniform Tyst-customized cells of sanctuary. I could smell their stale scent; I tasted their bitter essence and wanted them all.

Until death do we part, amen.

We approached the snaking black river, making our way down the grassy incline, slick with the evening mist off the deep water, to the gravel path below. The scent of the river was thick and sweet with silt and decaying plant life. The soft crunch of the tiny shards of stone beneath our feet melded with the chorus of the water's movements; an ancient opera whose author had now been forgotten by strangers such as us. The waves lapped rhythmically against the muddy shoreline and thick reeds. Neither of us spoke.

We walked further and further away from the golden promises of the oil lamps that hovered in their posts along the expanse of the bridge and into a sleeping black landscape. The last vestiges of summer four-o-clocks and night jasmine had begun to find their way along the bases of trees and the monolith structures of broken concrete that now lay hidden amongst the weeds and vines. The flowers' cloyingly sweet fragrance enveloped my heightened senses with their precocious innocence. Crickets and tree frogs hummed over the delicate music of the waves and the chime of those beautiful bells.

With a delicate pressure, I guided her down to the river's edge, to a place where the water and reeds gave way to soft dry sand. I let her fingers slip from mine as I removed my long black coat, spreading it on the ground in a great swirl of passing shadow. I knelt down before her lifting my hands in silence for her to hold. The last of her resistance buckled. I could hear the rushing thud of her heart against her chest even as she laid her palms against mine and let her knees slowly bend to meet me face to face.

Her golden brown skin was now a soft olive in the heavenly illumination, her deep hazel eyes almost black. I gazed deep into her eyes, nearly losing myself in the raw emotion I saw there, and opened my heart to her soul. I let the need and awareness of her that filled me echo into her. A small sharp gasp escaped her lips as a bitter understanding blossomed from the embers of desire I had planted in her heart and mind, without her consent.

Without losing her gaze, my fingers glided slowly over and up her arms, knowing the tingling electricity such a gesture could create. My fingers glanced over the flesh of her shoulders and to the delicate nape of her neck. Her eyelids fluttered softly and she moved closer to me, her body warm beneath the fabric. She pressed against me, wrapping her slender arms around my cold hard chest. Her face nuzzled my neck seductively, the crisp cool of the golden rings in her ears brushing my skin. I felt my eyes closing. I wanted to consume all her warmth and human needs.

I pressed my cheek against hers and whispered into the fragrant waves of her hair. "No fear..."

Nothing, no thoughts or dreams, no words, passed within me. All that I was now lay in the salt of the skin that I held: the perfumes of lilac and patchouli, smoke and blood, silk and satin. I felt my teeth sink into the soft flesh just below her jaw. Blood flooded my mouth, pungent and coppery sweet.

Flickers and flashes of her life shattered like a broken mirror across my soul, a confused patchwork of human experience that seemed fused together randomly with strings of what appeared to be Chronous architecture code. The dazzling flood of imagery assaulted me from every dimension, ebbing and flowing, at one with the tide of the river beside us, moving too quickly for my intellect to grasp and decipher. I let go completely, gathering her close to drink deeply. I felt her tense in cold my embrace, her nails biting deep between my shoulder blades.

Gradually, the strength faded from her grip. She became weaker and weaker, her hands slowly sliding down to my waist without the strength to lift them. Her fingers brushed the sides of my thighs as they drifted to the ground. Slowly, I pulled away from the wound torn in her neck and breathed. Her scent was no longer a force of nature; I had taken it into me along with the rest of her essence. For a long moment, I held her against me like a broken doll, her head resting against my chest with a heavy weight that brought tears to my eyes. Laying her down upon soft lining of my coat, I studied her features.

I stretched out beside her and placed her hand over my heart. The sky swam with stars that had escaped the illumination of the amagin's glow. I wanted to let go of the ruin around me and drift, but the energy of her blood burned inside my veins and anchored me to gritty reality with a frantic will of its own. I felt the residual warmth that clung to her skin begin to leave with the wind that caressed us.

I sank deep within my own thoughts. Tonight, I rested beside an angel slain by my own hands, just as I had countless times throughout the centuries. After all that time I was no better cured of my own sickness than before. What was there left for me to covet other than my own curse, a curse grown heavy and saturated by too many alien dreams?

It seemed I closed my eyes and dawn began to seep in. Slowly, achingly, I rose to bid farewell to my sleeping beauty. I lifted her with me, cradling her in my arms with pure and gentle respect. As if setting a lit luminaria upon the water's surface I laid her silently in the water on her back. She drifted for a while, suspended by the water, further and further out, and then, with an eerie grace, she gradually sank below the rippling mirror of the surface. I stood there staring at the spot where she had vanished, watching the water dance as if she had never disturbed its journey.

I breathed deeply the heavy scent of decaying foliage and river water, gazing back up the path at the city. The sky began to grow rich cobalt streaked with dark gray clouds.

I made my way home.

* * *

I awoke the following evening in the spartan confines of my apartment. Face down in the soft dark folds of my ragged, black couch, I realized I had made it only so far into the room before the Sleep conquered me. My brethren called me a fool to be so careless with my resting-place. I suppose, after years of hiding in dark, forbidden places, far from the warmth and security offered by mortal shelters, I had simply ceased to care. With such age comes the understanding that there is nothing you can do to avoid your moment of departure from this world, and to fear it is an utter waste of time. I would have rather spent a night in the comfort of a true home, than a century more in some dank crypt deep within the earth. If that made me soft, so be it. The young ones would understand one day.

Something soft and damp nudged the palm of my left hand as it lay on the cold concrete floor beneath me. I made to lift my arm, slowly feeling sensation return to it in a flood of metallic fire. Still face down on the moldy torn sofa cushions, my hand sought out the warm black fur. Without opening my eyes, I ran my fingers through the thick mane of the cat.

Lifting myself up a little, I peered over the edge of the cushion at the two golden eyes that gazed up at me expectantly. "Hello, Dune."

I gathered my strength and hoisted myself into an upright position. Dune took my place without hesitation, seeking out the warm indention on the couch where I had lain. His luminous golden eyes questioned me as he greeted me with a soft rolling chirp. Butting my elbow with the crown of his head, Dune directed my attention towards him. Soon he would become restless, as I did each evening, and desire to venture out for his own hunt. Creatures of habit, both, were we. Night in and night out, through our paces we crept with the common understanding that we would always follow through with our part of the deal. We were predators in our distinct reprehensible natures, though neither hunted the other. This mutual agreement was without judgment or the preoccupations of morals or standards. I never questioned his requests and in turn he never questioned the hours I kept.

My first year in the amagin had been a harsh, fast indoctrination not only of the new global political hierarchy with all of its cruel Machiavellian laws, but also the splintered subcultures that ran like a silent, invisible grid just beyond the peripheral vision of the Tyst. Humanity existed almost entirely beneath an impenetrable layer of suspicious survivalist segmentation. Though the fear of the Tyst and the Chronous still held a vicious grip on the masses, people had come to realize that it was impossible to be absolutely dependent on the government for everything they needed to survive in such a hostile world. They would die one way or another: slowly broken and starved or instantaneously before a firing squad. They worked together in an intricate network coined the "market", which was designed to safe house the true development of the amagin's societal face from infiltration by Tyst spies. During the daylight hours, this grid of interconnecting affiliated groups all but vanished, its activities completely untraceable as the city carried on in the proper mindless contentment desired by the Tyst elite. On the surface they milled about like complacent sheep, an elaborate play to fool the Tyst into looking the other way. However, each individual, no matter what their age or placement in society might be, was intricately involved in one deviant cell or another, whether it was smuggling, selling or stealing. Anything could be purchased for the right price.

The silent Market relied heavily on the willing pacification of the individuals who bent without resistance to the Tyst's persecution in order to maintain their anonymity. At night, however, the Market reactivated and the development and sale of both information and technology flowed freely amongst the affiliated groups. As I wandered the streets, listening to the faint whispers and rumblings with my vampire ears, pulling vaults of images and distilled knowledge from my victims' minds, my curiosity of this underground network overwhelmed me. No matter how diplomatic I was, I had only begun to crack the surface. Foreigners were not welcome, not unless they came bearing rare and extraordinary gifts of data wealth, which I had yet to acquire.

Except for cold glow of the computer screen in the far corner of the room, the apartment was still dark. It ran on the same solar-powered generator that electrified the rest of the complex. A working machine was a rare find in those days, as the ability to manufacture such a toy had been securely imprisoned by the Tyst. I had managed to purchase several items, however, from a soft-pirate whose reckless desire for money often preceded his desire for secrecy. The equipment had needed severe work, but after a week of long nights repairing the hardware and patching the system, I was able to stabilize it enough to begin my personal exploration of the computer matrices that mutated and thrived outside of the Chronous mainframe.

Since the invention of computers, I had always held a love-hate fascination with them. Though my rapidly evolving intellect accepted the progression of human innovation, there had always lingered the ancient superstition of my people that cursed such creations as evil. The dichotomy enthralled me.

Throughout the decades of the late 20th and early 21st centuries, I had spent hours in front of them, studying strings of code that rolled across the screen, testing the limitations of their system matrices; worshipping the power of raw electricity mutated and forced into the confines of a tiny titanium shell lighter than a human head. The accumulation of thousands of years of human thought tucked neatly away and bought with a few worthless sheets of paper. I could push buttons in silence to speak to someone without ever uttering a word or seeing their face, and all in a split second. I could steal billions and destroy lives at the speed of light. But computers had quickly lost their ability to seduce me, just as everything had eventually.

However, a century had created a vast new advance from the toys I had conquered and thus, my fascination had been quickened once again. The pirated hardware and crafted program hacks that leaked out through the black market was of an architecture and method quite different from the ones used in the 21st century. Technology was religion now and for those who revered it, there was no other air which they could breathe. The level of code surpassed that of even the most ambitious programmers of the 20th and 21st centuries; layer upon layer of numbers interlocking, swimming, breeding, it would seem, in a space that only they knew how to access.

The geniuses who did not submit to the Tyst were pariahs, wanted dead because of their skill and their understanding of the matrices they had created. In the previous century, I had been known as a bit of a hacker myself amongst the Immortals. However, even with my supernatural speed for learning, it took me nearly a year to grasp the true scope of the evolution, but soon it was as natural as breathing to me. Even then, it was a breath without sustenance. We had eliminated the human factor and become, instead, misanthropes.

I rubbed my face and sighed. I had left the florescent wall light on in the kitchen, a cold and alien landscape of metal and dark gray concrete. The refrigerator, salvaged from god knows where, sat silent and broken near the far wall. Except for this amenity there was little else to show that anyone actually lived here. The cupboards were bare of all human sustenance; the counters clean of mortal clutter. I had no need of these things. I allowed my mind to wander through the mists of the previous evening as my fingers caressed the fine black fur on the back of Dune's neck. At one point, there may have been a justice to my kills, a meaning attached to a greater purpose. Time had embittered me, though, causing them to appear pointlessly cruel and wicked. The essence of whom I had once been as a mortal had been mangled by pain and suffering and immortal coil.

My victim's blood had quieted the Thirst in me for the time being. As the years passed, the need to feed on a nightly basis lessened. I could go nights without sustenance now. However, when the Thirst came, it was unreal and left me feeling strange and disconnected the next night. There was something else as well, a longing for something I had yet to acknowledge, a trace of unexplainable residual yearning as if I had lost something dear to me. I felt, in fact, quite empty. I dismissed the feelings. Better to blame it on the dreams I could not remember.

I lifted myself from the couch and walked through the living room. I passed an ancient broadcast radio upon a low aluminum table nestled amongst piles of ancient books, their paper covers all but unreadable, Ethernet cables, copper wires, circuit boards, and other illegal items. I reached out and flicked the radio on. The anonymous, pirate broadcasts detailed much the same as ever: Death. Demons. Destruction. There was only one domestic station that existed legally and it was owned and controlled solely by the Tyst Empire. In essence, it reflected the overall state of the war-torn society decomposed and reconstructed beneath the guttural reinforcements of Tyst propaganda.

I sighed and pulled a worn fabric pouch of tobacco and thin parchment papers from the inside pocket of my coat. *So unbelievably sad,* I thought as I rolled a cigarette. I lit the end and let it hang lazily from the corner of my mouth. I switched the channel to an overseas signal, not sure why I thought I might find anything any more uplifting in the world news than in the domestic. I stood there in front of the little black box, hands in the pockets of my faded black pants, silently waiting to be amazed. A man's voice crackled through the fizz of static in Greek. I listened carefully, quickly recalling the language as I picked through the words that made it over the airwaves. A civil war that had erupted in what had once been the Corinth canal still raged on.

There was a sickening, frenzied desperation in the man's voice as if his hope was hanging by a single thread stretched dangerously thin, as he pleaded hysterically with a blind alien audience, begging those that listened to rise up and find the spirit of justice and compassion they had forgotten. I listened for a moment until the man's voice began to weaken, growing heavy with a realization that his efforts were futile. I switched off the radio, feeling my stomach begin to sour.

The world was overgrown with biases and prejudices bred from generations of war-induced fear. Truth had always been a tenuously justified definition in "civilized" politics, but now it had completely lost its meaning. The Tyst had outposts in every continent, in every country that had ever been established. Borders meant little to one great empire; what little tangible, visible method there had been to governmental diplomacy in previous centuries had been completely leveled and eliminated. It used to be that wars were raged between nations, not simply a global slaughter of one empowered group against the ragged remnants of a rebellion. Trapped within the same old sickly skin of bitterness and rage, we now fought to exterminate the child we helped deliver into existence.

I pulled long and hard on the smoke from the cigarette. The heat burned in my chest, the nicotine coursing through my veins and numbing me almost imperceptibly, but nothing swayed. Nothing dimmed. Nothing ever did.

I strolled over to the computer. I noticed a strange string of code flashing in the upper left-hand corner of the screen. Instantly, I recognized the pattern as an anonymous salutation. I evaluated the pattern for a moment for any unusual encryptions that might signify a Chronous spider. When I was content that I could register nothing sinister in the code, I returned the greeting with a curt "nod" of neutrality. I took another long drag from the cigarette, letting the smoke escape lazily from my nostrils like a tired old dragon, as the computer worked to peel away the encryption of the full message.

The letter pulled up onto the screen. It was from Phelan. I was stunned. In the year since my awakening he had not once acknowledged my return, much to both my surprise and relief. I fell into the chair next to me as if I had been shot. A cool draft of dread crept up my spine, its icy fingers winding serpentine around my insides. In my mind, I saw a gothic visage of brilliant amber hair and emerald eyes, an ancient messenger of death and destruction; a self-proclaimed defender of the weak and damned in flowing black velvet and ivory silk.

I forced my attention back to the neatly typed message. I felt numb as if I could accept it only from a place deep within me where nothing could possibly disturb me.

Tynan,
The time has come again for the Council to reconvene. Your presence is requested in the discussion of important matters. I trust you will join us.

Phelan

The vagueness of the message irritated me. I felt ill. Not terrified, as I had anticipated. Dread sent my stomach writhing as if filled with poisonous serpents, while the muscles in my neck stiffened painfully. Why did he suddenly believe that I would obey his summons without question? I was no beaten yard dog desperate for shelter, no shattered visionary bowing at his knee for absolution and redemption. I was not the same vampire that had slunk away from the judgment of my brethren to sleep away my life. There was not an ounce of my blood that I now felt belonged to Phelan.

Yet, something deep within me cringed and slunk back to the locked sanctuary of denial I still kept secreted within my soul. Council gatherings were always an omen of great tragedy to come. Only when our race was threatened on an unfathomable scale, did Phelan reach out to the Immortals to bring us together. I leaned back in my chair and stared up at the fine cracks in the concrete ceiling. Dune leapt into my lap.

He could sense my tension, my fear. I felt as if I was being sucked back into the black hole of Phelan's universe. In all honesty, I had done everything but join the Phuree to escape the judgment I knew was to come. I had never been one to take criticism very well and I did not relish the icy reception I was certain to receive from my peers. That was, if they deigned to acknowledge my presence at all.

At least I had one more evening before I was to be subject to the rules of the new apocalypse, whatever they were.

* * *

Rain. Soft drops of acidic liquid falling upon the dreams of the unsuspecting, touching things with a sensual grace as they vied for resting places upon the concrete substance of the tangible. The rain was a fine perspiration on the brow of the world. It spoke to itself in a whisper like the shredding of antique blue silk. Above the hiss of wind over asphalt grown deathly in the wake of the sky's pain, above the grumblings of the discontent wanderer who had forgotten how to see beauty, above the restless beat of my own heart.

I had shut down the computer, unplugging it from the generator, and now stood in the stark, cold bathroom. For the longest time I stared at my reflection in the large mirror above the sink. I saw a wraith in dusty rags hovering in the simple darkness of a realm I knew nothing of, a realm of truth, pure and painful.

In the strange ambient light that seeped down the hall from the kitchen, the image had startled me as I blundered into the room in search of a distraction to my internal misery. I appeared so cold and weary, so pale and worn. For a moment, I lost the will to breathe. The rich dark blond hair that fell to just below my chin was matted chaotically, the hazel eyes that stared back at me were wide and haunted, lined with dark brown lashes that curled as if from weeping. If there had ever remained a trace of color in the high cheekbones, it had vanished centuries ago.

I still wore the clothes of the night before; the long sleeved white shirt, the ragged black trench coat, the heavy black boots now caked with sand and mud as evidence of my crimes. I stood there unable to speak, unable to move. Entranced by my own miserable state, I felt myself sinking. I leaned against the cold hard marble of the counter, questioning suddenly the new strength and conviction I had thought were growing in me since my reawakening. Though it was still an unstable and volatile new aspect to my being, I had wanted desperately to believe I was no longer the wretched creature that now stared back at me from across the distance of a few dingy porcelain fixtures. But I was still not the proud fierce creature I had been in my youth, the man who had railed against injustice and won wars with his words. I was not a person who would die for a cause. The creature I saw was not poetic or lovely or even strong, and it had taken a mere few words from my Maker to shatter my resolve. I wanted to weep, but nothing was left inside of me to weep for. I reached out to the mirror, leaning ever closer to the image that hovered before my vision, wanting to know that what I saw there wasn't true. My fingers lighted upon the slick surface. Finding it solid and cold, the nightmare of paranoia became real.

I stepped away from the sink, finding the light switch with long and weary fingers. Artificial light flooded the tiny room bouncing off the silver faucets and ivory tiles. I squinted painfully into the light, rubbing my eyes as I ran my fingers through my tangled hair. I felt assaulted and shaken, robbed of my one infallible certainty that I knew who I was. I turned the tap on, stripping away the dusty trench coat and letting it fall to the floor behind me. A warm stream of water splashed over the rusting steel basin. Cupping my hands, I splashed it over the smooth skin of my forehead and cheeks. I sighed into the water wanting to drink it but knowing all too well how violently my body would reject it. Smoking was the one human habit I had managed to maintain over the centuries. Why was unexplainable, just as with so many other aspects of my existence.

I needed a mundane distraction. I turned from the sink, drying my damp skin with my sleeve, and bent to scoop up the small pile of dirty garments in the corner behind the door.

I stuffed the clothing into an army-issue canvas bag that had been hanging upon a hook behind the door. It was worn beyond belief, its thick material ragged and frayed around the edges and adorned with faded patches that had nearly outlived their years of service. I slipped my arm through the gray-green strap, slinging the satchel over my shoulder as if it contained the weight of the world. Without another glance at my secondary self, I exited the room, allowing my fingers to fall blindly on the light switch as I did.

It was a dance I had done so many times before; down three flights of concrete stairs, footsteps echoing in the middle of the night, to wash the same few articles again and again. Of the myriad warehouse studios that filled the building where we lived, Jasmine's was one of the very few that was large enough to hold an antique washing machine. Such luxuries were rare in those days. People were poor; much of the society based on a barter and trade system. Jasmine was a shrewd businesswoman though and called the game when luck was on her side. I admired her; she prospered where others floundered. She learned to adapt. She was a survivor.

And she was beautiful.

From the moment I had laid eyes on her, I had been entranced, drawn undeniably to the molten gold of her warmth. Our immediate, intense attraction was illogical and dangerous; it was irrational, but sometimes you meet someone and something deep inside of you simply says *trust them* despite all rationale. And I did, more so than anyone in centuries. She was my saving grace, my mortal angel, perfect and passionate and skilled at making me forget, with each kiss, with each chime of laughter, the world of darkness in which I dwelled.

Though she was an ally of the Immortals, she remained innocent of the true horrific nature of our darker side. And I was not about to be the first to shatter our angelic image for her. Something childish and terrified cowered within me, still ashamed of the merciless crimes I committed in the name of survival. In my heart, I know she instinctively sensed that there was something vicious about me, a brutality kept flawlessly hidden beneath a guise of shy silence and fierce lovemaking.

Never once, though, did she deny my tentative knocks on her door. Without question or judgment, she had welcomed me into her world and, in turn, I had clung to her, baring my soul to her with all its tender spots and wounds and falling into her warm embrace as if it was all I had ever searched for. A secret. A truth. A link to my human past embodied in the form of this youthful woman whose eyes were the deep brown of the forest's base, whose hair fell like falling autumn leaves just beyond her shoulders. I hesitated to say, she was my best friend.

How many times had I listened to the scoldings of my brethren? Besides Dune, Jasmine was all I had. I'd never let them know that, though. I wasn't supposed to need anything. Now, I wanted the drama of her concerns, the solid reality of her presence to distract me, to ignore my Maker's summoning and dismiss the lingering essence of my last victim. On waking, I had felt that perhaps I had forgotten the girl from the night before, but now she seemed to creep back into my consciousness, begging for a second chance at redemption. The thick reminder of patchouli and cloves was embedded within the thin tissues of my nose, the salt of that nameless beauty that was recklessly glossed upon my lips. I fought the urge to return to the sink and scrub my flesh until it was raw.

I passed through the darkened living room, with all of its deep and musty artificial scents, and into the kitchen. Dune was nowhere to be seen. It was unlike him to disappear so early and without cause. When my shadow went missing, it was a portent of bad times. He perceived things that were even beyond my awareness. He was my third eye.

I slipped the satchel off my shoulder and tossed it quietly into the living room. I wandered into the tiny bedroom and flicked on the light. It flooded the spartan room in a burst of harsh yellow-white. "Dune?" My melancholy state was beginning to be replaced by an overwhelming irritation. "Where are you? It is time for you to Hunt."

I flicked off the bedroom light and moved back into the kitchen, listening to the currents of energy humming through the building. Amidst the tangled extensions of living energy there was a vacant spot, a "hole" void of any perceptible wavelength or warmth. I tensed and quickly double-walled my defenses; something was shielding itself and doing a damn good job at it. That could only mean one of three things: it was either very old, very powerful, or both. Whichever way, it was extremely brash to disrespect my territory. Even Elders announced themselves.

I was incensed.

There is an unspoken code amongst vampires, much like that of a pack of wolves: to tread upon another's territory was a challenge, plain and simple. The hairs on the back of my neck bristled with the charge of anticipation. I leaned back on the arm of the couch and faced the front door. I was too old to run.

It moved languidly up the stairs, pausing briefly at the top before continuing on. Down the long, narrow cement hall to my door. It stopped. I sensed a mild hesitation, a preoccupation. There was no malicious intent here, but merely mischief. However, I did not entirely trust that judgment since the creature was so well cloaked from my investigation. The temperature in the room suddenly dropped, a rippling static crackling about the doorframe. Dune began to hiss violently from beneath the couch revealing his hideout. I did not move or take my eyes off the door. A bluish fog had begun to seep in around the edges where it did not quite meet the frame. Crackling sparks of bluish white electricity arced in and out of existence; there was a chaotic random purpose to it.

The smoke rose up, swirling and contorting, ripping the stale monotony that had previously occupied the four square feet of cold gray cement over which it now moved. For an instant I thought it would linger there forever a shadowy display of ethereal pyrotechnics, but then it expanded, contracted and in a soundless explosion, vanished. In its place stood Sea.

He was dressed in a strange silken suit of dark teal that seemed to trap the florescent light around him and hold it like a breath caught in one's throat. In another time, in another place it might just have had that effect on me. But I was hollow now. He stood there, poised with palms upraised, shoulders back on his waif frame, waiting for the deadpan applause he knew I would not give him.

"Such flourish." My voice was flat and unimpressed.

His hands dropped to his sides with an overly exasperated sigh. "Sleep well?" Sarcasm dripped from his glinting fangs.

I let it wash over me as I pulled my tobacco pouch from my chest pocket once again. "Well enough. How should I know?" Folding the thin white tissue between thumb and forefinger, I sprinkled the sweet brown tobacco into the crease. I did not raise my gaze as he began to move towards me languidly.

He sniffed the air around me arrogantly. "You stink of humans," he said, wiping the last static electricity from his sleeves in soft blue snaps. "Been associating with poet trash again?"

In his youth, Sea had languished in the decadence of the arts and a fine fascination with human debauchery and passion, but the years had soured him, gradually. Due to his secrecy and allegiance to Phelan, I did not fully know what had transpired in the century while I slept that had forced his final transformation into the chill, vain Immortal that stood before me now. In the year since my reawakening, Sea had kept his distance from me, associating with me superficially only when absolutely necessary. When we spoke, our conversations were stilted and sharp, filled with sarcastic barbs of suspicion. For all intents and purposes, he had become a complete stranger to me.

"One man's trash is another's treasure." I hoped he heard the ice in my voice.

I quickly changed the subject. "State your business here, soldier." I tried to remind myself that I still considered him a friend, if a tolerated one at best. Sometimes he could rub me the wrong way, like a blister just broken, even though I knew he would run to my side when others would flee. Our relationship had grown embittered like that.

I lit the end of my cigarette and folded my arms across my chest. A low guttural growl still sounded from beneath the couch every now and then, a constant reminder of Dune's disapproval.

"I've been sent to fetch you." Hands clasped behind his

back, he gazed down his aquiline nose at me. There was a slight smug smirk itching to spread across his wide narrow lips. The situation was obviously amusing him.

"Fetch me, eh? Been demoted to 'go-to boy' have we?" I paused to take a long drag on my cigarette. Sea gazed at me with cool analysis until I continued, "To whom do I owe this degradation?"

I couldn't help but smile as I exhaled the smoke slowly up into his face.

He didn't flinch; the smirk only became a shallow grin. There was a brief moment of complete silence in which I thought we might actually share a laugh again, then the seriousness seemed to creep back into his expression. I should have known by then that laughter was a thing of the past.

"We tried to contact you by more *traditional* means, but, apparently, you no longer listen to our calls. You are late to the Summoning." He turned away and began to walk slowly around the tiny living room, superficially inspecting the modest decor.

"Late? What are you talking about? It's not until tomorrow night...?" Anxiety squashed the air from my chest with a quick iron fist.

"No. It's tonight. In fact, it began at sundown. That was over an hour ago. We have been waiting on your worthless ass. Phelan is especially displeased..." He trailed off, peeking out the single small window covered in heavy black curtains.

"*Fuck Phelan!*"

"Oh, that's mature! That's the kind of attitude that keeps you in hot water all the time." He walked over to where I leaned against the arm of the couch, smoking sullenly. "Why do you have to fight everyone all the time?"

"It's my nature." My words barely audible, I rubbed my face with an exhausted sigh.

"That's pure, unadulterated rubbish and you know it!" He sighed heavily through his nose. "But all that aside, it still remains that we must leave immediately." He turned his back to me and strode quickly to the door. I stared after him, refusing to budge.

"And what if we don't? Will fire and brimstone rain down

on me? Will Phelan put a stake through my heart himself, or will he just put us over his knee like the children he sees us as? Just what will happen, Sea? Why must we run like licked pups every fucking time he snaps his fingers? I'm tired of it!" I hissed through clenched teeth, barely able to contain the rage that had suddenly spawned inside of me.

"Seafra, I'm tired." Just as quickly the anger fizzled away. I truly was simply *tired*. The past year had proven overwhelming; adjusting to the new way of life had made me feel all too human again, too many head-games, too many politics.

He rolled his eyes. "Tynan, please. Don't fight me now. This is important. Very important." He began to walk towards the door. "We have to go."

"He destroys lives, Sea." I hissed.

"He *saves* lives." Sea was blindly loyal.

"This is pointless." I threw my hands up and looked around for an ashtray. "I'm talking to Phelan's personal lapdog. I keep forgetting!"

I leaned over to flick ash into a small ceramic tray on the coffee table, but before I knew what was happening, Sea had me by the arm. He yanked me upwards from my sulking on the arm of the couch, bringing me face to face with him. For a moment we stared into each other's eyes fiercely, like wolves facing off at dusk. I thought he would lunge for my throat. There was something crazed and furious in his eyes. We were so close our noses almost touched. For a brief flash I thought of grabbing him by the scruff of the neck and kissing him hard to break his intensity, but before I could act he released his grip on my arm. He pushed me away from him with such force that I nearly stumbled over the coffee table.

"Get your things." Pure ice. He walked to the door and waited. I watched him somewhat warily as I extinguished the last of my cigarette.

Grabbing the army satchel that held my dirty laundry, I emptied it onto the floor. I retrieved a worn leather-bound notebook from the bedroom and tossed it into the bag. I had a strange feeling I wasn't coming back any time soon. I must have stood there for a long while, gazing hollowly about the apartment, for Sea began to snap about the urgent need for haste. I stared at him, a sudden cold descending on my soul as the realization that I might not return solidified within me.

I broke out of my reverie, "There's just one more thing..." I turned back to the couch. "Come on Dune. It's time to go."

I got down on my knees and peered under the couch. His big harvest moon eyes shone back at me full of questions. Animals have a strange sixth sense about their keepers; it is almost as if they understand more about your emotions than you do yourself. With vampires, it is as if our hearts and minds become interlinked with the animals. He knew I was leaving. He knew I wasn't coming back. I reached under the couch with both hands, slipping my long fingers around his warm soft torso. He protested little as I pulled him slowly from the shadows and brought him close up against my chest.

"Where are you going?" Sea asked.

Without a word I turned out the lights and walked past Sea into the hall. Down the stairs, three flights of echoing dismal concrete, whispering quiet reassurances into the velveteen fur between Dune's shoulder blades, I reached the ground floor. Sea was right behind me, a few paces back. He headed for the door even as I turned down the hall in the opposite direction; one last stop before my departure. I heard him pause.

"We don't have time for long goodbyes, Tynan." Sea growled behind me. "We have to go, now!"

I didn't acknowledge his remark but kept walking. I reached the end of the corridor and turned to the door on my right. Number 6. I reached out knocked on the slate gray door. It echoed menacingly through the building. I heard voices inside and then the clicks and scrapes of latches and bolts being drawn back. The door opened a crack. A young boy of about twelve peered cautiously around the edge and up at me. His skin was a deep golden tan framed by a shaggy mess of unruly brown hair.

"Hey, Danny. Your sis home?"

He smiled as he recognized me. Opening the door a little wider, he yelled back over his shoulder, "Jas, your friend is here."

"Which friend?" Her voice drifted to us from down the hall, over the soft sound of running water.

"Who do you think?" Danny looked back at me and rolled his eyes, sighing dramatically with youthful impatience.

I could hear her bare feet padding across the cool cement floors towards us. She rounded the corner quickly, slipping past her little brother to throw her arms around my neck. "Hey there, possum." Her southern accent was thick and warm.

Dune made a small squeak as she hugged me tightly. Her autumn hair was wet and smelled of homemade peppermint soap. She was wearing a long blue robe of soft linen, tied at the waist.

"Oh! Sorry Dune. Didn't see you there!" She pulled away from me a little to ruffle the fur on his head. She looked up at me, a smile as bright as the sun lighting her face. Her smile faded quickly as she saw the misery in my eyes. She reached up to touch my face with long gentle fingers. "What's wrong?" Her voice was no more than a whisper.

"I need you to take care of Dune for a while." I handed him to her.

She took him and clutched him to her chest like a baby. "How long is 'a while'?"

I let my gaze drop to Dune. I ran my fingers over his long jet-black fur. "Too long, I'm afraid." When I looked back up at Jasmine, there were tears streaming silently down her cheeks.

Her voice was strong and steady though, "We'll take good care of him."

I smiled weakly at her. "Thank you."

"I'll miss you." She tried to smile. I took her into my arms and kissed her on the forehead.

"I'll come back, I promise," I whispered into her hair as I let go of her, turning back down the hall to join Sea at the end of the corridor.

I never was a very good liar.

5

Sea and I took to the sky on invisible wings. It was a power I had not used in over a hundred years and I was hesitant to attempt it at first, but Sea insisted, noting repeatedly that we were now more than unfashionably late. Though the location of the secret manor was only a few hundred miles northeast of the amagin, Sea's agitation since his arrival at my apartment had grown from nearly imperceptible to overwhelmingly rude.

I was consumed enough by my own thoughts without his adding to the flames of apprehension that engulfed me. Strange haunting memories flooded through me in torrents. Memories that were engrained within my soul as if they were my own yet were far too old to be of my making. Adian's past had all but obliterated my identity when I killed him leaving me to fight off the ghosts that once haunted him. And after decades of struggling to decipher between the two realities, I eventually allowed them to consume me, dragging me down along with my other demons to destroy me. Images of *my* homeland and of *my* mortal father's castle, of battles and long hard winters clawed at my mind, trying to pull themselves up from the graves where they were buried. I saw the face of my father, proud and wise, his high cheeks lined with the black tribal tattoos of our clan. I saw the bodies of Catarine and Tegwaret, the sister and brother I had slain in my terrifying first nights as a vampire. I could not shake the visions and so I let my mind replay them as we soared through the sky.

I had sought my siblings out that fateful night, calling them from the castle and into the stable yard. There, I told them of what had befallen me and I begged for their forgiveness. They had cursed me calling me *evil*, believing I was a trickster spirit in the guise of their older brother. Angry and hurt and unable, yet, to control the Hunger within me, I took their lives violently. All the while my father had been a witness, helpless and frozen, from his bedroom window far above us.

There was no redemption or forgiveness left for me then. I took from the man who had given me life and love and honor, his legacy, his son and daughter. The terror and betrayal in my father's eyes was unbearable. I was dead to him, disowned and banished from his lands forever. I heard once that several years later his second wife bore him a healthy son, but by then my father, the once great lord, had lost control of his own lands, too mired in grief to be respected and feared as he once had been. History soon forgot him and all because of my murderous actions and cursed blood.

Feeling tears beginning to freeze on my cheeks, I forced my mind out of the past and concentrated on the journey ahead. The flight to Phelan's reminded me of my early years as an Immortal first coming into my powers; initially, unnerved and nauseated by the weightlessness, then enveloped by an indefinable sense of peace. We soared high above the weather and into the bejeweled pitch of eternity. I let go of my home. I let go of Dune and Jasmine. I let go of the sour taste of my last victim. It all faded fast, down, down, down...away from me until I was untouched.

It doesn't mean anything. It doesn't mean anything at all...

I flew on ahead of Sea. I knew the way all too well.

Spiraling down, birds of prey descending from the storm cloud-lined sky, we lighted silently on the rain glistening cobblestones amidst one of the grand gardens behind the manor. The temperature was much colder; the rain that poured from the sky fierce and angular in its descent. It struck the side of my face, tiny shards of glass. I winced at the tower of brown stone and glowing yellow windows that loomed up ahead of us. Sea was already walking up the pathway to the rear gate, his shoes tapping loudly over the hiss of the rain. I shivered and bowed my head, pulling my collar up for warmth.

I had not set foot in the grounds since that fateful night when I had fled and, yet, it appeared to have changed little in that long expanse of time. I frowned up at the towering stone building and wondered how it could have escaped the wrath of the war? It seemed that every other structure within a hundred miles had been destroyed. I knew Phelan had always been good at cloaking the existence of his lair, and had done so successfully for centuries, but everything has its limits. After a moment of hesitation, I was able to make my feet move beneath me. Every fiber in me told me to run. Sea had entered the house without me. I peered through the beveled glass panes in the door. Inside, the room was empty. I sensed the other Immortals though; an ancient solemn presence that sent a shiver up my spine. I opened the heavy oak door and entered the kitchen.

Again, I was overwhelmed by the timelessness of the house. It was as if the war that had waged outside had simply been a dream and all was whole and gleaming and surreal once again. It was all horribly wrong. Over the years, I had watched as the house evolved and grew, reshaped and expanded with each passing decade to accommodate Phelan's own growing power and the Immortals who sought shelter there in times of need. As I stood glaring at the shining steel and polished black marble surfaces, I felt as if I had walked into a dollhouse, a replica of the past pristinely preserved as it had been in the 21st century.

I was suddenly painfully aware of the sopping disarray of my own countenance. Leaving heavy wet footprints behind me, I wandered through the kitchen and into the hallway. It was a strange décor, a blend of Far East and industrial gothic art smash. The floors were of a highly polished dark maroon tile that gleamed seductively. Ambient light from gray metal wall sconces, pierced and twisted by haunting gothic designs, melted over angular dark wood and deep red walls. Every few feet were thrown soft eclectic rugs of the same dark reds, greens and grays. Tile, rug, tile, rug, the hall stretched on forever as I made my way to the open double doors at the end of the corridor.

I reached the library without ever looking up. Eyes locked on the floor, I lingered listening to the fierce voices inside. Anxiety strangled the air from my lungs as my hand found the doorframe to steady myself. The animal in me wanted to tuck tail and flee rather than face those old souls. I stared at the floor. I could feel their eyes on me, suddenly, a hundred of years of burning resentment and accusations. Some were refusing to acknowledge me at all.

Why am I here? I'm better off dead to them, I thought fighting back bitter blood red tears. A hand settled on my shoulder, cold and heavy as marble. I was shaking, suddenly acutely aware of the musty scent of incense and wood burning. Slowly, I looked up.

Phelan stood very close to me. He was dressed in a long oriental jacket of dark royal purple hemmed in gold over black linen pants. His feet were bare, his bright auburn hair neatly plaited in a single braid down his back. He gazed down at me with unreadable emerald eyes set in a flawless face of alabaster porcelain. His eyes glittered from the reflected firelight. I opened my mouth to speak, but found no voice within. He pulled me against him in a strong fatherly embrace.

"Welcome home," he whispered into my still dripping hair.

I was stunned. I felt my satchel slip off my shoulder. It hit the ceramic tiles with a dull thud. Where was the cold aloofness of abandonment? Where was the violent admonition I had dreaded for so long? Who was this creature that now embraced me with such compassion and sincerity? I was frozen, barely able to return the gesture. He pushed me away a little and locked me with his gaze. He was just as I had remembered him. His hands lingering on my waist, I stared at him in wide-eyed amazement, my lips parted in an unspoken question.

He touched the side of my face as a mother might do gazing upon a child. "It has been a long time."

"Yes..." The word was barely more than a hoarse whisper above the crackle of flames in the distant hearth. His power radiated from him like the Sun, infiltrating my defenses and causing me to want to confess all of my sins in a torrent of babbled apologies, but my voice was lost against the roar of my conscience.

He turned back to the room. "Come. We have much to talk about."

* * *

For what seemed like hours, I listened to the voices rise and fall, a frantic surf crashing upon a beach. Hidden amongst the shadows of a far corner, I had tucked myself within the dark leather embrace of an old claw-foot armchair. From there, I watched and waited in leery anticipation. Occasionally, a gaunt beautiful face would glance in my direction, its expression guarded against a backdrop of firelight. Eventually, I was forgotten entirely. I began to believe the languid Immortal souls that draped themselves about the room really had no concern for me anymore. I thought about sneaking out, but that was not really an option in a room full of telepaths. As if sensing my nervous energy, Phelan watched me warily from time to time. His expression told me it would not be wise to try running a second time.

At first, Phelan remained at the edge of the group, letting Sea direct the flow of the conversation. There were several moments of formal introductions and of the twenty or so vampires present, I recognized only a third of them. The remaining individuals were young, some even newly incepted. Something sharp shifted inside me as I realized, with a numbing shock, that a place in the Summoning was filled by one so young only when there were no Elders to take the position. I looked around the room counting the faces I knew: Phelan, Sea, Tatsu, Mara, Lillian... My urge to flee suddenly dissipated. I began to listen more closely as they spoke of the current state of Tyst politics.

Abruptly, Sea took his seat amongst the others. Since our arrival, the arrogant demeanor I had grown so accustomed to in him had vanished. It unnerved me the way he could switch it on and off with the shrug of a shoulder. While he had spoken before the group, Phelan lingered against the far wall, a pale silhouette against a tower of dusty leather-bound books and shadows, gazing out the looming bay window at the relentless storm. Now, he turned and slowly moved to the front of the room, near the fireplace. I say "moved" because he neither walked, nor glided, but seemed to simply be in one place and then another. He was an element within himself.

He stood for a moment, arms crossed over his chest, the forefinger of his right hand thoughtfully tapping his lower lip, as he considered each and every one of us. The orange glow of the fire behind him made him appear as if he were standing amongst the flames.

"In one way or another, you all know why you are here tonight." He paused to gauge our reactions. "For those of you who have not been with us for a while..." I shifted uncomfortably in my seat. "Or are fairly new to Immortality, take a good look around you. We are a dying race."

The silence was deafening.

A young vampire with short spiky maroon hair bolted up out of his chair, his fists clenched at his sides. "How can that be?! Some of us are so young!" His voice shook with a barely controlled fear and anger. Anger at a responsibility thrust upon him.

Phelan's expression was that of a sad sort of sympathy. "Traq, you should know better than any of us how this has come to pass. The Tyst has despised us since they discovered our existence. We cannot be controlled like the human masses they subdue. We do not exist within their laws and, thus, we are a threat unlike any other."

He made a sweeping gesture towards his captive audience, "You and I both know we couldn't care less what the Tyst Empire does. Mortal wars, for the most part, do not concern us. We used to be a proud fierce species, but now...there are few of us left and our numbers are dwindling further every night. Cardone and his followers have spent the last few decades exterminating us, one coven at a time. Those they do not kill immediately are interrogated and brutally tortured for their secrets. As long as we exist, the Tyst know that they are not completely in control of the world." He turned away, staring deeply into the flames dancing in the hearth beside him.

"I realize that." Traq's anxiety was visually growing. His black eyes wide with questions, he spoke again. "My own family was killed only a few weeks ago." His voice cracked as he struggled to repress the sadness in it. "I watched my own Maker beheaded and burned. Tyst militia scoured the mountains where we had been camping...I may be the only one that survived that attack..." His voice trailed off.

An uneasy murmur rippled through the room of similar stories of loss and expressions of condolence for Traq and his family.

"But, I know we are not all that remains." Traq shook his head, pulling himself out of the past. "I know others exist. I sensed them only last night. They are afraid and in hiding, but they are there." He looked around the room searching for an answer. "There have to be other Elders out there...somewhere?" As if shaken by his own words he slowly sank back into his seat, fidgeting nervously as he did.

Phelan shook his head slowly, amber strands of hair escaping his neat braid. "There are other vampires, yes. But they are too young and inexperienced. For knowledge of this world and the powers inherent to our race, we are all they have now to turn to for guidance. And I guarantee you, most do not even know we exist."

"Most of us never had proper guidance as fledglings. Hell, we were lucky if we knew our Makers at all!" It was Tatsu's turn to speak. "We are no more fit to give guidance to fledglings as say...Tynan over there." He flicked his hand in my general direction without looking at me.

I sank deeper into the shadows of my chair.

Tatsu was a Korean–English vampire of some four hundred years. He had spent the majority of his existence haunting the beaches of exotic coastal towns in Greece and Italy. He and I were like night and day. His long black hair was partially pulled back in a high topknot away from pale olive, feline features that contained a quiet predatory danger. He draped himself in his chair placing one arm casually over the back.

"Genocide is nothing new to our kind. We have endured such persecution throughout the millennia. We must simply learn to adapt more quickly to the new strategies of the Tyst Empire. This isn't the Church throwing holy water on us and chasing us with stakes. This is a militia who truly *understands* what we are. I'll be the first to admit that we have become very lazy when it comes to protecting ourselves. Perhaps it is merely elimination of the weak from the herd?" His chill demeanor was heartless.

"Shut up!" Traq lunged in his direction with a snarl. Phelan stepped forward and caught him by the arm.

Tatsu did not look up to acknowledge Traq. Inspecting the nails of one hand for imperfections, he continued. "So tell us, Phelan, why are we really here? I know you wouldn't drag me all the way from Sorrento just to brow-beat me on the responsibilities of being a good foster-parent."

Tatsu had a way of rubbing everyone the wrong way. His sarcasm and honesty often bit to the bone, unnerving those who would rather not disturb the waters with their own words. Phelan was unmovable. A thousand years made him a patient parent. He watched Tatsu with a vague detachment.

His eyes narrowed very slightly. "How are the beaches these days, Tatsu? Seems I remember you moaning only last month about how hard the Tyst has made life for you and your brood."

"I don't have a *brood*." Tatsu snapped defensively.

"Of course not." The corner of Phelan's mouth twitched as he repressed further commentary for diplomacy's sake.

The level of agitation was growing in the room, making the air stifling and oppressive. I uncurled myself from the chair. I hoped the movement would not draw attention to me, but it did not go unnoticed. Lillian, sitting near the hearth, turned her head to look at me. Even after three hundred years, she was still as enchanting as the day I had found her abandoned by her Maker in the hull of a trader ship off the coast of Ireland. For many years after that I had played the part of her mentor. We had shared a bond unlike any I had previously experienced. I knew I had hurt many when I left, but of all of them, Lillian was one I truly regretted. Her stormy blue eyes shone with a thousand unspoken questions. My heart constricted painfully. Suddenly, she smiled, bright and warm and forgiving as the summer sun. She turned away to watch Phelan once again and the moment vanished. It was the first time since my return that I had felt welcome.

Phelan was speaking again. "As much as I hate to admit it, Tatsu is right." He stood, hands clasped behind his back, gazing up at the high arched ceiling. "I did not bring you all here to instruct you on your future obligations as part of the Council. That lecture is for yet another time. No, what I have to say is of a much more grave matter altogether."

He continued. "It would appear global domination is no longer enough for our dear dictators. They want to become Immortal as well."

Tatsu laughed hysterically. "You're not fucking serious?!"

I had to admit it was a bizarre concept but, then and again, after conquering the physical world, it would be the logical next step in their acquisition of power.

Tatsu scoffed at the idea. "That's ridiculous! They want to be vampires?"

Sea shifted uncomfortably in his seat; his voice was barely audible. "Not exactly..."

"Well the only other way to become Immortal, that I recall, is to sell your soul to the Devil!" Tatsu's remark sent a ripple of nervous laughter across the room.

"Exactly." Sea's face was a smooth, unreadable mask, but below the surface the waters churned dark and deep.

I wondered how it was that he alone had been privy to whatever knowledge Phelan had of the Tyst's plans? The humor and pomp melted from Tatsu's exotic features to be replaced by a strangled confusion. A sinking pulled my stomach towards the center of the earth. During my travels, I had heard tales of a certain vampiric god, a master of chaos. However, they had only been whispered myths passed around the campfires of gypsy Immortals and nothing more. Or so, I had believed.

I leaned forward in my chair, head bowed in earnest thought. For the first time that evening, I raised my voice. "You speak of the Vicinus." The room was silent. I looked at Sea. "Do you not?"

Traq's wavering voice cut through the stifling silence. "What's the Vicinus?" The fledgling was more tightly wound than a harp string.

Phelan walked over and took his place behind Traq, resting his hands lightly on the boy's shoulders. "The Vicinus dates back to the dawn of all Immortality. It was the first of our kind and that from which all vampiric life evolved. Some say it was a spirit. Some claim it a demon. Some even came to worship it as a god. A god of restless storms and tormented dreams."

Rolling black clouds flashed across my mind's eye, the scream of the dying dragons faint in my ears. I shivered, shaking off the ghost of the dreams that had haunted me since my return. Phelan continued in a flat academic fashion. "Regardless of his title, the Vicinus was, is, an entity of immense unbound power. He is Chaos to Calm." He paused for dramatic effect. "That is not to say that this entity is *evil*. I do not believe in such a black and white concept as *evil* that is so gutturally human. However, in order for there to be balance, there must be opposites, and these opposites are forever at war with one another. It is a power struggle as old as time itself. And now is a time in which I fear we are dangerously close to destroying the fragile balance on which we depend."

"What is it to us if they become Immortal?" Tatsu challenged Phelan. "What should I care if a bunch of power-hungry idiots decide they want the Curse?"

"You really want those that slaughter us to truly have the same powers as we do?" Sea interjected, true astonishment in his tone.

Tatsu did not answer, but looked away into the fire with a scowl.

"That is very true." Phelan agreed. "Our enemies becoming equals with us would be a devastating and possibly final blow to us." He walked to the front of the room and sat delicately on the edge of a brown leather armchair. He suddenly seemed his age, the weight of his millennia pulling him down towards the earth. "But, what Lord Cardone and his Queen do not realize is that once the Vicinus is in a material form, their binding spells will no longer work on him. They will have no power over him to do their bidding. The Vicinus is desperate to be free of the prison his fellow gods placed him in. The lore is such that, eons ago the Vicinus took a mortal woman to his bed. He wanted to see what would come of such a coupling. He cared not for the mortal; it was an experiment to him. To his surprise and twisted fascination she became with child, the first of our kind."

"We were *birthed* by a *mortal?*"

I could not tell exactly who hissed the words, but the voice was soft and female.

Lillian moved her hand in front of her stomach protectively. "You mean we can bear children?" She seemed terrified, yet awe-struck, by the notion.

"A vampire child has not been brought into this world in over two thousand years. Perhaps evolution has saved us from the torment that comes with such a birth and the hideous, bloody way in which the mother dies, by giving us the ability to create fledglings through transfusions? We cannot say for sure, except that vampire births are extremely rare.

"The birth of that first vampire infuriated the gods. The Vicinus had not only meddled with the order of things, he had altered them forever. They stripped him of his physical form and the powers inherent and bound him to the ether. He has been a prisoner there for nearly 5,000 years. At least, that is how the story has been told over the eons."

I leaned back in my chair, disappearing into the heavy shadows. "And now he's found a loophole in the decree?" While I had witnessed countless unexplainable phenomena throughout the centuries, Phelan's tale felt too far-fetched even for me to accept. Hissing rattlesnakes of irritation began to seethe within me.

"In a manner of speaking, that is correct." Phelan seemed smugly pleased that I had decided to participate in the discussion. I suppose he had anticipated that I would slink off to avoid further confrontation.

"The Vicinus promised the Tyst what they desire most and like the predictable fools most mortals are, they believed him. He will destroy them, though, each and every one of them as revenge for his lengthy prison sentence. So, you see, if there are no humans, there are no vampires. The food chain collapses. That is, if he doesn't decide to take us out as well."

Phelan paused, drawing a long breath of fire-warmed air before continuing. "As with the first of our kind, the Vicinus must be reborn into his physical essence by a mortal woman.

The one that has been chosen by Cardone for this heinous and deadly honor is his very own Queen, Lady Moria Cardone. If what we have heard is accurate, they have been successful with their bizarre experiments and she is now *pregnant*."

Voices swelled in confusion and disbelief throughout the room. For what felt like an eternity, the chaos of frantic arguing and questioning waged on. I silently digested what Phelan had said, about how the Tyst's new quest for Immortality truly affected us.

After hundreds of years of contemplation, the new order of ruthless global politics varied little that I could gauge, from the countless other empires that had risen and fallen in the hands of humanity, with the exception of its absolute global scale. From pagan Rome to the fundamentalist United States of the late 21st century, global empires had slaughtered thousands, devastated the world's resources and coveted conquered lands in the name of various political or religious agendas.

However, the wars that had ravaged the Earth's surface had concerned us little because they were human wars. Their petty, arrogant squabbles had been beneath us, or so we thought; we had our own battles that waged from time to time within the cobalt shadows of night while the world of the living laid down their weapons and slept, but in mortal affairs we always kept our distance, standing eternal vigilance over the ages, the true historians of time.

That age of neutrality was over. We, Immortals, no longer existed beneath the protective surface of mortal society, buried deep within their dark desires and dreams. The Tyst had proven our existence and hated us, perhaps more than they hated the insurgent factions of human outlanders, for the mere fact that we possessed the one thing they could not take by force, the one thing they craved above and beyond anything they had managed to scrape from the core of the earth: true *immortality*.

Every ruler, since the beginnings of mankind, had fled from the notion that one day their reign would come to an end, that their empire would crumble, and their entire legacy and all that they had achieved be reduced to the scrawlings of a scribe collecting dust within a forgotten tomb till it, too, returned to the earth, forgotten. Every ruler had chased the notion of immortality by building higher and conquering further, but it had all been merely a façade of immortality. No government had ever had truly believed they could cheat death, until now.

We had always been hunted, though. That plight was nothing new. I suppose one grows numb to another's hatred and fear after centuries of watching them flail about with their hollow threats of annihilation and religious condemnation. The Immortals would always be the predators of mortals and, in turn, vampires would always fight to maintain their delusion that they were the rulers of the planet. We had no fear of the vampire slayers of old and if they did, by the pure stroke of luck, happen to catch and kill one of us, we simply looked at it as a *thinning of the herd*, a weeding out of the weak that we could not take into our own hands.

However, the occasional thinning had evolved into a decimation that, if the stories were true, had left our people upon the brink of extinction. The closest we had come to true genocide was during the Witch Hunts when anyone who deviated slightly from the rigid Christian norm would be hunted and burned. We had been smarter then, though. We had not involved ourselves so deeply in mortal affairs. When our kind began to dwindle in numbers, when clans were decimated or destroyed, we went underground, literally. Many of the elders had slept for decades while the young ones, the ones who could not exist so long without fresh blood, hunted only when absolutely necessary and only on the fringes of the larger cities where the derelicts and deranged would not be missed. It was a bleak era of starvation and solitude, but we survived.

Phelan remained silent, his face a cold, emotionless mask as he stared at the ground before his feet. I uncurled myself from my chair, moving to sit on the edge, my elbows upon my knees as I listened intently to the voices of my kindred. My jaw ached, my teeth clenched as I repressed the urge to simply stand up and walk away from the madness unfolding around me.

Then, over the din of horrified exclamations, Phelan spoke again. "We must stop the Tyst before they complete their plan. We have lingered too long in this new world allowing it to do as it wished with us. Now is our time to stand and fight."

It sounded too outrageous to be true. To think Phelan would suggest we endanger ourselves further infuriated me. "Where, exactly, are you getting this interesting batch of information from, if I may be so bold?" I crossed my arms over my chest. The rest of the gathering fell silent, turning to watch me curiously and I spoke.

Phelan's eyes narrowed. "The Phuree. And...other sources I cannot reveal at this time. Are you questioning the truth of my words, Tynan?"

"Yes, actually. I am." I said bluntly. Without waiting for his reply I continued with my questioning. "And the Phuree have absolutely no reason to fabricate this outrageous tale to serve their own cause? Seems rather convenient that they would enlist us to wage a cosmic battle against the Tyst Empire, don't you think?" I was trying desperately to control the edge in my voice. Though I felt compelled to challenge Phelan, I knew I now walked a perilously thin line. I had not been redeemed and, for all intents and purposes, was still a criminal in the eyes of many.

"I would know if they were lying. Just as I know you are challenging me for deeper reasons than not wanting to engage in war." Phelan studied me, a svelte marmalade cat from his place near the hearth.

"I see." I ignored his condescending comment. "So, what you're saying, and please do correct me if I'm wrong," I stood up and walked to the window, feeling like a caged lion suddenly, "Is that, based upon some fantastical allegation made by the Phuree, a group of unpredictable outlaw sorcerers and mystics, you're willing to bet our vagabond little crew of Immortals against a royally pissed off primordial vampiric god and the global dictatorship who will raise him?" The razor edge of my sarcasm cut deep into the silence of the room behind me as I stared out into the stormy night. I could see his reflection in the icy panes of glass.

Phelan was silent. His face had become dangerously calm, barely containing a bubbling anger within.

"Phelan, of all of the outlandish requests you have made over the years, this is by far the most ludicrous!" I shook my head, disgusted. Turning back to the others, I held out my hands to the room. "I know you all still hate me for one reason or another, but am I alone in this?"

The tension was stifling as they exchanged glances of disbelief and concern. Tatsu stood up and crossed the room to stand beside me. "I can't believe I'm saying this, but I'm with Tynan on this one. You can't possibly expect us to believe or back such an outrageous and obviously lost cause?" I had never liked Tatsu for his arrogance and extravagance, but it was nice to know someone else held my opinion.

"Well, I'm sorry to hear you have so little faith in me, Tatsu. Does anyone else share Tynan's sentiments?" Phelan's gaze challenged me with a deadly quiet.

"It's not that we have no faith in you, Phelan." Lillian rose from her seat, a tall form of seductive curves and shadows. Her voice was smooth and ran across my ears like water, "You are our leader, our Elder, but you speak of living mythology. Fairytales and war. War with a group no one has been able to defeat in a hundred years. A dictatorship that has taken painstaking strides to eradicate our race for our powers and our unwillingness to take sides." The firelight highlighted her high cheekbones and delicate full lips, shimmering on the liquid surfaces of her eyes. "In the last couple of years, even though they still attack from time to time, some of us have been able to form lives again...peaceful lives... You must be patient with our hesitancy to forsake everything for a cause we cannot see." Though her voice was strong and even, I could see her hands shaking where they lay clenched at her sides.

Phelan slowly unpinned me from his gaze and transferred his attention to Lillian. "I realize your concerns, but unless we do something, this 'fairytale' will become all too real, and we will become all too extinct." There was fear in his voice, a crumbling vein of exhaustion. He took a deep breath and exhaled slowly, "But honestly, there is only one of us who has the power to defeat the Vicinus and the skill to crack the Empire." I found his gaze once again locked on me.

My brow knitted; I narrowed my eyes, cocking my head a little to the side as if listening to a sound I couldn't quite make out, "Why are you looking at me like that?"

Phelan took a deep breath. "Face it, Tynan. You are the only one left among us with enough knowledge of the Tyst's Chronous technology matrices to get inside them. I know you have studied them intensely. The Phuree oracles have seen you..."

"Now, hold on just a minute!" I charged towards him, not sure what I intended on doing next. "This is outrageous!" I stopped, inches away from him. "Don't you dare put this on me like I'm some fucking prophet!" My heart careened against my ribs until my whole body shook with contained adrenalin. I swung my arm round in a wide arc, pointing at the other attendees in the room. "There are twenty vampires in this room just as capable of learning a few strings of code as I am. And don't tell me that they're not cause it's just fucking code. I don't care what anyone says about how *special* it is!"

"Yeah, what is this Phelan? Tynan pops up from the dead and now he's supposed to lead this war?" Mara stood up, crossing her long sinewy arms over her ample chest. An Amazon in midnight blue desert garb, she stood a head taller than I.

"Don't expect me to follow that pathetic martyr of an Immortal!" She glared at me with black eyes from across the room. "His insanity has already cost us too much as a race. I would never entrust my life, or those of my fledglings, to that schizophrenic."

Her words stung. I frowned at her, knowing she referred to my warped, muddled identity. She tossed her long black hair over her shoulder and stared back bitterly.

Phelan sighed with exhausted patience and pushed my accusatory hand away from his face. "It's not *just* about code. You're right. Anyone can learn code. A string of numbers, a language a child could learn with the right instruction, but this is the Chronous we speak of. The Tyst themselves barely understand their own technology now that it has evolved to such a level. It would take far too long to train anyone who hasn't already studied it intensely." Instantly, he seemed to tune me out again, turning to address the room. "However, it is quite late now. What must be discussed is at great length, but the sun is approaching. You will each play a part in this war. That is, if you will lend your strength to this cause."

Pale anxious faces watched him warily from all angles. The fire was growing weak in the hearth; outside the rain had stopped. "I am sure you all have a tremendous amount of questions that need answering, but it will all have to wait until tomorrow evening. Please, make yourself at home." He gestured grandly to the manor interior.

"Don't! No! You can't just shut us down like this! You can't shut me down again!" I shouted.

"*Tomorrow*," he said as if subduing an unruly child. "We will convene again here tomorrow evening. Please, if you have any loose ends to tie up in your lives, I would suggest you begin as soon as possible. The servants can show you to your quarters." He turned and, in a swirl of purple silk and amber hair, he *moved* out of the Great Hall.

I ran after him.

* * *

"*Why?*" My voice quavered behind wave after wave of raw emotion. Rage. Confusion. Betrayal. It washed over me, a Japanese blade twisting my innards. Never had I so hated another living thing as I hated him at that moment. I chased him up the grand marble staircase and into his master bedroom.

"Tynan, you truly exhaust me." He hung his head as if in defeat, lifting a pale slender hand to delicately rub his temples. "Do you think for one moment I would appoint this kind of power to you if I did not think there was solid evidence to back it up? The last thing on earth that I want to do is engage you in yet another battle of wills!"

"Power?! What power? You've drafted me into some sick little espionage game between the Phuree and the Tyst. Don't you see, the Phuree are using you, Phelan! They want an end to their war and they've finally figured out a way to do it.

There is no Vicinus, no end of the world. There is only a ragged group of sand-dwelling rebels who want to overthrow the government."

"I told you I have the evidence—"

"What evidence? Visions? Prophecies? Hearsay!" A sudden hyena laugh escaped my throat. It echoed off the high marble walls around us. I shook my head, breathing deeply. "I want some proof, dammit! I want some cold, solid, concrete evidence! Not this mumbo jumbo black magic crap."

"And you will have that, in time." He placed a soothing hand on my shoulder. I shrugged it off and stepped back a pace, out of his reach. He sighed, eyes falling to the floor. Behind him, the world was growing gray and violet with the coming dawn. My eyes shifted from him to the windowpanes and back, my agitation growing worse with every passing moment. I could feel the Sleep starting to draw at the center of my being. A heavy lead weight hung over my heart slowing me subtly with every step.

Phelan sighed again, shaking his head sadly. He turned and walked to a bedside table of intricately carved oriental mahogany. From there, he retrieved a small black remote. He pointed it at the windows. There was a soft click from either side of the room followed by the soft mechanical whirring of electrical gears as thin sheets of dark metal began to descend from the ceiling. I watched as the waking world turned to shadows and steel, feeling the last of my love for my Maker die with the light. With a hiss and a click, like the safety lifted on a handgun, the automated sheets locked into place.

Phelan crossed the room, passing by me without a glance. He sank into a large red velvet armchair near the dark stone hearth. As if summoning a water boy, he flicked his wrist at the fireplace. Flames roared to life, hot and angry. He looked up at me silently, orange flickers reflecting in his eyes, clouding any emotion lurking on the other side.

"Whether you believe me or not, you do have a choice in this matter."

I was aghast. My eyes widened, my lips moved, but no sound escaped. Before I could enunciate my disgust, he waved me to silence and continued.

"I will not hold you here against your will. Not again. If you cannot find the truth you need to convince yourself of the legitimacy of this cause...I have no choice but to leave the door open. All I ask is that you give me a little time to make my case. I think you owe me that much. You have all the time in the world...what is another night?"

I didn't answer. I was growing weaker with each passing second. I needed to find my quarters and fast. I stared into the hungry depths of the fire. I felt caged and scared. "Why should I trust you?"

"Because the cause will be pursued, with or without you. *We* have little choice in that matter. But I do feel for you, Tynan. You've been through a lot in your lifetime. However, unlike many of us, you have not grown hard in your years, but felt each and every one of the blows as if it were the first, as if you were still human. I can't say that I have always understood you, but I do feel for you. And thus, I cannot, as your Dark Father, condemn you to another battle."

I began to laugh. In my weariness, my psyche had become overwhelmed; I could feel my judgment and restraint slipping, words falling out of my mouth without hesitation. "You pity me. All of you. You treat me as humans do their senile aged ones. And you hate it. You hate the very fact that the Phuree have chosen me. Tynan, the demented. Tynan, the pathetically human, to lead your cause and save you!" A silent chuckle shook my entire frame.

"Tynan—?" He began to lift himself out of his chair, wary that perhaps I was truly loosing it after all.

I cut him off before he could begin again, "You're right! I do have the choice. And, it seems, I have the power as well! The power over...well... *Everything*! I guess you get to play by my rules for a while. That is, if you want your messiah to save your precious little world."

I gestured wildly with my hands at the room around me. I suddenly felt alive and wicked. The anger inside of me had transformed suddenly into a devious mischief. A sense of control over my own fate that I hadn't felt in hundreds of years surged through me. My heart was thundering in my chest. I turned to face him. "I'll tell you what. I won't just give you a night. I'll give you a whole week to show me something as moving as the Second Coming and if you do, I'll consider taking up the sword on your behalf. However, if I don't see proof by the time that last sun sets, I will leave and you will *never* contact me again. We will be finished." I turned and walked to the door.

On the other side, a young mortal woman attendant was waiting to show me to my quarters. I wondered how long she had been there, and what she had heard of our conversation. My concern did not last long for my attention turned back to my weakening state of being. Staring at the floor all the while, the young woman offered her arm for me to lean on. I was taken aback and stared at her for a long while before accepting. She began to lead me down the darkened hall.

Phelan called out to me from his place near the hearth, "You are a fool, Tynan, to be so brazen. A true fool."

The door swung shut behind us with a thick wooden echo and I was alone again. Alone with only a human girl to guide me through the darkness.

6

When you lose all hope you often have your greatest epiphanies. When you have nothing to lose, nothing is sacred and nothing is revered. You become omnipotent as the culprits of your demise witness your reckless insanity. That night I cut the last thread tethering me to my hope and lost myself in the numbness of nothingness.

If they wanted a messiah, a messiah they would get.

I awoke the following evening in a plush bed of dark blue velvet: silken sheets that only royalty should have been allowed to wallow in. I reveled in it. It was perfect for the new king of the end of the world. Not a devil. Not a saint or a martyr, but simply the one person who could make or break a war of worlds. I had never in my life felt so powerful. It was perfect. I sank deeper beneath the down comforter, realizing with a mild shock that I was naked. I peered over the edge of the heavy blankets at the room around me. My old clothes were nowhere in sight. In their place, I saw clean linen pants and a shirt folded neatly over the back of a chair near the window. I couldn't remember who had taken my clothes or when, but I cared little. I had lost my sense of modesty long ago.

The room was eerily still and dark. The steel shades had been raised on the windows to my left. The storms of the previous night had vanished. Moonlight poured in from a cloudless obsidian sky. Everything was sharper to the point of being surreal, the furniture more angular and pronounced, jutting from blue-black shadows and milky white light. The walls seemed to stretch upwards forever and yet, I felt I could reach out and touch the tiny details in the ceiling stucco. My head felt clearer than it had in centuries, focused and humming with energy. I lay awake for a long while simply watching the stars shimmering in the sky outside, something I hadn't done in a long, long time.

For reasons I couldn't explain, the anger and resentment that had surged through my veins for Phelan and the rest of my Immortal brethren had vanished. My heart felt hardened towards them. I pitied them for their complacency, just as they pitied me for my "humanity", for my strange madness. They wanted me to lead them, like cows to slaughter. Phelan had said I had a choice, that I was free to go. I knew better though. Nothing was ever that easy.

I stretched out like a cat, arching my back before slipping out of bed. The hardwood floors were cold beneath my bare feet. My skin prickled from the chill, sending quick shivers down my spine. To my right was an open door. The chamber beyond was heavy with black shadows. I could barely make out the glimmer of a porcelain sink and a mirror above it. I made my way to the bathroom, flicking the switch beside the door as I entered.

Light from a fixture above the mirror flooded the room, jarring my senses and causing my eyes to ache fiercely. The room was small and simple and elegant. Fresh towels had been stacked on the closed toilet seat. I sat on the edge of the white marble tub and turned the faucets on. The air filled with lazy white steam that drifted out into the bedroom. The rush of water was a strangely meditative sound, plunging from the duel gold plated fixtures and echoing off the dense marble below, constant and cleansing.

I turned the water off when the tub was about halfway full and slipped in. I sighed heavily as I felt the lingering tension melt from my muscles beneath the seductive caress of hot water. The steam invaded my pores making me feel lighter and cleaner. I closed my eyes and slid completely under the water. Like a womb, it surrounded me with an echoing silence. My own heartbeat filled my ears. Behind my eyes, images began to appear.

The dragons!

I had seen them again. They had visited me while I slept; their screeching echoed through my head; the red one and the white one, clawing their way to the surface. They were almost here. They had almost reached the surface. What was stopping them? A flash of black, steel scales passed through my mind's eye and with it, the water lost its warmth around me. A loud and sinister roar seized my heart with obsidian claws.

Could it be a third dragon? My mind raced frantically. Whatever it was, it was far older than the ones I had seen before. There was an angry venomous aura about the creature, one of vengeance centuries sought.

Coughing and gasping, I burst up out of the water. My lungs burned from the frantically inhaled water. I rubbed my eyes, trying to gain focus on the waking world again. I reached out and touched the black tiled wall with cold shaking fingers.

The dreams were coming to me more and more often. Usually, they were just as the original one had been, when I had first awoken to the new century. I often tried to hold onto the dream for as long as I could, to push beyond the repetitious ending. I wanted to know more, but my fear would force me to wake. This one was different though, I realized. I hadn't dreamed the day before. I hadn't dreamed at all.

I ran my fingers through my wet hair, gripping it to pull my head back. I stared at the ceiling; my heart thundered in my ears. A sharp chill clawed at my spine. I looked around the room. The nauseating feeling that someone was watching me was intense. The room was empty. With the exception of the gentle movement of water against marble, all was silent. I lifted myself from the tub and quickly dried off. The luxury and extravagance of the soft bath towels was lost now. I slipped into the new linen clothes that had been left for me. They fit perfectly, but I felt strange and uncomfortable in them. My worn army boots sat beneath the chair, cleaned of silt and mud. I pulled them on hurriedly. The clothes suddenly felt too insubstantial, the boots too heavy.

"Damn-it!" I hissed under my breath. I could barely control the shaking in my hands to finish lacing up the boots. I took a deep breath, trying to steady myself.

I considered the importance of the new dragon vision as I scanned the bedroom for my leather satchel. Like my clothes, it too had disappeared. Suddenly, I remembered the dull thud as it had fallen to the floor outside the library. Distracted by Phelan's embrace, I had left it there, unprotected. Panic gripped my throat. My innermost workings had been scrawled on those pages. From my hatred of my own kind to vicious confessions of my victims' last breaths, the words were secrets I would not even share with a soul mate. I kicked the chair across the room. It crashed into the dormant fireplace with a splintering thunder. I staggered to the mantelpiece. Leaning heavily on the marble shelf, I stared into the mammoth mirror above. I wanted to destroy it all, the mansion, the vampires, the humans, the ideals, the wars, myself.

"Just get yourself through the next few nights. Put your mask on and dance around them as you've done for years. Then you'll be free of it all...forever!" I whispered to my reflection. Deep slow breaths of stale air moved through my lungs. Stuffing the lashing hissing resentment back into its iron cage, I pulled back from the mantelpiece and smoothed down my wrinkled shirt. Damn the book and all of its secrets. They all thought I was mad anyway.

* * *

I slunk through the long red corridor past shut doors and tall black arched windows. The world was abstract and empty, devoid of life or light. Through the layers of brick and mortar, Persian silk and wrought iron, muffled voices began to seep from the edges of the house. Mara's quiet concern and Traq's restless fears. From the library wing I sensed Sea and Phelan in a heavily cloaked and heated debate. I picked up my pace, straining to break through their auric walls. The secretive pact between them still grated against my intuition like reverberating shrapnel from a car bomb.

The hallway came abruptly to an end, opening up to the cavernous greeting hall and cascading black marble staircase. I stared up at the wrought iron chandeliers suspended from vaulted ceilings painted like the night sky. A painted full moon watched me from its bed of stucco and wood. I listened, trying to pick out the subject of Sea and Phelan's debate, but their shields were a titanium fortress guarding them. A cool breeze caressed me, causing my clothes to ripple against my skin. I tore my eyes away from the moon and found a set of open

French doors to my right. As if in a trance, I followed the beckoning night air out onto the balcony.

My foot touched the stone terrace and the voices stopped. They had sensed me and withdrawn even further. Good. I wanted them to know I was listening. The night sky stretched out above me, the roof of an ancient sea cave. It rolled out forever over the undulating hills of the Texas landscape below, its dense clusters of dying worlds were like the diamonds of Persephone's hope chest.

"Beautiful, isn't it?"

I whirled around. Tatsu stepped out of the shadows at the far corner of the balcony, hands stuffed in the pockets of his black pants, his long hair whipping about his face. I had been so lost in my pursuit of Sea and Phelan that I had been oblivious to his presence.

Disconcerted, but not terribly concerned, I turned back to the nightscape behind me. "What do you want Tatsu?"

"You do have allies." He leaned against the balcony next to me, facing the French doors. "You're not the only one who thinks Phelan's overstepped his bounds."

"*Allies* is an abstract term. I find it too loosely used amongst this group." I continued to stare straight ahead at the dim horizon.

Tatsu laughed under his breath. "I'm not sure if that's wisdom or bitterness in your voice."

"Last time I checked it was called sarcasm." The last thing I wanted to do was place my faith in a fellow Immortal.

"At any other time I would tell you, you were taking all of this too seriously, but right now, you are completely correct in your evaluation of the situation. This is very serious. I'm not trying to earn your trust. Just know, there are those who are watching your back." Gently, he pushed away from the balcony and walked silently inside.

I lingered a while longer on the balcony. I dreaded the evening to come. I would be playing a guessing game with what each expression meant. Were they with me, were they against me? It was nothing but more torturous new information to eat away at the edges of my attention.

I made no attempt to disguise my presence as I slowly

walked down the polished stairs, my features frozen in a determined frown. I strolled back down the hall towards the Great Hall. To my left and right were open doors and archways leading to various rooms. Scattered throughout were the familiar grave faces of the previous evening. I could feel their eyes on me as I passed by, their conversations and movements ceasing until I was out of sight. It was as if I was on my way to the stake to be burned.

Dead man walking...

The hour hand on the grandfather clock reached nine and the hollow gong of metal reverberated through the house. My bones caught the dense ripple of sound and moved me forward. Without announcing myself, I entered the library and shut the door loudly behind me. Phelan sat behind his obscenely grand desk by the bay window. Sea leaned against one corner of the desk, his back to me. Phelan's head snapped sharply towards me when he heard the echo of the door. He whirled around, his eyes wide and angry at the intrusion. They had been intently discussing an open book upon the desk; it was my journal.

I felt the hackles bristle on the back of my neck. Phelan stood up slowly, palms flat on the desk before him. He watched me warily. "Why don't you have a seat, Tynan?"

"I prefer to stand." I strode over to them and snatched the journal off the desk, snapping it shut. "I told you I'd give you one chance to earn my trust. This isn't what I had in mind."

"You have certain knowledge we need," Sea chimed in.

"And that *knowledge* is in *this*?! What are you trying to do? Find more proof that I'm unstable?!" I hissed.

I could hear the retort forming in Sea's mind.

"Shut up!" I snapped at him before he had a chance to utter a word. He recoiled, hands raised in mock surprise, a sly smirk on his face.

"There are equations throughout that notebook, strings of code. Tynan, you already have a great deal of the information we need to strike at the Tyst." Phelan kept his tone low and even.

"What's in this book are scribblings, random notations,

nothing more!" I shook the book at him. "You lied! I don't have a choice in this at all. What I don't give you freely, you'll take anyway!"

Sea continued. "And the last victim you took, the girl on the river bank..."

"What about her?!" I stared at them, horrified. "How do you know about that? I didn't write that down..." The sense of violation was sickening.

"How we know is not important." Sea's tone became dark and serious.

"You've been following me!" I was aghast. I had never sensed being followed.

"The girl you took was the Tyst Queen's personal handmaid," Sea continued over my stuttering.

"What are you talking about? I read nothing of that when I met her." I knew deep within my soul that I lied as flashes of what I had absorbed of her past flickered across my mind, the broken strings of code and strange images of the fortress that I had dismissed as unimportant at the time. I was absolutely stunned that they could read such a thing through my words alone.

"Rumor has it that she was on her leave of duty for the evening and slipped out of the fortress. The last place she was seen was in the quarter where you were that evening." Phelan paused, trading uneasy glances with Sea.

"I don't understand. Why...what does it mean to you?" Confusion and rage were beginning to blur my vision.

Phelan took a careful step towards me, "It is nearly impossible for anyone within the center ring of the Tyst fortress to leave. Their security settings are locked into the Chronous matrix. It monitors their every move. A handmaiden would never have been taught, on any level, how to read or manipulate the matrix. If this girl was able to get out, she was not only devious, but she was a pure genius. You took her essence into you, which means, if you tried, you could retrieve her memories."

"That's it, I'm out of here." I turned and walked towards the door.

I reached for the doorknob and was met with the icy

sensation of Immortal flesh. Sea was standing before me, his hand blocking my one exit. "Tynan, don't." It was not a plea, but a warning of extreme caution. Our eyes locked in a match of wills.

I reached out with my mind, *Why do you do this to me? After everything we've been through, is our friendship truly that dead to you?*

He replied, his words like a shimmering razor blade across my soul, *There is no time for such sentimental friendship anymore.*

Without a word I turned on my heel and strode towards the fireplace. Before they could anticipate my actions, I hurled the journal into the flames. Sea dashed towards the hearth, grabbing the iron poker. With a strange desperation, he dug the journal out of the hot coals, dragging it out onto the floor where he stamped out the remaining smoldering edges with his boot. Gingerly, he picked it up and returned it to Phelan's open palm.

I stared at the two of them in disbelief. They were sinister angels in their conspiracy, gazing stonily at me through their flawless guise of perfection. I could not comprehend their egocentrical logic or their lawless sense of truth. When had I simply become another pawn?

"You forsook your status when you turned your back on our world." Phelan's tone was even and cool.

I said nothing and quickly put another layer of defense around my mental fortress. Inside, I cringed knowing how close I had been to believing Phelan's promises of free will the night before. I struggled to maintain my composure; deep down I was slipping, a wolf in a steel trap, ready to gnaw my own leg off to save myself. The hunter was standing over me. He watched me bleed, somewhat amused. All I could do was snarl and snap.

And then suddenly the ground was gone—I lunged at Phelan, fangs bared, pale fingers curled like claws, ready to rip into his alabaster flesh. It was instinctual and primeval, fight or flight, kill or be killed. I was blind, the world dissolving into a red haze. I felt my hands on his throat, my nails biting through his ancient skin. Fire burned in my veins fueling the surge of strength that lifted us from the ground and dominated my Maker. The smell of his blood awakened a sickening primal Thirst deep within me. Far below us, I could hear the shocked cries of my brethren as they ran into the room, muted and warped as if in slow motion. We struggled and flew high into the dark arched ceiling above, twin dragons bent on annihilation.

Phelan's roar echoed off the ceiling as I bit down hard on his throat. For a moment, the reverberating sound startled me, but the distraction was fleeting. I could feel his nails, tiny shards of glass, tearing through the thin linen of my shirt. Hot rivulets of blood snaked down my back from the shredded flesh beneath. I clutched at him, sucking hard on the punctured artery forcing the flesh to stay open as it frantically tried to mend itself. Oblivious, I drowned myself over and over again in his vital essence.

Suddenly, a blinding white lightning strike exploded between us. The force of the explosion ripped me away from Phelan, hurling me towards the earth. Electricity fizzed beneath my skin as Phelan's blood mingled with mine, the power of it restructuring my DNA, strengthening it, warping it. I stared up at the dark shadows above me as I fell. I could see myself reflected in Phelan's eyes, deranged and demented, white face smeared with blood. I fell fast towards the earth, a meteorite of gore-streaked flesh and bones.

My body slammed into the ground with a sharp crack. The sound echoed through the room and all became quiet. Outside the tall windows, a low wind moaned. I lay stunned, unable to move. Hot coppery liquid welled up into my mouth, filling my throat and choking off my attempts to breathe. I could feel my lungs slowly beginning to fill as the blood drained back down into my airways. I gasped and coughed sending a spray of crimson into the air. It fell in a glittering sheet of tiny liquid rubies around me. Pain starburst through my abdomen. I grasped at my stomach; my fingers touched something hard and slick with a warm sticky substance. Shaking, forcing myself not to succumb to shock, my hands traced the item down to where it disappeared into my stomach. I lifted my head slowly to inspect the damage.

Panic gripped me hard through my haze of delirium. I had struck one of the large wooden armchairs with enough force to obliterate it. Only one leg remained intact. It impaled through my stomach, a gore-slick death sentence. Blood pooled around me, seeping into the polished floorboards and Persian rugs, staining my dark blue clothes black. My heart thundered, dangerously draining my body of its vital essence. I gasped; I was drowning in the blood I had stolen from Phelan. For so many years, I had told the world that I had wanted to die, but now, faced with the sudden harsh reality of death, I found myself fighting to stay amongst the living.

Shaking nearly uncontrollably, I grasped the chair leg thinking I might pry it from my body. A pinned moth, my hands becoming skeletal and nearly translucent with each passing second, I barely had the strength to hold on for a fleeting second before they slipped off the shaft, falling to either side of me as if my strings had been cut.

I can't die like this, My mind raced as my vision began to fade, *It can't end like this!*

A fog was building around the corners of my eyes, leaching the light from the room. Phelan bent over me, studying me with a quiet hatred. I could barely make out the gouge in his neck where only moments before I had dominated him. In another few minutes, it wouldn't be visible at all.

"You are so foolish, my child." He shook his head in cold disbelief.

I tried to reply, but all that emerged was a gurgling of red fluid over my lips. Shadows upon darker shadows crowded my vision. I tightened my body forcing the blood up out of my lungs and into my mouth. With my last waking breath, I spit hard at Phelan, drenching him in the stagnant hot mixture of blood and saliva. He backed up cursing as if I had thrown holy water on him. I closed my eyes and felt my head hit the floor, a dull thud that sent me into darkness.

"Sea, get him out of here."

* * *

I had often wondered what the afterlife for our kind would be like and if there would even be one for creatures such as we? I had done my best with the lives I was given, both the one birthed by my mortal mother and the one dealt by my Immortal father. I had asked for neither. I had known many vampires who believed they were damned for merely existing. I suppose that in the later years of my life, before my long Sleep, I had begun to believe that myself, that eternity on earth was a sad sort of hell, that we were condemned to an existence where right and wrong were obscured by the dominance of instinct. I had searched in vain for a light to cling to, some justification for our existence; a philosophy that could give us a rightful claim to the earth.

I had merged the liberating philosophies of Existentialism with the theory of a holographic universe and the new earth magic of Witta and Wicca, of the Celtic and Norse paganisms of my ancestors that made anything and everything possible. I gave us a beginning, a purpose and an end. I called it Preternaturalism. It was beautiful, it was succinct and it justified every horrible crime we committed in the name of Nature. The others clung to it as I did. We were vampires and for the first time since our inception into creation we were not the Devil's minions. However, I had never found an answer that rang true to the great question of what lay beyond the physical realm for those of us who had finally been laid to rest: A heaven and a hell to divide up the sum total of our deeds? A netherworld to cross over to and find our peace? Reincarnation? After all of my earthly sins, I dreaded that, above all else. My greatest fear was that we would simply cease to exist, our powers relegated to a womb-like darkness to drift in and out of fathomless possibility for an eternity; our energy to be dispersed throughout the web of time and space like scattered ash in the wind...

Gradually, I became aware of a gentle swaying motion and the distant groan of an engine. Through a cold static of numbness, I began to recognize the outline of my body. As if they had fallen asleep, my limbs were alive with millions tiny electric sparks dancing chaotically like hungry frantic worms just below the surface of my skin. I could feel my fingers twitching as random electric impulses fired through the muscles. It was an odd sensation, as if I was plugged into an electric conduit and no longer controlled the flow.

"Tynan?" The voice startled me, cutting through the darkness. I felt my body twitch in response. The voice was familiar and warm, with my mortal mother's same sweet lilt. I drifted along the blanket of electric currents. Behind my eyes I searched for her, sinking back into the dream-like state.

"I think he's coming to?" Another whisper, sharp and male. I did not recognize it at first as I compared it to my memories. It was sharper with a soft Grecian accent.

"Check his wound." The male voice again, concern in his tone this time. There was a tugging sensation near where my waist should have been. Slowly, I became aware of my own breathing, heavy and deep, the rise and fall of my chest and the cold texture of my clothing.

How odd, I thought, *that my soul should wear clothing?*

The tugging sensation vanished and for a long moment there was nothing. Just as I began to sink back into my comfortable black sanctuary, there was a light pressure on my stomach, reeling my attention back. The sharp prickling radiated outwards to my chest and legs; the pushing became more forceful and in a blinding instant, pain exploded through me as if I had swallowed a live grenade. An eerie animalistic howl escaped my lips, jarring me into waking reality. Without thinking, I lashed out, striking hard at the thing that had been inspecting my wound.

"Goddammit! That hurt!" The female voice again, irritated and a bit angry. "I'd say he's coming to." Sarcasm. I recognized it suddenly as Lillian's and wondered just how hard I had hit her.

I wasn't dead! Fear, relief, disappointment, wonder; layer after layer of distorted emotion washed over me. I groaned. Clutching at my stomach, I rolled onto my side and curled into a tight protective fetal ball. I could hear an engine now, old and badly in need of a tune-up. Large heavy tires raced below the floor where I lay, hissing over wet pavement, catching every tiny bump and pothole. I cringed as we hit a rough patch, the jarring sensation sending arcs of fire through my chest and abdomen. I could only imagine, with a nauseating shudder, the shards of wooden splinters still embedded in my kidneys and intestines. The gods only knew how long it would be before my body dealt with that, breaking down the hard organic material bit by bit and forcing it out of the pores of my skin by means of blood sweat. I had a long painful road of healing ahead of me.

"At least the bleeding has stopped." The male voice had a face now: Tatsu. "He's healing quickly. Phelan's blood must have sped up the process a bit. I'm surprised he survived at all. Never seen anything live through something like that before."

"Yes, but he's going to need to feed, and soon." Lillian's tension was tangibly thick; I could feel her concern radiating from her as she knelt beside me. It grated my raw nerves, adding fuel to the fire of worry that burned already in my chest.

"Shhh! Not so loud," Tatsu hissed. "Remember the two louts driving this thing—"

"Hey, is everything alright back there?" A strong male voice shouted over the roar of the decrepit engine through the tiny sliding window above my head.

"Yes, we have it all under control," Tatsu shouted back.

There was a long tense pause penetrated only by the sound of the truck rumbling through the night. Then the window slammed shut with a hiss and a crack.

"If Tynan feeds, it has to look like he did it on his own. Phelan wants to keep him as harmless as possible and that means weak. If we're caught helping him, we'll be the ones with a hole through our guts!" Tatsu spoke so quickly and quietly that I had to strain to capture it all.

I opened my eyes. Gradually my surroundings came into focus. Metal walls merged with the small tinted concave windows above dusty blue gray carpet, scratchy and gritty against the side of my face. I could only see what was directly in front of me, but the vehicle we traveled in *felt* large and heavy, an army van or SUV from the 21st century. All of the

113

seats had been removed to make way for cargo. Tatsu was sitting on a large black metal crate near my knees, staring out of the tinted glass of the rear two windows. Like a dark raven on his perch, his moonlit form was tense and watchful. I slid my hand towards him, inching the skeletal digits over his hand-tooled Italian leather shoes to the cuff of his pants. I grabbed hold of the thin fabric; my hand began to shake from the exertion. Tatsu jumped like a frightened cat. He stared down at me, half horrified, half pitying. The expression was all too familiar; the strength vanished from my hand. It slipped slowly to the floor.

"Where—?" A hoarse rasp slid past my cracked lips. There wasn't air enough in my lungs to finish the thought, but Tatsu understood. His expression changed to a sad kindness.

He reached down and laid his hand on mine. "We go to meet the Phuree. But do not focus on that now."

"Yes, Tynan, you must rest and let your body heal itself." Lillian moved closer to me. She reached out and stroked the side of my face, gently pulling the hair back out of my eyes. I continued to stare at Tatsu, unblinking and wild as I tried to read what lay beneath the dark pools of his eyes.

I turned my hand over beneath Tatsu's wrapping my fingers around his. He squeezed my palm gently as if he were afraid he might break me if he gripped too hard. I could smell Lillian's delicate scent of sweet tea and parchment as she hovered over me. Dry heat and sand blew through my mind. The Phuree were merely legend to me. They now held the key to my fate, my future. I had attempted to change the course of my destiny by waging war with Phelan. I had lost that battle and I would not forget the consequences. It would be nights before I had the strength or courage to do so again.

I closed my eyes and let go with a deep ragged exhale.

T

I awoke, propped against the front grille of the truck, a hunting trophy about to be skinned and cleaned of its useless parts. The night was heavy, the metal cold against my back. A dense bluish fog had crept in, sweet and low and smelling of earth and ozone. I stared mutely ahead into the soundless motion of the ground clouds, my neck tilted to the side as if it were broken. I could not move; I had neither strength nor will to do so. My body felt weightless, so light that I wondered if it might drift away with the fog. I pictured myself spiraling off into the mist, a lost receipt of purchased experiences, dreams and desires. The pain that had tortured my body had vanished. In its place nestled an astounding clarity, a lucidity of mind and body that I had not experienced in centuries. I felt as if I had been fasting for years, blessed with a cleanliness that was strangely alive.

I became aware of the sand beneath me, every glassine crystal both soft and razor-edged. Molecules of moisture suspended in the fog danced before my eyes, amoebas spiraling beneath the clever lens of a microscope. I sat motionless, a discarded Halloween decoration, wrapped in my meditations, and listened to the echo of the night. I raised my eyes towards where the sky should have been, searching for the moon or the faintest twinkle of a dying planet; I could see nothing but rolling ground cloud and velvety pitch.

Crunchshh. Crunchshh. Crunchshh. Even and soft, the sound of heavy boots crushing the splinters of millions upon millions of miniscule fossils into a finer dust for the sun to bake again with a new day. *Crunchshhh. Crunchshh. Crunchshh.* A second pair, lighter than the first, treading softly on the bones of history. Voices drifted towards me, hushed and hard to locate in the oublean fog. The dialect was clipped and aggressive, every sentence a threat no matter the inflection.

115

Crunchshh. Crunchshh. Crunchshh. Two snakes hissing at each other across the sand, they moved towards me as if evolving from the fog. I watched them emerge from the shadows; heavy dark leather boots laced up to the knee, rough hewn leather pants of a lighter tan with long sleeved tunics of dusty dark hues. Thick dark blue cloaks swirled around their bodies, the wings of a stingray flying through the ocean's depths.

They stopped just short of my outstretched legs. Their voices fell silent, banished ghosts dissipating into the fog. The one to my right softly nudged my foot with the tip of his boot as if uncertain I was even alive. Slowly, I rolled my head back to lean it against the icy metal of the bumper. My eyes felt heavy and it was hard to focus; the movement made my head spin and stomach threaten to crawl up my throat. I watched the pair carefully; a man and a woman, both in their mid twenties, though it was hard to gauge for certain from their sun etched skin. They closely resembled each other with piercing storm blue eyes and sun-bleached hair. They watched me with veiled scrutiny; it was impossible to read their thoughts. The man, a good foot taller than his female counterpart, squatted down so that we were on the same eye level.

"Tynan Llywelyn?" His voice was strong and crisp, the sound of one who had led troops since a young age.

I wanted to speak, but when I moved my lips, no sound emerged. The man looked back up at his companion. The wind was beginning to pick up, vanquishing the fog with greater speed. As the clouds cleared, I began to notice other forms waiting silently in the dark at a distance. Their presence sent an eerie shiver across my skin.

He looked back at me and began to speak in heavily accented English. "I am Tiernan Eldrid the second, chieftain of the Phuree. This is my sister Khanna Eldrid." He gestured to the woman standing at his side. "This is not how we had expected to receive you, but we will try to make you as comfortable as possible."

Tiernan and Khanna quickly bent to lift me from my slack position. I sensed no fear in them, only urgency and duty.

Arms intertwined beneath my slack form, they lifted me from the ground. My head fell back with a snap over their interlaced limbs as they carried me, a sacrificial offering for the hidden agendas dictating my destiny. The sea of silent onlookers parted before us, closing in behind us with one fluid movement. I watched their inquisitive expressions through my half-lowered lids; the grave white faces of the Immortals, stark and guarded, beside the tan, weather and worry-etched features of the Phuree. The vampires moved in and out of the dark shadows of the crowd, snakes weaving their way through a murky river. So alien they appeared suddenly, meditative and wary ghosts chasing a past no longer obtainable. I closed my eyes and sighed into the fog and darkness.

The whispering of muddled unspoken thoughts bored their way through the sinew and muscle of my shell to the fragile web of my mind. Though I could not understand their language, the raw emotion contained within those foreign words sliced through the malaise of numbness to which my soul had retreated until my body healed. The Phuree were worried; the fear of extinction, the dread of further persecution, the weariness of a people at war for a hundred years. I could almost taste the bitter sadness that dripped from their thoughts as they questioned why they had decided to place their faith in me. A sour nausea rose in my stomach as the wretched current of their thoughts threatened to drown me. Each step my carriers took jarred my aching bones. I opened my eyes. A small girl watched me from behind the hem of her mother's skirt, pure blue eyes wide with wonder, and I suddenly remembered the morning sky on the day I was incepted, how true and sacred it had felt as I knew, without truly knowing, that I would never see it again.

The future of the Phuree now rested on their misguided oracle and the broken shell of a vampire, too weak to even walk. The world spun around me as we moved deeper into the heart of the Phuree base-camp. Torches burned solemn and motionless atop tall wooden stakes, stripped of their bark and carved deep with elegantly cryptic tribal designs painted in eerie red henna like the blood of their enemies. Long shadows stretched from the crowd, bleeding up and over the rippling

117

sides of the leather teepees, distorting the tanned animal flesh of the shelters so that it appeared alive and breathing. The heavy musk of men and animals coiled beneath the odor of campfire smoke, stinging the delicate lining of my nose and throat with its unaccustomed pungency. Deep beneath, mingled the earthy sweet scent of incense and pipe smoke embedded within the pores of salt rich flesh and sand dusted hair. All was silent except for the dull crunching of feet on sand and the restless pacing of the wind. The molten aura of magic permeated the world around me, emanating from the Phuree people, a hot breath against my skin. I closed my eyes and sank deeper into their sea.

Tiernan and Khanna stopped suddenly. I felt the crowd close in behind us, waiting apprehensively. Brief words were exchanged in low clipped tones. My curiosity was not enough to warrant the energy necessary to lift my head to see the party with which they spoke. I focused on the rushing of blood through my temples. The living power housed by the Phuree taunted me, luring me seductively to succumb to its ancient knowledge. Eons of worship had given the primal magic life, made it an entity which no longer needed its followers to survive.

Come, love me...use me...make me your own...

I wanted it. I wanted the strength and power, to be whole again.

The rustle of heavy fabric being lifted and dropped behind us woke me abruptly as the pull of the unseen diminished as if a door had been suddenly slammed in its face. Through the cobwebs that choked the light from my perception, I was faintly aware of the crowd outside beginning to disperse, people turning hesitantly back to the uncertainty of their own fragile lives. Tiernan and Khanna gently laid me on a thick pallet of woven fabrics and heavy soft furs. The interior of the teepee was hot and stifling after the chill humidity of the desert night.

Although a flap high on one side of the octagonal structure had been opened, the air was close and acrid from the small fire that burned inside a raised clay pit in the center. Like a broken china doll, limbs numb and lying inert and lifeless up on the bed, I watched my captors with a detached curiosity. My soul longed to wander with the ether and dance with the magic that called to it, but it was tethered inexorably to my broken frame. I could feel it straining against its chains, a feral dog on a new leash. I narrowed my eyes as I watched Tiernan kneeling before me, repressing the urge to growl at him.

Tiernan sat back on his heels, studying me silently. His thoughts conspired behind the iron gates of his mind, pacing furiously behind the shallow blue pools of his eyes. Khanna hurriedly retrieved a clay basin of water from a low wooden table on the far side of the tent. Alone, with only her brother to protect her from me, her cool reserve began to crumble quickly. Panic and fear radiated from her in jagged pulses of energy even as she tried to subdue them beneath of guise of calm determination. My presence deeply disturbed her, as it should have. Tiernan, remained unreadable. The evidence of his valor was etched into the lines around his eyes; a deep scar traced the length of his jaw, the palest pink and white in its newness against the golden bronze of his skin. The dark prophetic symbols of a tribal tattoo swirled along his scalp beneath his closely cropped blond hair. It vanished into the longer locks on top that curled forward against his forehead and snaked down his neck to disappear beneath his shirt. He reminded me of the young warriors of my homeland, fierce and unmovable, willing to die for their family and their gods and placing nobility and honor above all else. His nobility was lost on such an age as the one we lived in.

Khanna returned bearing the basin of water and a clean linen rag. With her eyes transfixed on the task at hand, she knelt beside me, accentuating the tense silence with the rustle of her clothes. I listened to the trickle and splash of water returning to the basin, wind through bamboo reeds, as she wrung the wet cloth of excess moisture. Nervously, she pressed the cloth to my temples. I could feel her trembling through the rag. Tiernan and I continued to watch each other with unwavering suspicion. In my peripheral vision, I could see Khanna's eyes darting nervously from one man to the other, searching for a means to end the silence.

"You do not trust us," Tiernan said quietly.

With shaking fingers, I reached down and pulled up the front of my torn blue shirt to reveal the swollen and raw puncture wound slowly knitting itself back together. "I do not trust my own people. What reason do I have to trust yours?"

Khanna turned her head away with a small gasp, unable to allow her gaze to linger further on my torn flesh. Tiernan stared down at the wound, his expression overcast and distant.

"You have no reason to trust us." He crossed his arms over his chest. "Just as we have no reason to trust you."

"What are you implying?" I was too weak to protest greatly.

Tiernan did not reply, but only watched me in careful silence.

I knew he had been told tales about me. Phelan and his lot would certainly have painted a picture of an unruly dangerous element.

I lowered my shirt back over the wound. I did not feel the need to justify my actions to yet another stranger. My voice was flat and cold. "You should be careful not take sides so quickly."

"I assure you, the only side I am on is my own. My only concern is for the lives of my people. I am still unsure what to make of you, your people or this new turn the war has taken." He paused for a long moment and I became aware of the distinct sensation of being *read*. I tried to mask my shock, quickly adding layer upon layer to my internal fortress to protect my weakened state. I stared into his eyes as they bored into me.

He severed the link suddenly with a snort rubbing the scar along his jaw in contemplation. "It is only under great persuasion that I have allowed you entrance to this tribe. Make no mistake, you are under close watch."

"I am as much a prisoner of this scam as you are."

"I am not a prisoner. Neither are you. But cross me, just once, and I'll kill you." Not a threat, but a simple matter of fact. He was his people's protector and I was a mere nuisance.

He turned to Khanna. "Give him the concoction Nahalo sent over. Join me when you are finished."

Khanna remained motionless at Tiernan's side. Her eyes darted back and forth between Tiernan and me like a cornered animal.

"Are you sure...?" Her voice trailed off as her eyes met mine, the same stormy blue as her brother's. She could smell death on me, the souls of the victims I had taken that would tinge the fabric of my being now and forever. Her instinct screamed for her to flee but her tragic pride held her in its grip.

He stroked the side of her face. "Where is the warrior in you, Khanna?" She didn't take her eyes off me. "This is different..."

Tiernan sighed heavily, slightly annoyed at being held up by her fear. "There are two guards posted right outside if you need anything." He gathered his cloak about him like folded wings as he stood.

Khanna nodded, suddenly ashamed of her display of weakness, and turned away to retrieve a steel and leather canteen from the small low table near the far wall. Tiernan walked quickly to the entrance of the tent. As his hand fell on the leather doorway, he paused hesitantly, casting one last furtive glance over his shoulder. His eyes flickered one last time from myself to his sister and back. Our gazes locked.

With my remaining reserve of strength, I spoke to him silently, *Do not worry. No harm will come to her.*

However meager, it seemed to be the assurance he needed and with a curt nod he disappeared through the tent's entrance. The leather flap fell after him with a whoosh, forcing a gust of cold night air into the stuffy tent. My body convulsed in a spasm of uncontrollable trembling as the air molested my skin through my thin torn garments. The exchange with Tiernan had squandered what little energy I had left. I craved the numb hollow womb of sleep and the promises of the whispering voices in the ether outside.

Beneath heavy lids, I watched Khanna as she worked, her back to me in a false air of security. Tiernan's challenge to her "warrior" spirit had obviously struck a sharp note. The amber light filtered through the fine curtains of her golden hair as she uncorked a bottle near the water pitcher and poured its thick dark contents into the canteen. From a small glass vial she added a silken white powder to the liquid.

Perhaps they do not know how a vampire's system works, I thought, *Or they would never offer me such to drink.*

She moved the canteen in small circles to swirl the mixture inside. Her shoulders rose and fell as she searched for strength before she turned back to face me.

She returned to my side, her footsteps soft on the woven jute mats. The flickering glow of the fire glittered off the polished metal of the canteen, igniting the delicate details of the ornamentation on the broad smooth sides. She held it close to her chest, a raw electricity of defensive tension crackling about her as she knelt beside me, shoulders back, spine ridged, as if supplicating before a king. I could smell her suddenly, beneath the heavy stink of campfire smoke and tanned animal flesh, a sweet earthy musk mixed with salt and cloves above the strong current of living blood. My body ached to take her life, to fill her mind with beautiful lies while I wrapped her in my skeletal arms and pulled her down to the mat beside me. The coppery perfume of youthful essence stung the delicate lining of my nose. My eyes began to tear as I struggled silently to restrain the beast within.

Khanna's stormy eyes darted over me as if sensing my growing unease. The fear that had immobilized her only moments before was now dampened by a magnetic and morbid fascination. She was being drawn in and drowned by the poisonous lure of the damned, the eerie silent dirge that could lead the most resolute of mortals like rats to their early demise. Questions danced on the tip of her tongue as reality and fantasy began to blur her vision till I glowed, a fallen angel in despair, before her. Her lips parted, her hand slowly reached out to stroke my blood-caked hair.

"Don't get too close," I whispered to her.

The words seemed to release her for a moment. A shiver, barely noticeable, ran through her body. She blinked as if awakening suddenly from an erotic dream. "What did you say?" she breathed, disoriented and embarrassed.

I said nothing.

She thrust the canteen towards me. It trembled in her

shaking hands. "Drink this."

I did not have the strength to receive it. Motionless, I stared at her. "What is it?" I asked between shallow hungry breaths.

"It will make you stronger. It will make you heal faster." Her voice shook delicately as she clipped her sentences. She knelt, her arms outstretched. "The Rayhee-Osm will visit you later to finish your healing."

"Is that what the Rayhee-whatever told you?" I sighed heavily through my nose and attempted to shift my position on the pallet to one a bit more comfortable, but it was useless. The fibers of my broken body screamed in agony no matter how it was laid. "If your healer knew anything about vampire anatomy, they would know that whatever you put in that canteen will only make things worse." My voice was edging on a growl as my irritation raked its glassine nails across my nerves.

Khanna said nothing. Her hands had begun to shake so badly that she could not hold the canteen any longer. She placed it on the pallet next to my waist. She snatched her hands away and stood up in one startled motion. "Please, we do not have time... Please drink." She could not form complete thoughts as her mind and heart raced out of sync with one another. "I must go." She gasped and raced from the tent.

With the powerful scent of her removed from the room, another pungent perfume snaked to my senses from the open mouth of the canteen. Blood. The strange sweetness that had lingered in the air while Khanna mixed the concoction was gone, leaving only the rich metallic scent of cooling life force. I grimaced, grinding my teeth together as every cell within my body struggled to break free of my humanity, to break free of my reasoning that the toxins she had added to the stagnant blood would do more harm than good. There was no warmth in the scent, no living pulse, but the hollow shell of an essence that dissipated with every passing moment. I wanted it, nonetheless.

Like a dry dead branch, something snapped inside of me. A throbbing shook my temples with a rhythm as old as the sun, blurring my vision with each pulse. Outside, the wind was picking up, rippling against the side of the tent with urgent curious fingers as it uttered a low sweet moan. Deep within me, the Hunger rolled its own sinister sound, bubbling up to slither between my clenched teeth. In the distance, the voices of men and women betrayed the chaotic state of distress that saturated the regal pride of the tribe, while the guards outside my tent exchanged hushed strings of gossip.

Nori chi ach Vampyre...

Fire burned beneath my skin as my breath broke in sharp short gasps. Gripped in a pulsing iron fist, my innards wrenched with the pain of starvation. My body would take it what needed to heal, with or without my consent. I pulled the canteen closer, a great, dark carrion bird circling someone else's kill, starved and depraved. I watched as my fingers coiled about the canteen, stumbling over the delicate engravings. The ice of metal on my lips brought a precious corruption I could not resist. I closed my eyes and surrendered. Cool thick liquid trickled over my tongue tasting of the residual aura of the dead, tainted with the bittersweet pungency of sacred herbs. Somewhere beneath the frenzied chittering of the Thirst, my mind wondered if the herbs Khanna had added would me. My body might reject them, leaving me weaker than before, but the idea was quickly washed away in the torrent of blood that flowed faster and faster from the canteen.

The blood passed directly into my parched tormented tissue. One million. Two million. Three million. Like tiny spiders hatching and scrambling through my veins, puncturing the tenuous tissue binding me to my skeleton, the tainted alien blood wrestled with my own. In echoing slow motion, the empty canteen slipped from my hands, tumbling off the pallet onto the ground. A scalding, acidic burn ripped through my brain as my body waged war on the toxins I had ingested, until it slowly surrendered to their strange power. My body twitched and jerked, broken bones melting into one another, tissue knitting and stretching where it had been rendered useless by the massive puncture wound. They fastened onto one another with a blinding speed, reconstructing lost marrow and hardening protein into an indestructible internal armor.

The small fragments of wood that still remained embedded deep within my spinal cord and delicate internal organs were quickly consumed like gunpowder beneath a flame as the alien blood digested and discarded the last remaining obstacles to my healing. The twitching in my limbs stopped and gradually the churning in my innards subsided, replaced by a calm, cool tingling just below the surface as if every nerve were awake and vibrating with the post-orgasmic thrill of being alive. I drew a deep breath as my frantic heartbeat began to slow, falling into a new rhythm, unfamiliar to me. My body no longer felt my own.

I stared up into the velvety shadows of the tent's high roof. The darkness, which had misted my vision since my injury, vanished. Angles of midnight and pitch black darted chaotically in a dance to escape the undulating firelight. I could feel traces of the blood I had taken from Phelan, which had not been consumed by the earth and wind as the others had carried me from the manor that night, but they seemed weaker now. It was as if the new blood I had consumed had scoured me from the inside out, stronger than even Phelan's ancient essence. I knew without a doubt that the new blood had not been animal or mortal. No human blood could heal a vampire with such lightning speed. It would have taken the blood of several victims and still several nights to reach my optimum health. Yet, no Immortal I knew had blood that could do this either. Such power came only with age and was legendary within our dwindling legions.

The wind was growing increasingly restless outside. A curious gust scampered beneath the bottom of the tent, testing my newly honed senses with serpentine tongues. I shivered, feeling each and every cold molesting finger upon me, chilling to ice the fine dew-like moisture that blanketed my body. I wiped my hand across my forehead. My fingertips glistened with droplets of rose-tinted blood sweat. I smiled as I stared at my fingers, knowing that my healing was nearly complete.

Slowly, I stood. My muscles felt full of taut strength eager to break free and exhaust itself. They trembled with restraint. I removed my shredded shirt. The fabric was heavily saturated. I tossed it absently aside, keeping my eyes fixed on the entrance where the guards outside had grown suspiciously quiet. I reached down and grabbed a blanket from the pallet next to me. Quickly, I wiped myself down to remove what moisture I could. I attempted to wring the sweat from my hair, but it had already begun to dry, matting the strands together in dark red clumps. Surges of mottled electricity fizzed and snapped behind my eyes. With my body nearly completely restored. There was nothing that could hinder me in my flight and yet, I lingered.

For some inexorable reason, I suddenly felt a bond with the Phuree that I could not explain, a silent river of kinship that ran deeper than my own subconscious could define. I stopped pacing, confusion curdling my racing rationale, muddling fact and fiction. Whoever's blood it had been in the canteen, they had most definitely been Phuree for I could feel their history burning through my veins. I stared at the dying fire in the center of the room. The low wavering flames burned steadily over embers of glowing amber and ash.

I related to the Phuree's struggles for independence and freedom. I suddenly understood their pain and their isolation, the looming fear of extinction that mired their every small attempt at joy and peace and kept them running forever without end. I did not want to abandon them. However, the moment I stepped past the two guards, I would once again be the property of Phelan Daray and his Great War. I still wanted desperately to flee, but I knew that he would eventually find me, and a lengthy social exile would not be punishment enough the next time around. I sighed and sank back down upon the pallet, my newfound strength crushed beneath the weight of my dismal future. Hunted or enslaved, those were my choices.

Death was no longer an option for me.

I heard the nervous breath and the low sound of boots grinding into sand as the guards outside shifted their positions uncomfortably. They had sensed the change within me subconsciously. I could see them with my mind's eye, readjusting the weight of their swords, fingering the hilts absently and exchanging questioning glances as they tried to define the bristling of the hairs on the backs of their necks or the sudden sour twist of their stomachs.

Panic surged within me again, my flight instinct overwhelming. I stepped quickly to the back of the tent and quietly lifted the bottom of the leather wall just enough to scan the world outside. My tent faced another similar, but slightly smaller hut. No fire burned inside, its occupants were away for the time being. To my left and right stretched an alleyway formed by additional teepees. Some were warm and glowing from well tended fires, others cold and angular. The structures plunged upwards into the black sky, backs facing each other forming a barrier of tanned flesh and wood against the lonely expanse of the desert night.

The hour felt near to midnight, restless and tense and deep. The Phuree camp vibrated with distant nocturnal activity. Even the voices of children ran wildly amongst the dire tones of the adults, their distinct cries of oblivious youth a woven golden thread between the baying of animals and the guttural mumblings of their parents. How beautiful they sounded, a cacophony of wind chimes in the violent moments before a wicked storm. It occurred to me that I had not heard the sound of such innocence in many years.

Within the rotten limitations of the Tyst's amagin children were rarely seen or heard, tucked away by their parents in cramped sterile apartments to hide them from the corruption of the city's stagnant breath. The children of the amagin were not persecuted or kidnapped and sold into slavery. Those children grew up sheltered and fed the manifested history taught to their parents by the Tyst. They were not brought into the world as the last hope for a dying people as the Phuree children were, yet the children I now heard ran through the nomadic encampments without care, loving each and every moment of their lives, however brief. How could I leave behind such promise and watch it die at the hands of a tyrannical empire?

The narrow alley outside my quarters appeared uninhabited, far enough away from the main congestion not to warrant regular traffic. With a quick glance over my shoulder, I slipped out into the night. If I were to stay, I would need allies. I crouched down between the two tents, melding

127

with the shadows as my mind danced across the currents of energy around me, careful not to disturb the finely honed senses of my enemies. Like an anteater searching an angry mound, I stretched out the tendrils of my mind to gently probe the night in search of Tatsu and Lillian.

The Phuree language swelled within my head, breeding flashes of conversation, wickedly riddled with suspicion and sincerity. The words that had once consisted only of incongruous sounds began to take shape. Consonants and vowels, subjects and pronouns, sharp edged poetry melded into sentences relaying conversations from every corner of the village. Eyes closed, I listened in awe, drawn into the spiraling storm of human communication as it pelted my soul with a sudden torrential rain of clarity.

The fear, the pain, the joy; it was no longer an ambiguous fluctuating miming of spirit, but concrete in tangible digestible philosophy that flowed into my being and saturated my brain. From the wickedly moralistic fairytales of the elderly to the hushed and heated exchange between lovers, the gritty essence of the Phuree people congealed. My heart careened against my ribcage as the synthesis slammed into me with the force of a derailed train. Trembling, I tried not to buckle beneath the onslaught. With deep breaths, I steadied myself enough to comb through the raucousness of souls baring stories until, at last, I found the familiar Grecian accent of Tatsu as he spoke in hushed English. I honed in on him, trying to pinpoint his location. The voices of the village began to subside until they were no more than the low grumble of a distant storm.

In a liquid flicker, I found myself moving though the maze of tanned walls as if my soul had melted into the chill desert wind. Muscles flowed effortlessly without the slightest thought impulse, leaving my heart racing, not from exertion, but exhilaration.

Stop!

Without a rustle, without a whisper, movement ceased. I stared down at my hands in disbelief. I appeared no different, but I knew I had *evolved*. I looked up at my surroundings, realizing with a sudden horror that I was unsure of my location. I had stopped between two tents, just short of the center gathering area. Ten more feet and I would have plunged headlong into the milling social tumult of the Phuree. I crouched down again amidst the shadows cast by the harsh wavering glow of distant torchlight between the tents.

Wonder and fear stifled me with translucent fingers. I clenched and unclenched my hands. My skin sung with the harmonic vibrations of the universe; my eyes saw with an electric crystalline perfection unparalleled with anything I had ever witnessed. The details of the world around me crawled across the surface of reality like tiny glittering beetles. The dirt and grime that weighed down the world had been stripped away revealing an animated skeleton of existence too brilliant for the fragile common psyche to absorb. I ran my fingers over the ground that now writhed beneath me as atoms bounced off one another with an ethereal boiling of microscopic matter. It was almost as if I sat apart from myself, somewhere deep within, watching as I scooped a small amount of sand into my hand. The dry desert sand and packed clay earth turned to shimmering silk as they slipped back through my fingers, a sensation that sent a rush of electric chills scurrying up my arm and down my back. My heart raced: I thought it might disintegrate and the faster it beat, the more the world seemed to dismantle before me.

Please, dear gods, make it stop! Terror and confusion held fast to my mind with dagger teeth. I squeezed my eyes shut, rubbing their closed lids viciously as if I could drive the visions from my head.

I drew a deep breath, rocking back and forth on my heels. I could hear the dragons in the earth, rumbling far below. They were clawing their way to surface, so very close now that I could almost feel the heat of their breath through the thick soles of my boots. They would kill me when they reached the surface, render my body of its flesh and bone. Was it their roar, or the rush of the hundreds of heartbeats of the Phuree that pummeled my eardrums until they felt as if they might burst? The line of distinction between reality and delusion was slipping quickly.

I must...control...this... Hands over my ears... Another

deep breath.

Slowly, the white noise of the universe began to fade. I realized suddenly that I had fallen forward, my forehead pressed into the dirt as a dying man might pray for the last chance at absolution. I had clamped my hands tightly over my ears. Every muscle in my body trembled as they began to loosen, one by one. I wiped the sand from my face and opened my eyes. Though each grain of earth was still sharply defined in its multi colored beauty, the ground had stopped its convulsions. I listened to the wind for a long moment. I sighed cherishing the peace.

You have been reborn...

I started, falling backwards over my feet. The thought was not my own.

Scrambling backwards, further into the shadows of the towering tent, I realized suddenly that the world had ceased all motion just beyond where I cowered. Frozen, as if suspended in time, the lean strong faces of the crowd studied me with caution, brows knit in discernment of danger, lips parted without speech. An eerie silence had fallen over the center of the camp. I stared at the crowd, unable to breathe, as I found my feet beneath me. Slowly, carefully for I knew not what I was now capable of, I rose to my feet, my eyes never leaving the penetrating focus of the crowd.

Do not worry. They will not harm you.

The voice echoed through the chambers of my mind, sending a child-like fear ricocheting through my soul. I could feel my soul being tugged upon. Something was drawing me back to the tent where I had been healed. As a deer starts at the sound of a shotgun, I bolted, fleeing blindly towards the crowd of onlookers.

I wove in and out of them, silent and swift as time itself. An unseen ghost blending with the fabric of the universe, I passed the men and women. In the split second in which sight becomes understanding, I had reached the far side of the circle. For a moment, I watched in amazement as the gathered Phuree continued to stare at the alley between the tents where I had collapsed. Slowly, recognition set in. They turned and looked at each other for explanations. The tide of their voices began to rise, swelling to shouting as confusion mounted to panic. I quickly headed deeper into the maze of tents.

Sand sifted quietly beneath the worn tread of my boots as I crept along the narrow separations between huts. I listened to each and every muscle as I moved, struggling to harness the violent torrent of vitality that still raced through my body. Tatsu was nearby. I could sense his cool blue aura spiraling above the rolling thunder of the mortal earthen energy. As I neared his quarters, I sensed another within the tent, a female energy.

I recognized it instantly as Lillian. Her aura vibrated with barely contained apprehension. Beneath the delicate tea of her skin, I could smell her fear like the sweet sour residue of sweat after a fever. I could not quite make out their words through the stolid dome of defense that they had erected about them. However, the flexing of their emotions lent emphasis to the severity of the subject. I moved closer till I lingered just beyond the rippling fabric of their tent walls. There, I could listen without the use of my powers. They were on the verge of draining me and I dared not stretch myself too thin, for I felt I was already dangerously close to burning out my central nervous system.

"I think we should head back to the city and do a little investigating of our own." Tatsu spoke quickly. I could hear his fast light footsteps scuffing the jute mats and earth as he paced about the tent like a caged panther.

"Tonight?!" Lillian's surprise caused her to speak a little louder than she meant and Tatsu stopped his pacing. There was a long pause filled with the sound of the wind winding between the Phuree tents. They still had not sensed me, as close as I was.

Tatsu continued hesitantly, still listening to the world outside, "We should..." he began then stopped as he heard the rumblings from the center of the encampment, his attention torn by the confusion he sensed. I could tell he had also noticed something amiss in the ether, though it was not me he honed in on. I, too, sensed it, a strange ripple in the flow of energy within the village, an absence of solidity, which I could not pinpoint.

With one ear tuned to the village, he tried to focus on his conversation with Lillian. "It would be better to slip away while they are still consumed with their negotiations with the Phuree. Tynan may be a very good distraction, one that may allow us enough time to get a head start back."

"What kind of information do you think you can gain from going back? Wouldn't we gather more from the Phuree than from whatever we can dredge up from the amagin?" Lillian whispered heatedly.

"The Phuree are useless for an unbiased opinion. They want to save their asses at any cost. If their leaders say war, it's war." Tatsu spat his words as if they disgusted him.

"And who will give you an unbiased opinion within the city?" She laughed a laugh of weary exasperation. "You are either for the Tyst or you're against them."

"Bullshit. And there are those who will always be up for sale. Information is not cheap, but it is still available." Tatsu seemed overly confident in his predictions.

"That's disgusting." Her resistance was wearing thin.

"But true," he quipped.

There was another small pause before Lillian replied. "And what about Tynan?"

"What about Tynan?" Tatsu sighed wearily.

"We're just going to leave him here? He can't defend himself in the condition he's in."

"I'm afraid we have no choice but to leave him here." He spoke as if to a child, his tone forced into an unnatural softness.

"What if they are telling the truth?" Her words trembled slightly.

He had no reply to this. Silence filled the room, echoing out into the night around me. Cautiously, I moved to the front entrance and lingered for a moment longer to see if their conversation was done. Tension barbed the lines between them, but neither pondered Lillian's question aloud. Without the slightest whisper of wind, I slipped into the tent.

Lillian sat cross-legged on a large leather encased pillow upon the ground. Her head was bowed; lips pursed against the fingers of her hands. She seemed so small and delicate, the amber glow of the candlelight softening her already flawless pale features. Tatsu stood to her right, his back to her, arms crossed over his chest, head hung in thought. Though I could not hear their thoughts, I could feel the fear within them, the confusion and the panic. My heart constricted painfully as I was overcome with guilt. They did not deserve this sentencing. My predicament had landed my fellow brethren in my same dark cell by association of blood alone.

Time seemed frozen as I stood and watched them, removed as if I dreamed. They were oblivious to my presence. I realized suddenly that I was still wrapped within my own cloaking. Slowly, I forced the voices from my mind, struggling to find my own voice amongst the din and focused on removing the wall around me. Bit by tiny bit, I dismantled my guard till I was sure I could be seen, yet still, they did not notice.

I lifted my hand from my side, taking great care to move as a mortal might. Lillian gasped and leapt to her feet. She stood before me shaking, shocked beyond words, her mouth slack with amazement.

Tatsu spun around. "What the—?!" His words fell away in the quicksand of his own disbelief. He took a step towards me and then stopped, still unsure of his own safety. "Tynan? How did you—?"

"You're healed!?" Lillian's voice, a mixture of wonder and disbelief, drowned out Tatsu's stumbling question. She made no move towards me, rooted in place by her own twisting fear.

I stared at them both, wondering what it was that they saw standing before them. My body felt wickedly alive, my hands burning as if on fire. I lifted my palms up before my face, clenching and unclenching my fists. I was shaking. I lowered them to my sides and looked up at Tatsu, "I don't know. They've changed me…"

"I can see that from here." Tatsu replied, his voice low and steady. He grabbed a long woolen cloak that was draped across a wooden chest behind him. He held it out to me with an outstretched arm, as if he was scared to move any closer. "You're shivering."

"Am I?" I looked down at my body and realized that my pants were still soaked in blood sweat and coated in dust and mud from where I had fallen earlier. The chill of the night had turned the damp fabric bitter cold against my body. I looked back at the cloak Tatsu was offering, feeling helplessly lost and embarrassed by my condition.

"Thank you." I pulled the heavy fabric around my shoulders. The coarse fibers of the hand-woven material bit into my skin like steel wool. It was as if the top layer of my flesh had been seared away, exposing the raw, electrified nerves below. I quickly removed the cloak and handed it back to Tatsu.

"It hurts," I mumbled under my breath.

"What does?" Tatsu gingerly received the cloak and placed it on the table behind him. He took a step towards me, studying me closely.

"Everything." The words slid past my gritted teeth. The voices were returning, the harsh sharp blade of the Phuree language transversing time and space to pry open my mind and lay its seeds of confusion there. I pressed my palms to my temples. My arms trembled from the pressure until I thought I might crush my own skull in my desperation for silence.

"The blood... I can see everything... feel everything... I drank it and now I can't control it." I was rambling, my words stumbling over each other and slurring as if I could not voice them quick enough. I reached out and grasped Tatsu's forearm, dragging him closer to me as if I was afraid the voices in my head might hear me if I spoke too loudly.

"Please make it stop!" I hissed, my tone somewhere between a vicious snarl and a pathetic whine. The overwhelming awareness wrapped around me like a starved python, slowly squeezing the air from my lungs. I wanted to scream but feared the whole world might shatter.

I could not tell if I were moving or standing still, the universe vibrated around me pelting me with its unorchestrated rhythm. "Please help me."

Tatsu's eyes flashed between my frantic gaze and my hands wrapped about his forearm. My nails had begun to draw blood. The sharp scent caused me to shake even harder till my teeth chattered. He tried to keep his tone even and calm as he pried my fingers from his wrist.

"Tynan, you have to calm down." He freed his arm and, taking my hands in both of his, he led me to the table and sat me down on one of the leather cushions.

A silken coolness against my forehead brought me crashing back from the fluttering edge of insanity. Lillian pressed the palm of her hand against my brow and a cool ebb of soothing energy flowed from her to me, banishing the demons that shredded my soul. A deep welling breath filled my chest and I sank into her arms, exhausted. She stroked my hair, pulling the matted clumps back out of my face as she slowly rocked me back and forth.

Tatsu knelt beside us. "Tynan, can you hear me?"

I nodded.

He sighed and glanced at his forearm. The wounds had already healed, the blood vanished. He looked back at me. "Can you tell us what happened?"

I took a deep breath. The dream began to pour out of me in sharp edged whispers. I rambled like a madman as I tried to differentiate between illusion and reality. "It feels as if they are changing me into something I cannot control. It comes and goes without warning. I can't tell what is real anymore."

"Do you know whose blood it was?" Lillian's voice was heavy with concern.

I shook my head. "The Rayhee-Osm, whoever that is, was supposed to come visit me after I drank their potion." I looked up at Tatsu. "I came here, to find you, to make sure you and Lillian were not in harm's way. I should have stayed there for the answers to my questions..." I stood up and began to pace about the tent's cramped interior.

"They will be looking for me soon. If only I had time to master these new powers, but I am as good as insane right now. I can't trust myself." My agitation was beginning to claw at me again. I stopped, frozen like a deer listening for the rustle of a mountain lion. There it was again, that strange dip in the atmosphere. My heart began to race again; *it* was looking for me. I could sense it prying into the eyes and minds of the village denizens.

Tatsu sat back on his heels and eyed me suspiciously. He didn't speak, but I could hear his doubts as he dissected my ramblings with a clinical chill. He wanted to believe me, but hesitated now in the alliance he had offered the night before. I turned and walked slowly back to where he stood till we were mere inches apart. He did not flinch, though I could see the muscles in his jaw tighten warily.

I spoke low and carefully, my breath short and cold, "I need you to believe me." I paused, shaking my head slowly, "Without you and Lillian I am truly alone. And if that is the case, so be it. It would not be the first time in my life. But I would hate to think it has come to that again."

With a sigh he laid his hands on my shoulders. "You are not alone."

He met my gaze and held it, unwavering, "Forgive my hesitation to embrace your words. It is fear alone that clouds my mind with doubt. We are all in this together, Brother."

His mind opened to me revealing his innermost thoughts and feelings. In the lightning flash of psychic connection, he showed me that his deepest intentions were to help me. The raw display of vulnerability his doubts and fears showed me left me reeling. In a world where devils' masks were always a necessity, it was the ultimate sign of respect for a vampire to show his true face to another.

I hesitated for a moment in silence, unable to move. When I finally spoke, it was no more than a whisper. "Thank you."

He accepted my gratitude with a quick nod, and turned back to Lillian. I could tell by her puzzled expression that she did not completely understand what had transpired between Tatsu and I, but she did not pry, sensing the depth of sanctity of the situation. They sat cross-legged on the ground. Tatsu held out his hand, beckoning me to join them. I looked back at the doorway; the leather swelled and sank as if it were breathing, each movement issuing a soft sigh. The fine hairs on the back of my neck bristled at the sounds. The entity that pursued me was closing in. I could all but smell the crackling of ozone beneath its steps, its aura becoming distinctly male, though recognizable as neither human nor vampire.

"*He* is looking for me..." I spoke more to myself than the others, my eyes locked on the entrance.

Tatsu and Lillian said nothing. I turned back to them. "You have to go."

"What?" Tatsu snapped in confusion.

"The city. Head back to the amagin as you were planning." I pulled them to their feet and ushered them to the door. There wasn't much time left. "You have to go now."

Tatsu was loosing his patience with me. He had shown me the truth of his heart and I still kept secrets from him. Anger brimmed behind the dark moons of his eyes. He shook me off. "What the hell is going on, Tynan!? You need to tell me, now!"

I shook my head, unable to verbalize the sensation of being stalked. "All I know is that whatever it is will be here soon." I met his gaze with desperation in my eyes. "I trust you. Now it's your turn to trust me. If you are going to leave it's now or never. Please..."

Tatsu and Lillian exchanged uneasy glances.

I took Lillian's hands in my own. "Go back to the city with Tatsu. Find out what information you can about the Tyst's plans. I'll meet up with both of you in a couple of nights." I began to pace again, head down, hands clenching and unclenching in time with my rapid heartbeat. I paused in mid-stride. "Tatsu...?"

I looked up.

They had gone. I shivered.

Left alone again with the raging currents of my new power, I focused hard on the present, forcing the material reality before my eyes to remain intact. An overwhelming sense of isolation filled me; my only two allies were gone leaving me alone in a forest of secrets and lies. Intoxicated by the energy that vibrated within me, I stumbled to one of the leather cushions and sank to the ground. I turned to face the doorway. In my mind, I relinquished my last defense to the will of the gods.

That which sought me lingered so close, I could almost feel its breath on my face. Cold and wise beyond the essence of time itself, it watched me through the riddles of metaphysics. I knelt, head bowed, focusing on the center of my being till I felt rooted deep with the earth's core. A cool breath of desert air caressed my naked torso and I heard the entrance to the tent silently open.

"Hello, Tynan." A deep soft voice resonated through the tenuous fibers of my soul.

It touched my heart, a dragonfly alighting upon the water, stripping away the centuries of anguish and torment with a magnificent simplicity and eloquence. I rose to my feet. My heart still feared whatever stood before me, as though seeing it would make legend inescapable.

"Tynan, what are you afraid of?" The voice again, absent of all earthly sin or malicious pride, absent of the shackles of mortal condemnation or regret. It flowed over me like silk upon a statue.

My words came in shattered syllables. "I don't know." And I knew without knowing there was no truth in those words, for that which I feared hung heavy over my heart. My stolen past howled through my soul, vengeful and bitter. I was twenty-one again, standing before my father as he disowned me for slaying of Catarine and Tegwaret. I trembled, fearing the sentence of damnation from the being before me, whatever it was.

Fingers touched my face, cold and flawless like polished marble. "Do not fear me, Tynan." He lifted my face as he spoke, "I have not the power nor the right to judge you."

And what he spoke was *truth*. Not the "truth" by which my Dark Father had tricked me into the jaws of his plan, but the simple honesty only the universe could provide. My breath escaped my lungs in a deep shuddering sigh as I let go of the ropes that bound me to my guilt. My body felt insubstantial, the only sensation the pressure of his palms against my cheeks. Slowly, I opened my eyes.

Nahalo... A shimmering of auric essence congealed upon the tip of my tongue. The spell, it seemed, had been broken and I was no longer the man-child trembling before the furious sorrow of his father. In its place was a sense of limitless grounding as if the roots of an ancient tree had woven around me while I slept; it was a peace as I had never felt before.

"Nahalo...?" I whispered his name aloud and he smiled with perfect cherub lips beneath a beard of sun-flecked brown and white.

"Yes, my son." He continued to smile. His eyes were dark slate bleeding to white encircling a haunting circle of black. I wondered for a brief moment if he might be blind.

He chuckled and released my face. "I can see as well as you can, better, if what I've been told is true."

There was a lightness about his tone, which made me wonder if what he said was to be taken seriously. He was a full head shorter than I, his form slight but muscular beneath long robes of sea salt white, his hair the same dappling of sun and snow gathered in a leather tie at the base of his head. However, his presence filled the room, powerful and undeniable.

I found my voice. "Who are you?"

Another smile as bright as the summer dawn. "I am the Rayhee-Osm."

8

A smile still etched silently upon his face, Nahalo turned away and, in a swirl of alabaster robes, walked out of the tent. My feet moved of their own volition, carrying me out into the night in the shadow of his footsteps. He seemed removed from the earthly grime of the encampment, floating within a sphere of gently vibrating energy with the same marvelous choir of magic that had called to me on my arrival. I wanted to touch him, to confirm that there was indeed substance beneath his robes, but the few small steps between us never seemed to close. The world around me dissolved into a nebulous darkness until only the glow of the Rayhee-Osm pierced my sight, a light at the end of a constantly fluxing tunnel. We walked on for what seemed an eternity.

"We are here." Nahalo's gentle voice severed the cord of energy between us.

The trance that had held me prisoner shattered into a million tiny crystal shards, each reflecting a different aspect of shimmering reality. Cold wind slammed into my lungs causing me to stagger backwards. Nahalo caught my upper arms, holding me till my balance returned. My vision contracted as the world sharpened. We stood at the edge of a vast canyon. The gaping maw of the earth stretched for miles before us, fading into the velvety blue-black darkness of the desert night. The fathomless depths stared back at us omniscient, unseeing, dead.

For the first time in centuries, I longed for the interrogating blister of the sun, for the relentless heat and light to scour the shadows below us. The wail of the wind wound from the depths of the bottomless gorge, climbing the eroded walls of stone and earth to claw at our clothes and hair with desperate icy fingers. Nahalo continued to hold onto my arm, stopping me from plunging over the edge of the cliff. I could feel his strong steady heartbeat in the cool smooth of flesh of his fingers. The sensation drew me back from the shadows of the canyon, anchoring me. I tore my eyes away from the darkness and found Nahalo staring out at the scar, his expression distant and somehow sad as if he stood vigilance over the grave of a love one long past.

"Where are we?" I shouted over the howl of the wind.

You need not shout. Speak without your voice. I will hear you. Nahalo's words were clear and cool, rippling over the whorls of my mind.

I said nothing, but waited. He let go of my arm, folding his hands behind his back. Slowly, the wind began to subside, the wail of the damned spiraling away, pulled down into the earth until it was no more than a whisper. Nahalo turned from the gorge and walked away.

My confusion grew restless and I turned back to the crater, staring down into its depths. "How did you...?"

I looked up again, searching for Nahalo, but he had already traveled too far to hear my whispered words. Finding my feet, I followed his path to a distant boulder that faced the canyon. As I walked, the sand and dusty red earth beneath my boots hissed, loud in the absence of the wind. My mind was blank, filled only with the slow thunder of my heart and the shallow rhythm of breath through my lungs. There were simply too many questions that cancelled one another out in a frantic chaos equation, leaving me devoid of a beginning or end.

I closed the gap to the boulder quickly. As if awakening from sleep walking, I found myself at its gargantuan granite base. The wall I stood in front of stretched upwards with looming majesty. Nahalo had already begun his ascent up the side of the boulder, moving nimbly from crevice to overhang. He stopped on a tiny ledge and beckoned me to follow with one free hand.

Nahalo watched me from high up on the granite face. The icy halo of the moon outlined his features in unbreakable angles: his robes swirled about his legs from lingering tendrils of wind. With my newly heightened sight, the stone about him danced and shimmered, each and every compacted grain of crystal reflecting the moonlight. The movement made my vision swim. I tried to focus on Nahalo's robes instead, but the fibers of his garments were like bamboo reeds bending back and forth in the throws of a storm.

I stared at the section of stone in front of me; my body felt as if it were on fire from the new energy it contained. Slowly, I reached up and placed my palms against the stone. I gasped. The ancient heartbeat of the earth resonated a steady strong note beneath my hands, a gently humming sonata of life. I sighed. I had never before felt such a profound connection with the Keepers of the Earth; I could no longer feel the stone beneath my fingertips, but only the soft healing flow of energy.

Tynan. Come, Nahalo's words pulled at the center of my chest like a receding tidal wave. I looked towards the night sky. Nahalo stood watching me patiently, like a saint chiseled from the mortar of a tomb. His expression was one of deep understanding, as if he, too, heard the song of the earth. He turned away and continued his ascent of the rock.

I followed him. The bridge that had connected me with the earth had settled me somehow, planting a new unquestionable seed of faith in this strange man who had led me into the wild. I skirted the rock face with ease, my fingers and boot tips finding purchase in the crevices and cracks. Beneath my hands, the reddish stone still cooled. The residual warmth pulsed its ancient dawn song through the marrow of my bones. It was as if the heart of the Earth beat on the outside of its skin for the heavens above to marvel at. *I will be here long after you are gone,* it said.

I reached the top of the boulder and found Nahalo sitting cross-legged upon the highest point. A gentle wind teased his hair and garments, pulling at them inquisitively. He was so still that he seemed like a statue of a monk, his unblinking gaze transfixed on the gaping black hole hundreds of feet below us. Though he appeared perfectly human on the surface, there was something otherworldly about him that I simply could not pin down. He confused my senses, igniting both fear and intense curiosity in me. I hesitated to move, hating to intrude on the reverence he was paying to what was lost forever.

A delicate invisible strand kissed my cheek, adhering to the bridge of my nose as it was gently pulled by the breeze. I did not to remove it, but let my eyes focus and trace the tiny gossamer thread as it undulated with tranquility in the light of the moon. There at the end of the strand was attached the fragile translucent body of a tiny spider, no bigger than a grain of sand. She floated on the desert wind, her willowy limbs limp and resigned. I reached up and separated her line from my face. For a moment I held her fate pressed between my thumb and forefinger.

She will be okay. It is a spider's life to go where the wind tells her. Nahalo's voice touched my mind like a comforting hand on my shoulder.

I released the silk anchor line into the wind and watched in silent awe as the tiny fragile being spun away into the darkness. I wanted to follow her, to learn from her instinctual ease of adaptation. I watched until the spider had disappeared from my sight before turning to face Nahalo. He patted the ground lightly beside him.

Come. Join me. You have questions that I must attend to.

Did Nahalo speak, or was it the ancient stone beneath my feet? With a deep breath, I found my strength and crossed the remaining few yards between us. I took my place beside him. From our perch, I could see the full outline of the crater, though I still could not gauge where the bottom lay. It must have stretched at least five miles in diameter, the edges blackened in the starburst pattern of an ancient blast.

I don't remember this. The thought flickered across my mind like a dragonfly.

You were still slumbering when this atrocity happened. Nahalo's words caressed my soul with a mysterious yet comforting purr. *It has been nearly 80 years since the bombing of Fredericksburg.*

I felt my brow furrow in confusion; I turned to stare at him, stunned to silence. "Did you say, Fredericksburg?" The words passed my lips and were all but lost to the wind. My memories of the quaint peaceful town of craftspeople and retirees became muddled as images of the horrific blast

143

invaded and destroyed the serenity. The streets of twinkling Christmas lights were now reduced to cinders, bones and the dust that now stung my eyes. I could not distinguish between imagination and reality; were the thoughts my own, Nahalo's or of the ghosts that surely haunted this dismal graveyard? I could not tell.

Nahalo placed his hand upon my forearm. His expression was one of sympathy and sadness. "You knew the town?"

I turned back to the barren black crater. "Yes." I paused. "I visited it on occasion. It was a sanctuary of peace where I could escape the lights and noise of the city." I shook my head in shock. "I just can't believe it's gone. Completely gone..."

I turned back to him. "Did anyone survive?"

"No," he said simply.

"Why? How? Who did this?" I tried to blot the images of the fiery blast from my vision, but they continued to flood my soul. I wrapped my arms tightly about my body to keep from shaking. The reality of the war I had heard so much about was beginning to truly hit home.

Nahalo took a deep breath. "The Tyst had gotten wind of a rumor that Phuree intelligence officers were secretly meeting in a basement of the Fredericksburg town hall. The true tragedy of this event was that we were nowhere near Fredericksburg at the time.

"However, instead of substantiating the gossip, the venom spread quickly through the Tyst ranks until Cardone II decided it was best to just take out the entire town. It wasn't worth his time to spare such a small community. 'Fumigating', I believe, is what they call it." Nahalo's expression had become unreadable, his eyes misted over in deep reflection. "It's truly amazing how little our lives are worth now."

I felt pinned under his gaze as he studied me as if he was searching for flaws in his newest creation. My stomach churned, my skin felt transparent and vulnerable beneath his scrutiny. I could hear his thoughts.

You are one of us now...

"No." My defenses rose, bristling. "I am not Phuree." The words slammed into the wind as I shut the gates to my mind, forcing him out.

"Perhaps not of sworn oath, but no matter, you will be condemned now, just as the people of this town were condemned. Not for what you've been before this night, but for the mere possibility of what you might become."

His words clawed at my innards. I had been hunted my entire life for one reason or another. Mortals had hunted me as a vampire and my own kind had persecuted me as a traitor, as a martyr. Now an entire regime would hunt me for crimes I had not yet committed. I buried my head in my hands, angry tears welling up beneath my closed eyelids.

"Why...Why did you bring me here?" I whispered, the coppery salt of blood tears dripping from my eyes to the granite below me.

There was a long moment of deafening silence before he answered. "Why do you think we brought you here?"

The question stung. "Because I'm damned and this is Hell." The sarcasm pooled in the back of my throat. I wanted to give up.

Nahalo was silent, as I wallowed in my agonizing desolation. When he spoke it was as if to a child, soft and slow. "Is that really what you believe?"

"I don't know what I believe anymore. I am being told that I am some sort of *messiah*, a preordained assassin to end a hundred year war. I have no evidence to believe that anything I've been told up until this moment is true. People speak in riddles and broken phrases as if they expect me to accept and submit to anything they dictate, without question. Deception and pain is what has brought me here, and against my will." I glared at him through a haze of bitter tears. "Which placating lie would you like to hear first?" I paused, shaking my head angrily. "I don't care anymore. It doesn't matter."

Nahalo was unmoved by my anger. He remained in his lotus position, his face calm and distant. "I don't believe that."

Simple and sharp, his words cut quick and deep. The hackles on the back of my neck bristled

"You care more than any other being, mortal or Immortal, could ever care," he said. In the moonlight his icy pale eyes seemed to shine with a fierce inner fire.

I looked away. Caught within the strands of my own lie,

the pain of the truth was a strangling vine, making me want to cower in a silent dark cave until the rest of the world had faded into oblivion.

He continued to speak. "It is why your existence is such a burden to you. You see an injustice like this," He waved his hand at the crater before us, "and you feel the suffering of each and every person that died that day. The brutality is beyond your comprehension.

"That is why we have brought you here. You *feel* as no other vampire has ever been able to feel before. There is power in what you see only as needless pain." He paused, searching for the words. "Do you not remember the devotion and peace you inspired in the Immortal world when you comforted their souls with hope and redemption?"

"There is no redemption." The words were hard and cold as slate in winter. I turned back to face him. My tears had dried to thin tracks of salt on my cheeks. I could feel the walls of my inner fortress turning to steel. "If you're looking for someone to *inspire* your people and lead them to victory, as much as I already care for them, I am afraid I am not your man."

I stood, wanting to pry myself free of barbs with which he tried to trap me, and began to walk towards the edge of the boulder.

"Apathy calls to you like a siren. I know. I have been there before myself. It would be so much easier to fade into oblivion, to become as impassible and unnoticeable as a mountain ledge." His words were tinged with a weary sadness, welling up from a place deep inside. "But the choice is no longer ours to make. The Immortals are the true protectors of this earth. We are part of this war and we must end it before it destroys us all."

I stopped dead in my tracks. My back still facing him I spoke. "Did you just say *we*?"

He did not answer.

I turned slowly back to face him. "You...you look so *human*?!" My mouth hung open, my brow furrowed, as I waited in stunned silence for his reply. *Why did I not sense that about him...?*

A ghostly smile skipped across his lips, revealing a brief flash of ivory fangs. He sighed heavily. "My apologies for such deception. It is a guise I have created in order to put the humans more at ease in my presence. I have spent so many years amongst them that it has all but become a part of me."

He closed his eyes and settled himself as if sinking into a trance. I watched, mesmerized, as the illusion slowly dissolved. The tan, weather-beaten skin melted like wax. In the blue white glow of the moon, the lines and creases etched into his brow and cheeks faded to reveal a flawless countenance rivaling the luminescence of glacier ice. The full beard receded to a thin mustache and goatee, the gray disappearing beneath a rich golden brown. His smooth alien beauty seemed to remove him from the coarse granite and sand of our surroundings. I found myself drifting cautiously towards him, a jaguar approaching the statue of a god.

He did not move, but watched as I sank slowly to my knees an arm's length away.

You are a vampire...?

Yes. He heard my thoughts and smiled, a small faint gesture.

With the illusion of humanity discarded, the true magnificence of his power radiated from him. The whispering *voice* of Phuree magic gathered around him; I could hear the rhythm of its pulsing life force in my soul, a symphony of deep tribal drums echoing discordantly. I wanted to reach out and touch him to make sure that what I saw before me was not a phantom of my mind, but I dared not out of respect and fear.

I am nothing to be feared. Least of all by you, my young one. He took my right hand and held it firmly between his hands. The sensation of his touch was electric. Lightning currents of adrenaline shot up my arm and through my body; I tried desperately to keep from shaking. Before me sat a true Ancient of such immense age, it seemed that time had truly stopped for him in his existence on the Earth. The Ancients were the material of legend; those who had not been killed were believed to have had forsaken their kindred and their brood to live solitary lives of hermitage and meditation. It had been nearly a millennia since the last Ancient had faded from

147

civilization. A spark of hope ignited somewhere deep inside me, hope that others like him still survived somewhere, that Phelan and his vagabond band were not all that remained of our race.

A sudden thrilling yet, terrifying realization struck me. *It was your blood in the canteen. Your blood that healed me!* I could feel it coursing within my veins, a bond with the Ancient that I could not sever. A blessing, a curse, an indefinable gift, a damnation into eternal servitude. His silence confirmed the roiling sea of revelation, my heart waxing and waning between a hateful resentment and the deepest gratitude. His eyes, now a shimmering gold, gazed upon me revealing nothing and drenched in wisdom.

"I was not worthy..." The words choked in my throat as I thought of the deception that had brought me to that moment. He knew that I would never have accepted such power willingly. "Why did you pick one so weak as I?"

"Weak?" He chuckled knowingly. "By the gods, Tynan, you are the most strong-willed Darkling I have ever laid eyes upon in all of my three thousand years. Misguided, perhaps. A bit mad yes, but weak, no."

"I am a coward, an Immortal lacking both the conviction and the wisdom to be the messiah you need." I shook my head slowly. "I have committed great sins against our race...I tried to take the life of my own Maker..."

My confusion festered in bitterness as I stared into the liquid gold of his eyes. "Why would you absolve me of such atrocities? ... Why?"

I did not want absolution from an Ancient; I wanted his fury. I wanted disgust, I wanted merciless judgment as it should have been, and as I had been told it would be by every Elder that had had a hand in my path.

He watched me for a long while. The wind wound through the shadows of the canyon below, howling painfully of its sorrowful loss. "I cannot condemn you as you long to be condemned. Though your judgment may have been flawed, your wrath was not unwarranted."

"Again, you justify what you want where you see a need. I do not believe that you would be so merciful with one who did not serve a purpose in your crusade." I did not want his absolution.

He did not flinch at my words; his love for me as a Child of Darkness continued to radiate from him, completely void of judgment. "I wish I could explain it simply. I wish there were a few words I could say to put your heart and mind at ease, to make you trust me. But you have been woven into a tangled web." He sighed, contemplating me as if I were a storm brewing on the horizon.

He lowered himself into a cross-legged position facing me and placed his palms together as if in prayer, elbows upon his knees, and rested his chin on his fingertips. After a time he spoke, his voice soft, yet full of passionate emotion and conviction. "I have seen things that I cannot speak of to any living being, mortal or Immortal. Wondrous and horrible visions I can only explain as having been delivered from the Gods themselves.

"Before I found my path here among the Phuree, I, like many of the Ancients, retreated to the far corners of the earth. We removed ourselves, as we always had, from the petty squabblings of humanity. Only this time, the war did not end after a decade, and it spread like a virus about the planet. There was nothing we could do but watch in horrified silence as the world burned around us.

"We were no longer the silent guardians of the Earth as we had been for eons; our power had been stripped from us. Many of the Ancients began to fade in their despair, dying slowly in the shadows resigned to the idea that their time of reign had come to pass and the world no longer had a use for them. We had witnessed such vast conscienceless cruelty that even our hardened souls were crushed by its sorrow. In truth, we were losing our will to endure existence any longer..." Nahalo's voice trailed off into the restless currents of wind.

"I prayed to the Gods foolishly seeking an explanation for such cruelty. I humbly begged for strength and guidance. I did not expect them to answer for I thought it was to an empty void that I now prayed.

"What I received was far more than I could ever have dreamed. They showed me the future." He took a deep breath

149

to steady himself. The revisiting of his memories obviously gave him great grief as he was reminded again of the burden he carried on his back.

I lifted my head and opened my eyes, watching him carefully with renewed curiosity. *He speaks the truth...* I could not tell if the thought was my own or another whisper of the Phuree magic as it breezed through my being like a hawk's cry.

His eyes were glazed over, lost in reflection of the past. "Two possible futures, they revealed. In the first, I wandered away from the world of the living to seek solace and refuge alone as the remainder of civilization crumbled around me. I watched as the Tyst destroyed what as left of the Immortals and the Phuree. I watched as the Vicinus was born into our world, violently ripping apart the mortal woman whom carried him to term for nine long months. Helpless, I witnessed as he enslaved the last strands of the living. He toyed with them for hundreds of years, wallowing in their pain, until, bored with this world, he destroyed it, obliterating the earth and its millions of years of sorrowful history. There is something incredibly humbling about watching your very planet reduced to little more than dust drifting in an eerie silent void between heavenly bodies. It was a painful reminder of just how ephemeral this all is, just how precious..."

Nahalo turned his gaze back to me, his eyes brimming with blood red tears that shimmered in the moonlight. "In the second vision, I made the long journey from my hiding place deep within the opal caves of Australia. I became a holy man amongst the Phuree, a teacher of powerful secrets all but forgotten since my days as a Druid priest in the old lands of Britain. But as time passed, the quest of independence, so strong in the beginning of the dream, was dampened once again as the new generation of Tyst legions attacked the world again with a renewed vengeance. The Tyst leader elevated to power sought Immortality as well as ultimate rule over the earth.

"The few Ancients that had scattered about the world to work with the exiled peoples were now no longer enough to combat the impending evil. Our battle was beginning to fail once again in the face of Cardone III's regime. In my vision, the world called for another one of the Dark Blood, an Immortal of great wisdom and honesty and strength. An unsuspected leader who would guide the Phuree to freedom and stop the Vicinus from his hateful scourge of the earth."

Nahalo's eyes came back into focus suddenly and fixed on me. "The Immortal in my vision was you. The gods whispered your name in my ears with the promise that all would be set right if you were brought here. You, and you alone, would have the power to stop the nightmare that was destined to unfold."

He shook his head sadly. "I am so sorry for the pain and deception with which you were forced to make this journey. The Gods warned me that it would not be an easy road to follow, for anyone involved, but there was no other way."

I knelt in silence, unable to respond. My mind raced; all words felt profoundly inadequate. His words were true and honest and undeniable. This I knew without a doubt. The suspicion and resentment I had harbored for him and his people began slowly to melt, replaced by a weariness that was soul-deep. I wanted to hear more from the Ancient that sat before me. I felt his words were truth, the first actual truth I had heard. However, the hollow void remained within me where my own convictions once had blossomed.

How can I inspire the Phuree if I do not even believe in myself?

He heard my thought and reached out to touch the side of my face. This time the icy solidity of his hand did not startle me. "Tynan, I have watched you since you were a small child, knowing that you were meant for great things."

I felt something inside me twitch with confusion. "You have been *watching* me?" It felt as if the last of my secrets were being stripped away from me, leaving me naked and trembling.

He continued carefully, knowing he had disturbed something fragile. "I have lived a long life. There are many that have held my curiosity, but most turned out to disappoint me or have simply faded from my attention as the years waned. You, though, were different. I watched your painful

Gabrielle Faust

transformation to the Dark Blood. I saw you rise above it to
embrace your true potential. You constantly astounded me
with your dreams and hopes, your endless exploration of the
world and yourself." Nahalo placed his hand gently on my
shoulder, startling me out of my shocked reverie.

"You saw it all?" The pain of shame twisted sharp in my
heart once again.

"We have all made mistakes. It is part of our rebirth as
Immortal. But you, as the strong ones do, you were able to
create something beautiful from the ashes of your past."

"But I didn't rise above it." I shook my head, staring into
Nahalo's golden eyes. "It haunts me every night and every day
when I sleep." I wanted to be free, but I simply did not see
how it would ever be. My crimes were my burden to carry
through this life until death.

"One may rise above something without completely
letting go." His voice was soft and scholarly. "You took your
pain and your inner turmoil and you wandered the earth in
search of an answer. The glimpses of truth you gleaned, you
gathered close to you and wove into a beautiful tapestry for
others to come and worship. In a time when you were
desperate for something to believe in, when our people had
become tattered and threatened to sink into complete
oblivion, you offered a talisman of philosophy, of faith, to pull
us back to the surface. You cannot say that you were not
somehow healed by your own words?"

I said nothing. My words had been made into a religion
before they could be tested by Time. How could I find healing
in my own delusions? And now they came to me asking me to
weave another tapestry, even greater than the one before,
great enough to fool both vampire and human alike. It made
no sense to me.

He heard my thoughts and sighed. "We are not asking
such a thing of you."

"No?" Acidic sarcasm crept back up my throat. I laughed
under my breath to keep it at bay. I shook my head and
rubbed my tired eyes with my fingertips. "No. You only wish
me to take arms against an empire and lead the Phuree into
what very well might be their last great stand." I sighed. "And

152

what if I fail, again? What if I am not the leader, the savior, you so desperately desire? What then? If I fail this time, it could mean the death of life as we know it!"

"Then it will be as it should be, and we will go knowing that all that could be done was done." Nahalo tried to smile, but the motion was tired and strained. "We must trust in the gods. It is all we have now."

I thought about the pain and poverty that permeated the city I had awoken to, the city that had once stood graceful and proud, its granite capital silently watching guard over its passionately colorful people. It now lay black and broken like the shattered remains of a battleship deep below the sea, its denizens darting in and out of the shadows fearful of discovery. I thought of the Phuree and the subtle beauty that had washed over me in the few small hours I had been among them. I thought of their lives lived in persecution and war and fear; how kindred my people were to theirs. We shared a broken refugee existence; those that did not understand us feared us, and those that feared us hunted us. I knew in my soul I could not say no to them.

Nahalo knew it too.

Images of my own life flashed before my mind's eye. For the first time in my recollection, it seemed the circle was coming to fulfillment; perhaps this was what my true destiny, *my Fate*, was to be. Perhaps this was to be my purpose, and in that might there be a way to wash myself of the sins of my past? Was there nobility in war? Was there redemption in revolution?

A profound sense of hope filled me suddenly, making me want to weep.

Welcome home.... The Phuree magic whispered to me in her sultry sweet voice beneath the low howl of the desert wind. I buried my head in my hands, overwhelmed.

The Sleep was beginning to call to me.

"The sky grows light." Nahalo whispered softly, more to himself than to me. He rose to his feet, offering his hand to me as I still sat upon the rock.

"Nahalo...?"

"Yes, my child?"

"When was the last time you saw the Sun rise?" I stared out at the gradually lightening horizon as it faded from pitch to royal blue.

He smiled, a sad faint curl of his lips. "Everyday...In my dreams."

9

Dreams. Fragmented imagery of haunted Dali landscapes filled with the lost words of a shredded letter, schizophrenically fluttering lightning behind the bone and gristle of my face. I wrestled with them, their hydra voices beating me down like the buzz of angry hornets dripping from a nest. I could not grasp the slippery prophecy of the dreams, and woke amidst the darkness of the following night with a thin veil of blood sweat upon my brow. As my eyes sought a tangible definition of space, the call of my own name hissed reptilian in my ears. *Tynnnaannn.....*

I stumbled from the sleeping pallet, disoriented for a moment as my senses settled and disengaged themselves. Groggily, I surveyed my surroundings; as far as I could tell, I had returned to the tent I had been brought to the previous evening. I stumbled to a small, low wooden table on the far side of the tent and dropped to my knees before it.

Light. I wanted suddenly to fill the tent with light, to chase away the lingering remnants of the serpentine whisper that still echoed in my ears. To my right stood a short, wide, three-wick tallow candle upon a simple circular tray of tarnished silver. I scanned the table quickly for something to light it with but there was nothing. I stared at the candle in silence, longing for the warmth and familiar beauty of the candle flame. Something twitched inside my chest. I watched as the wicks wavered for a moment before my eyes. The world seemed to collapse in on itself in the blink of an eye as all of the power within me focused and funneled forward towards the candle, an instinctual impulse as natural as exhaling. Flames kissed the blackened wicks and bloomed into three brilliant teardrop halos of golden light, chasing the blue-black shadows of the room back to the far corners of the landscape of the dream world.

I fell back with a gasp, my wide-eyed gaze fixed
unblinking upon the flames. They danced and swayed with the
currents of air that scampered in under the sides of the tent. I
glanced quickly about the room, but it was eerily empty, the
tall animal skin walls gracefully undulating with the fluxing
night air. High above, where the tent poles met in a conical
point, the shadows gathered. They clustered like daddy-long-
legs on a cave ceiling, pulsing occasionally with their fear of
the fire below them.

I looked back to the candle. Cautiously, I returned to my
knees, moving hesitantly closer to inspect it. I knew without a
doubt, in the same foreign fathomless way a woman
sometimes knows the sex of her child before it is born, that I
had created the fire with my new powers. I reached out my
right hand and waved my fingers through the flame; the heat
of the candle flickered hot and painful across my skin. I stared
at my fingertips, laughing quietly under my breath. To think
that I now possessed the ability to control the fire element, a
preternatural level I had not expected to achieve for at least
another hundred years, was thrilling, dangerously intoxicating.
My mind spun out of control with the limitless possibilities.
How easy it would be to become drunk on such a profound
gift, how simple to lose myself in the new physical
manifestation of all that is philosophical. I pulled the candle
closer to me so I could feel its heat.

I smiled silently to myself. Phelan and Sea could no more
control me now than they could control the tides of the ocean.
In that new revelation, there was a strange sort of freedom
mixed with a bittersweet loneliness, an alien emptiness of a
burden lifted; a cross had been removed from my back, but
the rusted nails of my new conviction still bit deeply. The trivial
sophomoric squabblings of my past life were buried beneath
the weight of my rebirth in Nahalo's blood and Phuree magic;
I was a part of something far bigger than such menial
preoccupations and resentments. But it would not be without
its own price, of that I was quite sure.

From one skin into another... I thought silently.

The candle flames danced in their holy trinity of amber
warmth. I wiped the blood-sweat from my brow with the back

of my hand. On the table, next to the wide pillar candle, stood a tall pitcher and large shallow bowl of unglazed brown clay. With my newly heightened sight, the mineral impurities in the earthenware glistened and shimmered with a dusting of powdered copper across its surface. I marveled at its simple elegance. This ability to be seduced by the smallest fragment of existence was intoxicating, a drug to be savored.

I sighed, wishing I had the luxury to explore the world as I had done in my early first years as a fledgling vampire. I had roamed the hillsides of Scotland and Wales, England and Ireland, transfixed by the comforting perfume of the earth and ocean, of life and decay, and complex languages of each nocturnal creature. Hour upon hour, I would stare into the depths of a babbling brook brimming with ancient liquid mysteries, lost within the constant melodic chaos of its eternal quest for the ocean, until Phelan would retrieve me and drag me to our lair.

I picked up the pitcher and lifted it to my nose. The crisp scent of clean water combined with anise and cloves drifted to my nose. The sweet perfume was alluring, sharpening the abrasion of the stale blood-sweat and grime that coated my limbs. I filled the bowl, watching the rippling mirror of the surface bending my reflection in and out. Outside the tent where I knelt, I sensed two human guards posted at the entrance, an offering of protection from Tiernan. In another time, their presence would have annoyed me to the point of anger, but now I felt strangely centered, my mind too preoccupied with my state of being to pay heed to the mortal world. I wanted a moment longer to linger in my new existence, a moment before the universe broke down my door with its greedy demands.

I stared into the glittering shallows of the bowl till the tiny waves had subsided, thinking of my last moments at the apartment before Sea had come to summon me. How different my reflection appeared now from the gaunt hopeless soul that had stared back at me from the bathroom mirror. The desert wind howled outside my quarters, making the sterile world of concrete and steel of my apartment seem like a distant memory. My hazel eyes glowed with a shimmering fire that emanated from deep within me. The self I witnessed was wilder, stronger, though still very much alone, and in it, I thought I began to see a semblance of the person I had left behind centuries ago.

I pushed the bowl aside with my right hand and laid my cheek upon the table below. Cool and solid, the grain of the heavy dark wood was smooth against my skin, deeply oiled with the lacquer of long years of use. Hand-made with the love and the determination of necessity, not temptation, there seemed a soul embedded within the wood, a gently hummed melody of memories from generations of fingerprints laid down in love and labor and war. That was what I had longed to return to; a history, a place amongst a heritage of purpose. I had lingered too long within the stuccoed walls of the city. I would accept my new path and embrace the hands and hearts of those that had laid it.

I lifted my face from the table, sinking back on my heels, pulling the bowl of water in front of me. However my great transformation had begun, it had not yet entirely erased the strands of violation and mistrust that had suspended my heart for so long. They had begun to be healed by the golden glow of the new blood that now coursed through my veins, but my former reservations were now being replaced with a buzzing swarm of questions in dire need of answers.

I wanted to go to Phelan, to confront him and pry the black pearl of answers, but I knew I had to be delicate. No matter how strong I had become, there were still too many facets I could not yet grasp to go blundering in demanding answers. Like an orb spider in its well, I knew I had to wait until I had spun the perfect web.

I dipped my hands into the still mirror surface of the fragrant water before me and lifted it to my face. The grit, sand and stale blood-sweat began to melt away. I unlaced my boots, removing them, and stripped away the ragged black pants I wore, stained and stiff with blood and mud. Naked, I knelt back down before the table as if it were an altar to the gods. I closed my eyes as I slowly washed my limbs. Each small handful of water kissed my cold flesh as a blessing of purity singing of sacred mountain streams till, at last, the cruel realities of the former evenings had been erased.

A small amount of clean water remained in the pitcher and I lifted it, pouring its contents over my head in one final cleansing waterfall. Pulling free the tangles of my hair. I tried to imagine my lingering resentments and concerns dissolving beneath the trickling rivulets of water streaming down my face and body. The ghostly whispers of the Phuree magic caressed my soul with velvety persuasion. Eyes closed, empty pitcher loosely interlaced between my slack fingers, I allowed the power to wrap its seductress arms about my body, placing its cool sweet lips against the back of my neck. My lover, my mother, my demise...

She whispered in my ear, *Welcome home....*

I opened my eyes and *she* retreated, slipping her serpentine lucidity from about my body. The sensation electrified each and every nerve in my body like a woman's warm wet tongue. I sighed and shivered, feeling myself aroused in a way no woman had been able to do in over two hundred years. The sensation was empowering, clearing the fog of material reality from my perception with razor precision. I was both slave and master to this new power that fluxed an unpredictable cosmic current beneath my skin. This unseen army was mine to control, just as I was its pawn in a war I had not yet fully grasped.

Using one of the many thin blankets from the bedding to dry my body and hair, I turned to search the tent for fresh clothing. In the far left corner, beside the bed-pallet, I found a small wooden trunk containing an assortment of clothing in a myriad of earthen dyed hues. Quickly, I slipped into a pair of roan colored linen pants, pulling the drawstring waist low upon my narrow hips. Over my head I pulled a hand-sewn shirt the color of sun-bleached sand. The sleeves were comfortably loose and fell just below my elbows, the hem, just below my thighs. Indeed, the clothes were a perfect fit, as if the seamstress who had stitched them had known me intimately my entire life. Silently, I pulled my boots back on.

Outside my quarters, the world had begun to stir; the muted shuffling and mumbling of the waking camp wound its way upon the cold currents of desert air. The stoic unyielding realm of the city and its bitter disemboweled legacy seemed a thing of myth, a thing to be told to children to keep them from misbehaving; a perpetuation of human grief and insanity to scoff at, and yet a dream that continued to wake grown men at night in a cold sweat and screaming. I wondered if I myself had been one such man, now truly awake for the very first time.

Suddenly, the dull ache pulsed again from deep within my chest where I had been speared, a quick sharp twisting pain that seemed to fade as quickly as it had begun. Apparently, my healing was not as complete as I had thought. I clutched my stomach with my right hand, as I doubled over, unable to breathe in my surprise. The ripples of the phantom pain spread through my body as they dissipated, radiating through me with each beat of my heart, reminding me that my past had been no mythological nightmare. It lingered all too near, laughing wickedly in the face of my newfound resolve, riddling it with venomous black suspicions.

Voices outside my tent entrance drew my attention away from the fading pain.

"I will see him when and where I choose." A female voice, young and determined. "My brother has sent me with message for our guest. Are you questioning his word?" Her question was a final warning.

"My lady, I'm sorry, but we cannot let you enter unaccompanied." A deep male voice to the right made me wonder just how many people stood outside my quarters. "It is not safe for you to be with *them* alone."

I knew he referred to our ragged band of vampires. We were still dangerous strangers to many of the Phuree, even though we supposedly came in peace. I opened my mind slightly and listened to the guard standing beside him. Quickly, I shut my mind off again from the outside world to protect my thoughts from any prying Immortal minds.

"*Step aside*, gentlemen. I am not afraid of our guest and neither should you be. He is here to help us, or so I am told." Her angry urgent whisper barely concealed the fear she herself felt.

The clanking of metal against metal suggested her path

had just been blocked.

"Get out of my way!" Her voice rose to an angry bark as she lost her patience with the two men. The metal shifted again. The entrance to my tent opened with an unceremonial commotion.

"And don't follow me." Khanna entered the tent, spitting the words back over her shoulder as the leather door fell closed behind her with a whoosh of cold air. "Damned idiots," she muttered under her breath.

She stopped at the entrance with a heavy sigh and turned her gaze to the interior of the tent. Her eyes widened and the lean sculpted curves of her body became taut with alarm as she realized I stood only a few small feet away, in the center of the room. A huntress herself in many respects, she was taken off guard by her lack of awareness of my whereabouts. Unconsciously, her right hand gripped the pommel of the short sword that hung from a heavy leather belt around her narrow waist.

In the warm amber glow of the three candle flames her icy eyes sparkled with an intense fierceness that spoke of a woman who had proven herself in war. Her youthful beauty was as unique as a piece of rose quartz glistening in the sunlight, her rich bronze skin warm beneath pale blonde hair that hung loosely about her shoulders, untamed and tussled by the elements. Woven into her hair were glass beads and silver charms in the shapes of runes. The magical trinkets glittered as the flames danced upon the table behind us.

Without quite knowing why, I wished suddenly to know the story of her warrior heart, but when I reached out to her mind with my own, I found an iron gate similar to the impenetrable fortress that I had sensed surrounding Tiernan's soul. I knew I could break such a human barrier easily now with my strengthened gifts, but I wouldn't. When humans guarded themselves so dearly, it meant that they had secrets that would surely shatter them, if pried into the light.

I could hear her heart fluttering within her chest as a wash of fear, wonder and desire kept her still and mute; I had seen the look before on many a mortal's face as they gazed upon that which they could not rationalize. I found that her flood of unfounded adoration made me uneasy, for I was as unworthy as I had ever been. She shifted her gaze to the floor embarrassed by her show of weakness, a flush of red rose to her face making her seem even younger.

"Tiernan asks that you join him, if you are feeling well enough for company." She strained to steady her voice as she spoke.

I did not like the fear I inspired in the strong woman before me. Slowly, silently, I crossed the few feet that separated us. Gently, I placed my fingers beneath her chin and tilted her face up towards mine. Through my fingertips, I could feel the subtle uncontrollable tremors that shook her slight frame. For a long while I stared into her wide blue eyes searching for a way to banish her trepidation.

I leant forward and placed my lips on her forehead and whispered, "*Do not fear.*"

Beneath my lips, I felt her trembling cease as she settled into a cool quiet calm. Though I did not feel the Hunger, the rich coppery perfume of blood coursing through her, mingling with the salty sweet scent of her skin was deeply alluring, drawing me dangerously close to the edge of my will.

Perhaps the guards were right, I thought.

I took a step back to break the spell, letting my hand fall to my side. I watched her in silence as she touched the spot where I had placed my kiss, her expression collected but still wondering.

As if she had forgotten she had already delivered her message, she spoke again. "Umm... My brother...He asks that you join—"

"It would be my pleasure," I gently interrupted, taking her hands in my own.

She stared at my hands for a long while in silence. I could feel the guards becoming restless outside, unable to hear what transpired between us. Their anxiety and fear were a thorn of distraction.

"You are so cold." Her gaze traveled back to meet mine. "Are you always this cold?"

The question shot through my heart with its piercing honesty. I placed an arm around her shoulders and gestured to

162

the tent entrance. "Come. Your brother is waiting."

Applying a gentle pressure to her shoulders, I led her out of the tent and past the guards. The crisp night air burst into my lungs, refreshing and exhilarating after the close stale containment of the tent.

I could hear the chatter of the guards' unprotected thoughts rearing like a scared steed. For years, I had lingered amongst mortals in anonymity, safe from their fears and prejudices because of their ignorance of what I truly was. The raw urgency that radiated from the guards reminded me intensely that my cover was no more. They knew they were now in the presence of a beast of prey. No matter what my intentions were, I would always be feared.

I thought suddenly of Nahalo and the guise he had adopted in order to meld into the world of mortals. He had chosen to sooth their simple minds with lies. I knew in my heart I was not capable of such deception. The guards were paralyzed by their own preconceptions; I could feel them watching us, motionless, as we walked away from the tent. I let my arm fall away from Khanna's shoulders. She did not seem to notice, lost within her own thoughts.

"Are all of your guards as skittish as those two?" My inquiry was part jest, part true concern.

She looked back over her shoulder at the two guards. They followed us now at a respectful distance. I assumed they were protective of Khanna. "Yes, they are rather useless."

She glanced at me nervously from the corner of her eyes. "My apologies. You should have had a better detail."

I laughed, pretending not to notice her suspicious observation. "I do not need, nor do I *deserve* a detail at all."

"My brother insists you are guarded at all times." Was there a tinge of irritation in her voice, or was it jealousy? I glanced at her trying to read her true emotions, but her aura was a swarm of fluxing energy. In the moonlight, I noticed suddenly the various weapons she carried; the short sword and holstered handgun on her belt were accompanied by daggers in leather sheaths tied to the outside of each thigh.

I did not reply, feeling cagey and restless under the close watch of the two men behind us. Suddenly, I sensed another soul following us closely, somewhere on the other side of the tents to my left. Though he did his best to conceal his identity, with my heightened perception I knew the smug, anxious aura instantly to be Sea's. He moved quickly through the maze of leather structures. I knew he searched for me and his frustration at being unable to read my location was growing. For a moment, I toyed with the idea of sending him false signals to direct him to the opposite end of the camp. I was not sure I was ready to meet with him face to face just yet. His presence would only be a reminder of the treachery that was still brewing.

I slowed my pace beside Khanna; she did not seem to notice, too lost in her own thoughts. Carefully, so as not to give away my location, I reached further into Sea's mind to listen to the individual thoughts that rambled in a bratish fervor. He cursed Phelan for sending him on this errand, that he was above such menial tasks. He cursed me jealously for being the *chosen one,* wishing that my obliteration from the earth would come quickly. He cursed the Phuree for being filthy nomadic refugees. He cursed the moon, the wind; he longed for the lush, extravagant comforts of Phelan's warm mansion nestled within the hills. He longed for the embrace of his little telepath, Alessandra.

I withdrew quickly and quietly from his mind so as not to alert him to my prying. I was shocked at what I had heard in those brief few seconds; Sea's petty, childish annoyance had reached a level that bordered on bigotry and hatred. His aura was foul, reeking of greed and vanity.

Whatever it was, this message that Phelan had sent Sea to deliver, it must be important to annoy him so. For a brief moment I lowered my guard, breaking down the wall I had sculpted to protect me from the maddening torrents of the world around me. Almost immediately, Sea sensed my presence like an angry hornet honing in on my location. Along with his attention, came the flood of ethereal white noise that had almost destroyed me the night before: the voices of the Phuree, blending chaotically with the under currents of the pure song of Life.

I gasped aloud and, pressing my palms to my temples, I

quickly rebuilt the psychic barrier around my mind. It would take time to learn how to control my new powers enough to tolerate such heightened perception, if I learned to tolerate it at all. Slowly, I realized Khanna was speaking to me, her voice echoing as if down a long corridor. It grew louder as the static of the universe subsided, bringing me back to the present.

I shook my head and breathed deeply.

"Are you okay?"

I looked up. Khanna was staring at me with alarm, her hand on my upper arm. My gaze traveled to her hand. She jerked it back to her side.

"I'm fine." I took another deep breath. "Still a little weak, that's all. Nothing for you to worry about."

I peered over my shoulder at the guards behind us. They stood in mid-stride gripping their swords, ready for battle, their expressions confused and terrified. I wondered how two so ruled by their primal emotions had survived so long in such a violent world.

"Tynan. We need to speak." Sea's voice startled me as he appeared as if from thin air before us.

Khanna jumped at the sudden noise, whirling to face him, sword drawn and ready for conflict. He caught her wrist in mid swing, barely escaping her decapitating blow. I was highly impressed by her speed and skill with the sword. It was no small wonder she commanded such respect from soldiers twice her size and strength. They stared at each other in perfect stunned silence. Behind us, the soldiers, their fear of Immortals consumed by their devout loyalty to Khanna, quickly began to advance on Sea. Sea tightened his grip on Khanna's wrist until she began to grimace in pain.

With her free hand, Khanna motioned for the guards to stop. I could feel her pain; it was taking every ounce of will power for her to keep from screaming.

Without releasing her, Sea turned his gaze on me, hissing contemptuously. "In private, please."

"Let her go," I demanded, my voice low and deadly. I knew then that I could kill him easily and without remorse. It was a disturbing calm, such knowledge.

His gaze locked with mine with narrowed eyes. He

opened the hand that held her. Khanna dropped her sword and clutched her wrist as if it were broken.

Khanna scowled angrily at Sea, her aura glowing deep reddish orange. "How dare you touch me! I should kill you in your sleep."

Sea snorted with a mixture of irritation and amusement.

His belittlement of her outrage only incensed her further. "You may think you're *immortal*, but I know ways in which you will never piece yourself back together again!"

Sea rolled his eyes. "Tynan, I don't have time for this!" He crossed his arms over his chest. His long silk coat swirled about him like dark waves of the blue green sea. How polished and perfect he appeared with his spotlessly elegant white shirt and stunning white blonde hair, a sore slick contrast to the hard grit that surrounded us. My stomach churned with animosity.

I could feel him trying to read my mind; I could sense his mounting frustration when he found nothing but a blank slate staring back at him. The Phuree camp was brewing with life around us as people set to their nightly tasks of survival. Their emotions and conversations swirled around us with the perfume of horses and sweat and leather. I turned to Khanna. She would not take her eyes off Sea. Her sword still lay at her feet.

"Khanna, go and join Tiernan. Tell him I will be there shortly." I placed a gentle hand on her shoulder.

She did not reply. Her confrontation with Sea had unearthed something far deeper than I could gauge. Though I still could not penetrate her thoughts, I had the distinct feeling that it was not the first time that they had met. The idea made me uneasy.

"Khanna?" I asked quietly.

"Do not linger too long." She continued to glare at Sea. "We have much to discuss that we cannot delay."

Khanna stooped to retrieve her sword with her good hand. She gestured for the guards to follow her as she stepped past Sea and continued on down the path to her brother's quarters. Sea and I waited in silence until we were convinced they were out of earshot.

"My, my. You're looking well." The words were black and riddled with poison as they slithered from his lips. A tinge of unsteadiness seeped through the venom, giving away his true surprise.

"No thanks to you." I was in no mood for idle banter. "What do you have to say to me that you cannot say in front of the Phuree? They are, after all, the reason why we are all here, are they not?" I kept my tone even and cool.

He eyed me suspiciously. "Where are Tatsu and Lillian?"

"They're gone? I would figure they'd be with you and the rest of the Immortals. I've been a little too *preoccupied* to keep up with them." I held his gaze.

Sea angrily moved towards me till he was only a few inches away. "You do not want to toy with me, Tynan. We know you sent them somewhere."

He peered at me as if he could find the answers within the green and brown flecks of my eyes. The wind toyed with his white blonde hair, lifting the delicate strands so that they flowed like cobwebs around his long thin face. "You are playing a precarious game, Tynan."

I realized, suddenly, as I watched him, that he honestly knew nothing of the blood that I had been given or the transformation I had undergone thereafter. He could sense that there was something dangerously different about me, that I had grown paler and harder in my appearance, that my wounds had healed all too quickly, but he could not identify just what it was about me that made him so uneasy. I smiled a bitter smile to myself, knowing that I had begun to control the flow of power that, the night before, had almost consumed me.

It frustrated him that he could not delve into my mind to gather the information he desired. His emotions fluxed, a solar storm raging across his being. Such animosity was dangerous if not kept in check and I worried suddenly for Tatsu and Lillian's safety. I dared not reach out over the ether to link minds with them, fearing Sea might sense the open gate and slip in to read my thoughts.

"Whatever it is that you're thinking, your silence is not helping. We will find them." Checking his anger to keep it from boiling over, Sea took a step back from me. Although the cold did not affect him, he pulled the collar of his coat up high as if to protect him from the wind.

"I'm not saying I know where they are, but if they no longer want to be a part of this," I made a sweeping gesture at the tents around me, "then let them go.

"Besides, I'm the one you wanted, am I not? And now that this pawn is in place what need of any other vampire could you possibly have?" The sarcasm was smooth and cold as I spoke. There was a long moment of tense silence. I closed the gap between us with a few slow steps.

I leaned in close till my lips were beside his ear and whispered. "Go back to Phelan and give him this message: *In every messiah there is either a martyr, a monster or a savior. He has given me the power to decide which it will be.*"

Sea's eyes became wide, his white blonde brows knitting with a confusion and fear he could not comprehend. I held his gaze, our faces mere inches away from each other. He said nothing.

I placed my hands on either side of his face and placed a kiss on each cheek. "You were once like a brother to me, Sea. In spirit as well as Dark Blood." I continued to hold his face in my hands as I spoke. "But you have betrayed my trust in so many ways that I cannot speak of them all."

I kissed him on his stone-white forehead. "All you can do now is pray. Pray that good will be born of your deceit and your malice."

A kiss upon his lips. "Pray," I breathed the words into his mouth, a ghost of a whisper.

I released his face and without a sound, stepped past him, leaving him dazed and mute with confusion. I did not look back as I continued onwards to join Tiernan and Khanna. There was a part of me that craved satisfaction from the cryptic words I had breathed to Sea, but instead a sorrowful defeat swam in my heart. In truth, I felt that I had severed the final ties to my once Dark Brother. The melancholy despair blossomed with poison thorns through my soul, rendering it painfully.

Behind me, I heard a faint *whoosh* of air as Sea swiftly

disappeared into the maze of tents. He would return to Phelan with my message and his words would anger my Maker deeply. I did not fear him though. He no longer controlled my destiny.

10

I wandered the maze of pale brown sand that separated the tents, allowing my intuition guide me towards Tiernan's quarters. I felt no hurry to find those that waited patiently for my arrival. My heart was scorched by the lies and deceit of my Dark Brother, my soul was propelled forward by the call of freedom from the past. Betrayal was not a new thorn. Yet, somehow, the turning of one so delicately intertwined with my existence had stung deeper than the others, poisoned with the desperate malice that spawned when Dark Brothers divide.

Sea's sudden and inexplicable ability to hate me with such heartless hostility was a phenomenon I could not dwell upon too closely, or it would shatter my last remaining threads of humanity, threads I needed now more than ever to hold me together. I studied the ground as I walked. It was hard packed from horse hooves and leather boots and soon I came upon the torch-lit central circle of the Phuree encampment. I lingered on the perimeter of the circle in the heavy shadows cast by the towering tents that surrounded me, soaking in the love, pride and fear that radiated from the Phuree. They hurried about their nightly preparations, oblivious to my presence. The budding evening brimmed with anticipation of an imminent war. Their hushed voices sheltered the hidden chaos of their personal internal struggles to find peace and acceptance. The evening before, the combined weight of their subconscious had nearly crushed my psyche, but the agony I had experienced then was now no more than a minor sting. I realized with relief that I was quickly settling into my new powers; if I could control the strength Nahalo had given me, I knew I could control anything.

Carefully I listened, concentrating to separate and absorb the essence of each current of intellect that swarmed about me. Every individual had lost a family member, if not several, that were close to them; most had resigned themselves to the fact that they would be lucky if they lived past thirty. I watched as the Phuree tended to the necessary chores of existence; men and women alike shared in everything from mending clothes and cooking meals to shoeing horses and smithing weapons. It was a society where equality was balanced effortlessly, as if the world had never shown them otherwise. I marveled at the peaceful societal dance, somewhat unnerved by the knowledge of their secret cunning and skill in the art of war. Though I had not yet seen them firsthand in battle, I knew they were a force to be reckoned with.

What little conversation flowed was, for the most part, casual, referring only to their tasks at hand. Here and there, however, there sparked philosophical questions between the adolescents, impassioned and wise beyond their years. They kept their youthful vigor to a whisper out of fear of reproach from the adults. It reached me as a single violin note, flowing between the storm of thought and quiet ebb of conversation. I felt a communion with the young minds and desired suddenly to gather them close to me, to protect them and teach them the ways of the world. To show them that all was not the gloom that seemed to linger forever upon their lives, tainting each and every note and nerve of their existence. Perhaps that aspect of me had not died completely? Perhaps, Nahalo had been right?

I tucked the feeling away in a niche of my soul to ponder at another time, and focused my attention upon my destination. Tiernan's tent, though proportionately no larger than the other Phuree quarters was instantly recognizable as that of a man of great importance. The slanting sides of sun-bleached brown leather were adorned with ancient swirling tribal symbols of protection and power in black and red. The markings were of an ancient magic whose roots in the beliefs of the old gods spanned centuries, older than even I could remember.

Interlaced about the seals in delicate white, danced strings of a language I could only assume was the Phuree tongue. Though well versed in five languages, I found I could not decipher the text. It seemed to be a derivative of ancient

Gaelic, but the markings it coupled with were a mystery to me. I counted my blessings that I could now understand the spoken form easily.

The entrance to Tiernan's quarters was closed. Amber light seeped out into the night from around its loose edges, illuminating the backs of the two motionless guards posted to either side. I gathered my courage about me, settling the nerves that still resonated with lingering anxiety, knowing I would have to cross the crowd of humans. I could have easily cloaked myself so that no one saw my passing, but some strangely narcissistic part of me wanted to be seen. I thought suddenly of Khanna's seductive nervousness, the way the sight of me had reduced the hot-tempered little warrior to a fragile woman overcome by desire. The power in that moment was dangerously addictive. Secretly, I wanted the people who had brought me to their prairie wasteland with blood and deceit to bow down to me. I wanted to rule them.

I gasped, taken aback by my own desire for power. It left me shaken as I hurriedly brushed the welling of vice away from my soul. I could not let it consume me for it would make me weak. With a deep breath, I ran my fingers through my hair, pulling it back from my forehead. I stepped out into the crowd. The idle chatter slipped into oblivion as they stopped their chores to turn to watch the pale, ageless man drifting through their midst. I could sense their paralysis; they wanted to approach me, to question me about the future, as if I held the secret within my heart and would not share it. The power I still struggled to contain kept them at bay, though; they could sense its furious instability and my own torn acceptance of my new destiny. They were uncertain of their own consensus to bring me here.

I kept my eyes downcast, wishing I had simply skirted around the edges of the circle and slipped into Tiernan's tent unnoticed. I wasn't ready for such analysis, such scrutiny by so many hungry souls. At the tent's entrance, I looked up and found myself locking gazes with Tiernan. The Phuree leader had noticed the sudden hush that had overcome his people and had come outside to watch.

He placed his arm about my shoulder. "Come. We have

been expecting you."

Though his expression was stoic, the same confused apprehension I had sensed from the gathering of humans behind us trickled through his hard calloused fingers. Subconsciously, he was the questioning his personal conviction to the war and his ability to lead his people to freedom. I wanted to take him by the shoulders and tell him of my newfound faith in him and his people. I wanted to reassure him and give to him from my own dark reservoir of strength. But I dared not. He would never be ready to admit his own misgivings; such a confession could destroy a leader. In stunted cold silence, I waited.

Such a burden for one so young... the fate of an entire people.

Tiernan's blue gaze dropped away from mine as if he could hear my thoughts. He wanted to remove his arm from my cold shoulders, but he couldn't. The muscles in his jaw tightened as his thoughts flowed through him, recklessly exposed to my prying mind. *You must not fear Tynan. You are a warrior. You have led your people through countless battles... You do not even fear Cardone and his men. One man should not affect you so...but one man should not contain such power, either.*

I knew I could not comfort him. I could not even comfort myself.

Silently, the guard to our left pulled back the tent's entrance.

Stifling heat and amber light assaulted my perilously tuned senses and for a moment I was blinded. Quickly, I shielded my eyes with the back of my hand until the initial intensity faded. Peering through my fingers, I took a step into the tent and felt Tiernan's hand fall away from my shoulder. Behind me, I heard the tent's doorway fall shut with a whoosh. Slowly, I let my hand fall to my side and allowed my gaze to take in the new space and its inhabitants.

Tiernan's quarters were barely larger than the tent I had awoken in and spartanly furnished, containing but a few necessary personal belongings. A roaring fire burned, barely contained within a ring of large prairie stones in center of the room. Above the fire, a rack for hanging a kettle had been built from scrap pieces of iron, artfully welded by hand to be easily and quickly disassembled. I listened to the updraft of the fire as its smoke and flames were lured towards the heavens through the hole at the top of the tent where the great wooden support poles joined. In the sudden silence of the close quarters, the roar transformed to a low howl, resounding in my ears like the desperate laments of the lost caught in the constant spiral between worlds. I was drawn to it, longing to warm myself beside its hearty flames, but something stilled me.

I surveyed the remainder of the tent with haste. Beside Tiernan's sleeping pallet was a large wooden trunk upon which was unceremoniously placed his shield and cloak. Aside from this, the only other piece of furniture in the tent was a long, low table of roughly finished mesquite wood. In the center of the table stood a tarnished, silver three-pronged candelabra and a large earthenware pitcher with several mugs. Around the table sat the few attendees of our private meeting. They waited patiently, sitting upon large plush pillows of patchwork materials and a sturdy jute mat spread on the ground to keep the sand from invading their clothing.

At the head of the table, furthest away from me, sat Nahalo, his back perfectly straight, his human guise intact once again as he played the Phuree oracle for one more night. His calm expression betrayed nothing of our evening together upon the great granite boulder. The dancing orange and yellow flames of the fire shimmered liquidly in his eyes hinting at the raw molten power that flowed beneath.

Welcome... His voice drifted across the plains of my awareness, an eagle gliding on the high currents of wind. I nodded my acknowledgment, a small movement only the Immortal eye could detect.

To his left sat Khanna. Cross-legged, she leaned forward, propping her elbows on the table, her fingers interlaced and pressed against her chin. Her injured wrist had been bandaged with torn strips of wide unbleached linen to aide with support, no doubt against her wishes. She watched me intently, seeming to glow in her perfect rugged and sculpted beauty, her wind tangled blond hair now tied back from her face with a thick length of dark brown leather..

I tried to read her thoughts, but they were sealed within the catacombs of her being. My ability to slip into that vault had been a momentary anomaly that she had quickly and permanently rectified; I would not be privy to her unwitting confessions again. Though the words that flowed through her mind no longer danced before me, her body language betrayed her desire to remain strong and stoic for the powerful men in her presence. Khanna was tense and guarded, acutely aware of her status. Her icy detached stare pierced through me, intense but unfocused.

Her eyes darted briefly to the man beside her. A familiar connection existed there that penetrated deeper than mere business acquaintances. He leaned lazily against the table beside her with an arrogant boredom. His hair was a wild mane of coarse wavy black, shot through with hints of silvery gray. It tumbled past his shoulders to reach his waist. Beneath it was a face of wickedly chiseled beauty with dark blue eyes rimmed with long lashes of jet. I could tell instantly that he was not Phuree, nor did he attempt to blend in. Instead, he wore dusty black cargo pants and a simple rough-knit gray sweater, heavily frayed about the collar and distinctly militia-grade, though from what decade it was hard to say. A glimmer of tarnished gold at the base of his naked throat caught my eye, a short, thinly beaten gold chain holding a small gold disk engraved with the Illuminati Eye.

His chest rose and fell slowly with his breath and the coin disappeared beneath the collar of his sweater. Absently stroking the small black goatee below his bottom lip, he evaluated me like a gambler banking heavily on his next move. Nervous, secretive energy rippled about him, erratic and electrical. I felt the hackles on the back of my neck bristle with intuitive defense. He sensed my unease, his wide full lips curling up to one side in a small knowing gesture that appeared like a challenge.

"This is Malakai Devolton." Tiernan's voice was calm and steady as he stood beside me, broken of the spell that had rendered him impotent outside the tent. "He has been quite valuable at keeping us supplied with weaponry and

175

information for the past few years." Though Tiernan's words were complimentary there was something subtle lingering between them, a tinge of disapproval mixed with indebtedness.

"Sounds like a good man to have on your side." I tried to make my voice light, but the darkness would not stay at bay.

Tiernan breathed heavily through his nose, "Yes, I suppose you could say that."

Again, the strained diplomacy of leadership filtered his true opinions. I listened gently to melancholy truths of his soul. War is skilled at disintegrating the fragile shell that holds one's better judgment. Its talons shred the fine fabric that cradle nations to the breast of humanity, reducing visionary leaders to starving coyotes and the civilians they are sworn to protect to scurrying field mice. The world mutates with a viciousness born of desperation, polluting humanity's ability to know right from wrong, and all too often forced the hand of the good into uncomfortable positions of corruption.

Tiernan's duty to protect his people had forced an alliance with Malakai. For all the ancient Phuree magic into which he had been born, I could tell by his expression that Tiernan did not like mysteries when it came to politics. Malakai represented the obscured line of justice that had become faded and dismantled. Malakai was a man with no past, no future, and no side. Or so he would have it seem. Tiernan, however, was not fooled by his arrogant guise of neutrality. Neither was I.

Tiernan's mental defenses were now no challenge to me and I continued to peel away the layers of truth from his soul. He struggled with his desire to banish Malakai from the Phuree. His sister had begun to jeopardize her ability to maintain focus in battle: her attention was torn between her tortured heart and the war. For the most part he kept his opinions to himself knowing all too well that his words would be lost upon his strong-willed sister, but the tension had begun to eat away at his restraint. It was only a matter of time before the dam broke, and Malakai now knew too much about the Phuree to be allowed to live; he could not be trusted to not profit from the secrets in some devious fashion.

I closed the door to Tiernan's soul. My brief insight into the tangled triangle had left me disconcerted. I continued to watch Malakai as he smiled at me. I wanted to read his soul, to lay it out upon the table like a crime scene autopsy, but the prying tendrils of my mind were met with immense panels of cold gray steel. The shock of the inhumanly icy sensation riveted through my mind as I recoiled into the protective depths of myself.

"A pleasure to meet you, Malakai." My voice was a blade cloaked in congeniality.

Malakai's liquidly sensual smile broadened, his eyes narrowing to sly feline slits. "Oh no, the *pleasure* is all mine." His gaze slid to Khanna. "Khanna has told me quite a bit about you," he paused and looked back at me, raising a black eyebrow, "and your...*talents?*" He could barely contain his amusement.

I felt my brows knit in confused irritation. Khanna stared directly ahead at the fire ring, lost within the spiral of her own inner turmoil. She tried to conceal the anxiety rising in her chest, but the nervous tightening of the muscles in her throat exposed her weakness to the room.

Nahalo's gaze flickered between the two humans disapprovingly. He, too, appeared not to trust Malakai. My gaze latched onto Nahalo as a sudden seed of uncertainty quickened in my heart. The seething distrust amongst the gathering made me wonder if I had been too hasty in my decision to join the Phuree's cause.

Do not worry child. Nahalo's voice rippled through my mind as he caught wind of my mounting anxiety. *I am watching him closely...and he knows it all too well.*

His words did little to soothe my racing mind. I looked back to Malakai. He was, after all, merely a mortal. I took a deep breath through my nose and centered myself.

"Please..." As he spoke, Tiernan touched my arm lightly, startling me. He gestured for me to take my place at the table.

I could still feel the hairs on the backs of my forearms bristling slightly as I sat down across from Khanna. As I came into her line of sight, breaking her concentration upon the fire behind me, she blinked as if startled out of a dream. Unable to meet my gaze, her eyes quickly darted to her folded hands upon the table. Unconsciously, she slid them slightly closer to her body as if afraid I might attempt to touch her again. Her unease bristled around her. It stung me deeply, this retreat into herself, though I knew it was not I alone she wished to distance herself from.

The air within the tent was close and hot, pressing down upon me. Tiernan settled his tall muscular frame into the seat opposite Nahalo. Two empty seats still remained and my curiosity demanded to know who would fill them. I kept quiet though, not wishing to draw any more attention to myself than necessary. Silence weighed heavy as Tiernan shuffled through a stack of maps before him, organizing them. A few of the maps were recently acquired rough sketches in black ink on thinly tanned deer skin; others were ancient originals from the 21st century, their once expensive white paper now yellowing with age and cracking about the edges. Tiernan handled these priceless references with great care, gingerly holding them by the edges as if they were made of gold.

Across the table, Malakai lounged, seemingly uninterested in his surroundings. With his left hand, he dug deep into the pocket of the black duster draped across his lap, retrieving a small silver container. He popped the top off it. The sweet scent of dried tobacco danced above the table, tugging at my mortal addiction with ease. I watched as he slid a leather pouch holding dried leaves and a small packet of handmade rolling papers out onto the table before him. With deft fingers, he sprinkled tobacco into a creased paper and casually rolled it between his thumb and forefinger. As he did so, he noticed my scrutiny of his work. He smiled, narrowing his eyes slightly.

"I didn't think your kind could partake of this nasty little human vice?" Without lifting his elbows from the table, he offered the cigarette to me clasped between the fore and middle fingers of his right hand.

My gaze locked with Malakai's piercing blue eyes. "There is a lot you don't know about *our kind.*"

It occurred to me suddenly that it had been several nights since my last Hunt. Though the blood supplied to me by

Nahalo had sustained me for a night, the innate predatory desire to take life was stirring within me. My jaw tightened as I thought of the taboo satisfaction I would have in draining the coppery stream of life from Malakai's body; I could smell his blood coursing through the complex scents of tobacco, patchouli and sweat. My abdomen tightened as I struggled to keep my grip on the Beast as it strained against my humanity.

I focused on the cigarette to distract myself from the mounting blood lust. I craved the comforting weight of the rolled tobacco between my fingers, the calming warmth of smoke in my lungs, believing for a moment it might keep the beast at bay for a while longer, allowing me the civility I required to make it through the evening calmly. I plucked the cigarette from his extended fingers. Placing it between my parted lips. I lit the end using my new power of fire.

My nervous system twitched. I turned away from Malakai, listening carefully to the buzzing of the dark desert world outside. Two vampires were nearing our meeting place. I instantly identified them as Sea and Phelan, their auras arrogantly on display for the world to view.

It made sense that they would be in attendance that evening, but, no matter the rationale, their sudden intrusion into my world still grated on my nerves. I realized I was not ready to see Phelan so soon after our battle, so soon after my brush with death. I worried I would not be able to control my temper if I was crossed and, with my new powers, I knew I could easily destroy him.

Tread carefully now, Tynan. Do not let anger rule your reason. He is part of this as much as you are now. Nahalo's soundless council was a heavy hand upon my shoulder. *You know why you are here. Let no one move you from your conviction.*

I slammed shut the shutters to my mind with a reverberating echo that made Nahalo visibly flinch. I meant no insult to him, but no matter the intention, Nahalo's unsolicited advice did nothing to bridge the cavernous gorge that now existed between my Maker and I. That rift was irreparable, the wound too deep. Not even Nahalo's magic could revive what was dead and quickly returning to the darkness and dust from

179

which it was born.

The tent's leather entrance parted shattering the warm stale silence with a cold gust from the bustling world outside. The fire within the ring of stones beside me shuddered and bowed away from the open door as if trying to flee its earth-bound tether. The scent of incense, horses and roasting meat spiraled past me and up to the open smoke vent high above.

I wished to follow the smoke up into the heavens.

The guard posted to the left of the doorway nervously held the entrance open for Phelan and Sea as they entered. Their movements were elegantly fluid and silent as they slipped through the doorway pausing before us all as if in expectation of a grand reception.

Phelan's feline beauty shimmered, gleaming in the amber firelight; his glowing auburn hair, loose and flowing in long straight coppery sheets about him. His emerald green eyes seemed to separate his physical being from the earthen shades and rough-hewn edges surrounding him. He was flawless and regal in his fine silken garments of the deepest midnight blue and black. I felt my heart twinge as I remembered the unquestioning adoration with which I had once worshiped him. Those were the years before I began to perceive the illusion.

Phelan's eyes settled on me, his expression mysteriously devoid of emotion. I could not gauge his reaction to my swift recovery, or if he cared at all. Half hidden beneath the long belled sleeves of his silk shirt, he held a small scorched book of leather and parchment. It was my journal.

Instantly, every muscle in my body tensed, ready to tear the book from his pale cold fingers. Behind them, the large leather panel hissed as it fell back into place, instantly shutting off the outside world and, once again, leaving us enclosed with only our demons for company. I looked away feeling the sting of anger beginning to boil beneath my skin.

So he owns my past? I thought bitterly. *He can have it. He cannot claim my future. I will be certain of that.*

Tiernan quickly stood to receive Phelan and Sea. He held his hand out to Phelan and the two men clasped forearms in welcome. "Sir Daray, thank you so much for joining—"

"You're late, Phelan Daray." Nahalo's smooth tone interrupted Tiernan with its riddle of velveteen accusatory scolding.

I drew hard on the cigarette between my lips and held the smoke in my lungs as my attention returned to the ancient blood drinkers in the doorway.

Phelan's posture had tightened subtly, the small muscles of his delicate jaw trembling as he momentarily clenched his teeth to control his anger. What were these mortals to him but mere inconveniences he must contend with out of his own desire for the greater cause? They were nothing to him and yet one was so bold to demand of him the respect of punctuality.

With a sudden shock, I realized he did not know Nahalo to be other than a mortal. The knowledge of Nahalo's powerful Immortal legacy was as much a mystery to Phelan and Sea as it was to Tiernan and Khanna.

Why, I wondered, *would he keep such intimate knowledge secret from the blood brethren fighting for his cause? Why have I been ushered into his Dark vault of knowledge and not my Maker? Am I the only one who knows?*

Surely there are others... I exhaled the tobacco smoke slowly through my nose. I did not want this secret. I did not like what the secret insinuated. I tightened the lock on my mind for safe measure. Whatever Nahalo's intentions were, it was not my place to move the next piece in this chess game.

Phelan's gaze was unwavering, his eyes swimming with a silent lust to swiftly kill his accuser. His lips twitched into a small forced smile. "We were detained with...*personal* issues."

"Your *issues* are of no interest to me at this time," Nahalo spoke softly, his words at war with his seemingly simple tone. "What is of interest is the fact that the hour grows late and we have much to discuss tonight."

Phelan transferred his attention momentarily to Sea, his eyebrows raised slightly in disbelief. Sea remained silent, his pale brows knitted in a small display of confusion and concern. His mismatched eyes flickered only momentarily to Phelan's, unwilling to let Nahalo out of his sight for too long. Unlike

Phelan, he had sensed something amiss in the exchange, something he could not place but which struck his soul with a melancholy note that was both ancient and dangerous.

Phelan immediately noticed the predatory tension that paralyzed Sea. His eyes narrowed suspiciously as he turned back to face us. He tilted his head slightly to the side and forced a small sharp smile onto his lips. "Our *sincerest* apologies."

He turned to Tiernan who, having been caught off guard as much as the others now stood uncomfortably, his eyes darting between Phelan and Nahalo in a desperate attempt to decipher the venomous undercurrent coursing dangerously beneath their strained civility.

"Your *oracle* is quite outspoken." Phelan's words slithered with an iridescent sheen to lash at the Phuree leader, "Forgive me if I have kept you waiting."

His eyes drifted back to me. "Two of our own have gone missing. We were only *concerned* for their safety."

My soul went cold. The cigarette crushed between my curled fingers began to tremble as my fury and my fear arced blue-white lightning through my veins. I wanted desperately to let my mind race from the tent to wander over the prairie lands and back to the city in search of Tatsu and Lillian, but I didn't dare crack open the fortress. My instinct made me more than certain that they had reached the boundaries of the amagin unscathed, but what had transpired since then was a mystery. If they had attempted to reach out to me, I had not received their message.

Tiernan quickly broke the silence. His strong clear voice showed that he was determined to regain the group's attention. "I mean no disrespect, but every moment we waste is another moment given to the enemy." He dared not touch Phelan or Sea as he had done with me, not out of respect, but out of fear. He gestured to the table with an open palm. "Please, let us all be seated so that we may begin."

The enemy. Yes, it seemed we had become so consumed by our petty feuds that we had all but forgotten about the Tyst and the malignant seed that split and mutated within the cold walls of their fortress. I wanted desperately to put aside the lust for revenge that poisoned my soul, but how could I when those that seethed and stalked my existence remained an irrefutable constant within the universe?

"Yes. Let us be seated." Phelan's posture transformed subtly as he reigned in the rage that sharpened his words.

Phelan and Sea split, a cell dividing, each flowing around Tiernan in soundless harmony to seat themselves on opposite sides of the table.

Sea lowered himself into a cross-legged position upon the pillow beside me. His aura was tucked tightly about him, his defenses fiercely armed for the uncertainty that plagued his mind. My close proximity was of little concern to him, I realized suddenly, as I saw his eyes remained fixed upon Nahalo.

Across the table Phelan settled delicately into his place. He placed my journal in front of him and folded his long white hands over it. Against the roughly worn and soot stained leather, the absolute pristine flawlessness of his skin glowed eerily, his nails gleaming glass in the firelight. His perfect white features were devoid of all traces of emotion or humanity, smoothed like a river stone by the endless centuries.

The healing hole in my chest twitched painfully as the muscles tightened with the poison of hateful bitterness I could not relinquish.

Tiernan returned to his place at the head of the table. I could see the confusion and caution he desperately attempted to conceal was wearing thin on his hard chiseled features. He had not anticipated the swarm of hostility that accompanied the gathering. Indeed, I sensed that he had envisioned a much smoother intermingling of companies. The subtle silent layers of communication to which he was not privy worried him profoundly. He needed his recruits to have one solid agenda and their hearts to be aligned for the greater good of his cause.

Instead, he stood a silent witness to a catastrophic fragmentation of relations, centuries in the making. I watched his brow furrow slightly in consternation as he wavered between his dual roles of warrior-king and peacekeeper, both of which seemed utterly lost on such ageless entities as Phelan and myself. Tiernan's fragile governing laws washed over us as we moved, warring Titans through his simple realm. Did he dare try to rein us in and tame our ferocity, or should he carefully craft a treaty to appeal to the remainder of our humanity and pray it bridged the lake of fire across which we hurled our silent spears?

His eyes flickered to me. They had grown slate grey.

He gathered the loose maps together neatly before him to give him a moment more to settle himself before beginning. When he spoke his voice was deep and steady.

11

"I cannot begin to tell you how long I have dreamed of this night." He paused for a moment before continuing, "I realize that you have all made great sacrifices," his gaze lingered for a moment on me as he surveyed the apprehensive faces around him, "and traveled great distances to lend your wisdom and your strength to our cause. I wish that words alone could express to you the depth of my appreciation."

His resolve was returning from the shaken confusion of the moments before, his voice growing stronger as it emanated from the depths of his heart. "Many have told me that what I strive for is impossible, a fool's ambition of unobtainable peace. I cannot accept that notion. I cannot accept the idea that our fates are sealed. The years weigh heavily as I think of my father's struggles and his father before him.

"At times it seems as if this reign of bloodshed is endless. Even the stories passed down speak of countless wars even before the time of the Tyst...I wonder if there has ever been an age of true peace upon this earth at all?" He paused for a long moment in reflection. "But that does not mean that it cannot exist one day."

I shifted uncomfortably in my seat as I felt the full weight of his fragile dreams settle into the tent's close quarters. It was true, there had never been a time in which races were not persecuted, lands were not pillaged, and kingdoms were not burned. I had watched empires rise and fall and the beauty of life crushed beneath the greedy ambitions of humanity's quest for expansion and progress. Utopia was a dream for romantics and revolutionaries. There would never be such a state where humans were concerned.

Even if mortals could put aside their differences and live in harmony and acceptance, what about we vampires? They

185

knew about us now; we were no longer myth and mist. We were flesh and blood and we were their predators. Could Tiernan look me in the eye and tell me he would not take up arms against us once his mortal foes were felled? I shuddered to think of such a confrontation. My adoration for the purity of the Phuree way of life seemed tainted now. I listened carefully to Tiernan's deep voice, searching for a flaw of some sort, a lie or deep-seeded doubt within his words that could change my mind and force me to leave. Dread had begun to roost again in the rafters of my consciousness. It fluttered and scurried, folding and unfolding its black wings to the beat of my heart.

"Tonight we begin to see the light returning, the light that left our world for so many years. Let there be no doubt though, the next few months ahead of us will be our darkest. The sacrifices of the past one hundred years will pale in comparison to the loss we will incur as we make our final stand against the Tyst." He paused letting the last words ring in our ears like a death knell.

My desperate fear twisted itself into a tighter coil about my spine. *Run*, it hissed icily, *run while you still have time to find sanctuary deep within the earth where they cannot find you.* The siren's song of cowardice sang sweetly of the oblivion of denial, obliterating the guidance of Nahalo's visions. But I knew there was no such thing as oblivion; there was only a state of numbness that eventually crumbled beneath the icy waves of guilt and regret. Even in my long Sleep, I had not found the utopian fields of redemption and forgiveness; I had not escaped the steel talons of my demons no matter what crevice of the earth I burrowed into. Death alone could, perhaps, bring such a sweet silence, but even that I could not be sure of.

Glassily, I stared at Tiernan overwhelmed by the divide in my soul, between my desire to help liberate a persecuted tribe and my fearful disgust for mortal conflict. Their fight had kept them alive, but only barely clinging to existence.

And now, as I listened to Tiernan's strong, heavily accented voice, I realized that he truly believed it would all reach a resolution in a matter of months, if not sooner.

"Though our loss will be great, so will our victory. I know it is hard to believe such a thing is possible, that we could very soon be utterly and completely free of the persecution that has haunted us for so many years, but my instinct tells me to believe, and my instinct has yet to fail me." Tiernan paused and took a deep breath. "We will bring the Tyst to its knees. We will end the genocide of the Phuree peoples. We will bring an end to the Cardone regime and when it has fallen, so will begin an era of peace which the world has not seen. Nahalo and his mages have received the gift of vision from the gods."

Malakai snorted a short cynical laugh beneath his breath. The room fell silent, all eyes turning to him with daggers drawn. He did not look up from the cigarette he rolled between his calloused fingers; he did not care if he were judged.

"Please elaborate upon your commentary." Nahalo's voice was deceptively smooth and neutral as the artic ice of his eyes glimmered fiercely.

Malakai laughed again, scoffing mockingly low. "It's just the irony of all of this." He lifted the cigarette to his parted lips and ran his tongue over the edge of the white parchment paper to seal it. "The use of blood hunters and guns to bring about peace." He drew a crude match from a small tarnished silver tin and lit the cigarette. Drawing deeply upon the harsh acrid smoke, he leaned back nonchalantly and turned his insolent gaze to Tiernan. "Even if you were to win, what makes you think that your regime will be any more peaceful than Cardone's?"

He paused and smiled a wickedly slick smile. "And what makes you think these guys aren't here to reap the benefits of your struggles?" He gestured flippantly with one dismissive hand towards Phelan and Sea.

Malakai turned back to face me, folding his hands on the table before him, cigarette between his fingers, as if he were about to make me a proposal I could not refuse. "And then there's you. Tell me, *savior o' mine*, just why are you helping the Phuree? I hear they practically had to kill you in order to get you here, yet now you sit here at this table as if it was of your own free will. I don't buy it." He lowered his voice, leaning towards me. "Just what is your game blood-hunter?" He had no fear of the Immortals.

Khanna placed her left hand on Malakai's forearm and whispered pleadingly, "Please don't, Malakai." Her eyes were full of anger mixed with a desperate fear. "They may leave..."

I was taken aback. The periphery of my vision closed in, tunneling black to Malakai's blue eyes. I remained silent; in truth I had no answer for him. The reasons as to why I had remained were a tumultuous reactionary blur. Nor could I know what motivated Phelan, Sea and the others to act with such seeming loyalty to Tiernan and his people. The world around me was spinning too quickly for me to find my feet. My newfound fascination with the Phuree was passionate, but founded in the haste of tragic circumstances. As for my perception of the Tyst, I had only my own fractured and selfish observations from the year past. For less than twelve months, amidst the dark caverns of my inner philosophical struggles, I had honestly given the Cardone regime little consideration.

If there was truth in the story of the Vicinus and his barter with Cardone, then perhaps the new regime was indeed more dangerous than those that had ruled in the past, and much more foolish. If it was real, the Vicinus would surely seek revenge upon all of humanity to prove to the gods he would not be confined again. If it was not real, if the myth was simply a mad rumor stirred by war, the Tyst still posed a very real threat to the existence of the Immortal race.

But did I truly care if the world was obliterated? Would I mourn the destruction of my race, the same eccentric egomaniacal beings that had stolen my mortality? Did the earth not deserve a time of rest from the inflictions of the living? What man, woman or child could honestly testify that we, mortal and Immortal, had not committed such atrocities as were fit to be judged by the gods? Even the Phuree, with all of their talk of *peace*, had committed atrocities against the Tyst in their struggles for freedom. For every strike the Tyst had made against the Phuree, the rebels had responded with equal viciousness, slaughtering entire Tyst platoons and mercilessly torturing Tyst allies for information.

There was truth in Malakai's flippant accusations. After all, if one regime fell, another would only rise to take its place.

The heavy bitter sensation of valuable knowledge beneath the oily surface of his sarcastic inquiry made my soul cringe, but when I scanned his mind for details he had banished the secrets revealing only what he wanted me to see and naught more. It was a game for him. The Tyst, the Phuree, the war, the world; it was all an elaborate sport in which he played both sides with deft dexterity. I both admired and detested him. I certainly did not trust him.

His sensual lips curled up, his eyes narrowing as he sensed my probing. "Don't think you're the first to try to get at the gold I hold." He tapped the side of his head. "The Tyst trained me well to guard against your kind." It was not hatred that dripped from his words, though the challenge was bitter nonetheless.

The Thirst shuddered within me. I wanted to drink from him, to break the eggshell enigma of his past and spill its contents into the dust. No one knew the truth as this one did, of that I was certain.

"I'm done tolerating you and your insolence," Tiernan growled deep and low, ready to tear Malakai limb from limb with his bare hands. He moved towards Malakai with unrestrained malice.

Malakai leapt to his feet in a swift feline movement, unafraid and ready to do battle with Tiernan, a man twice his size and seeming strength. "What would you do, Tiernan?" His fingers twitched at his side with a psychotic eagerness to reach for a weapon. "You need me and what I can offer, what I have always offered. You need my weapons, my maps, the connections with other defectors and sleepers. Without me, you're blind in this war. Face it, you've run out of time to cultivate another informant, if one such as myself exists."

"You egotistical bastard!" Tiernan hissed in Phuree.

"Stop!" Khanna's angry shout cut through the red mist between the two men. "Stop it, both of you! In the name of the gods, what the hell is wrong with you?" She was shaking, her hands clutching the sides of her head as if it would explode. Nahalo and I watched her carefully each of us praying silently that the waters would remain at bay; I feared the force of the conflicted anguish she mastered might destroy us all if released in one flood.

Khanna took a deep breath and stood. Exhaling slowly she moved between the two men who stood frozen, glaring at each other with tangible malice.

She turned to Malakai, placing her hands upon his rigid shoulders. "You're right. We do need you now. We need you and your skills more than ever. However, you should remember that the only reason you are still allowed within the parameters of this encampment is because of me and unless you would like our guards to march you to the front gates of Cardone's compound and deliver you back into the hands of the Tyst army, I would advise you not to forget that. Now, kindly sit down!" She hissed through clenched teeth.

Malakai's eyes darted between hers and Tiernan's unflinching rage. A flicker of genuine concern for her state of distress danced across his features as he was torn between his woman and his pride. For a moment, his mental guard fractured allowing fragments of his identity to seep out. Silently, swiftly, I gathered the tiny precious gems into my own consciousness.

Until three years before, Malakai had lived entrenched in the culture of an elite wing of the Tyst's secret intelligence militia dubbed the Third Eye. The Third Eye were legends; their intellects honed to razor perfection by the world's most brilliant scholars and specialists while their bodies were chiseled to withstand the most severe circumstances. The men and women of the Third Eye were considered gods in their own right, indestructible and feared by all.

In the year since my reawakening, as I had prowled the dark city streets, a phantom in search of blood and poetry, I had heard only fractured whispered rumors of the militia, quickly silenced for fear of the omnipresent fiber-optic monitoring of the Tyst. Unfortunately, I had listened little to the rumors, as it seemed that most of the mortals I mingled with found it hard to differentiate between truth and fiction, their hearts too enraged, their souls too lost and afraid. Now Malakai's brief unwitting unveiling of his past stitched together the words of the strangers, a dirge weaving through the mists.

Members of the Third Eye were born into the service or, in a few rare instances such as with Malakai, selected at birth based on the political assignments of the parents. In either instance, the individual was not given a choice in the matter and once indoctrinated, they were in essence property of the Tyst. They became no more than ghosts, dead to the mortal world, as they were mechanically and ruthlessly stripped of their free will and trained as automatons for the sole purpose of gathering intelligence and slaying the high ranking political enemies of Cardone's inner circle. Silent and emotionless as cold gray slate, their existence was a lightless hollow world of brutal bloody executions and cold archival dockets. So it had been Malakai's world for twenty-nine years.

He had risen quickly to the highest ranks of the Third Eye, becoming instantly infamous for his cunning telepathic capabilities. He utilized his talents mercilessly to lay bare the pleading souls of the captured in windowless cells far below the surface of the amagins. There was no secret that could be kept from him, no kernel of sanctity he could not rape from the whorls of one's mind. That was, if one were mortal. For the preternatural species, he had different ways of breaking minds as well as bodies.

A cold chill of dread raked its nails across my back as the faces of the dead glowed in silent endless lines on the cliffs of the otherworlds. Some guilty and deserving of their fates, most innocent and broken in haste and hatred.

His soul cannot be redeemed...it is lost, I thought silently to myself. *And he knows this all too well.*

I tucked the thought away and quickly scoured through the remainder of my stolen memories.

Malakai Devolton had been born to the Lady Cherica Maltess, the third and oldest sister of the Queen's mother, Her Royal Highness Tatiana Maltess Cardone. His father, Jacob Devolton had been merely a Captain in the North American Tyst navy and would never have graced the pages of history, had he not fallen madly in love with the Lady Cherica, whom he met by happenstance as he passed her in the halls of the Tyst fortress on his way to deliver the latest surveys from his vessel. Their courtship had been brief but passionate enough to produce a child, Malakai Maltess Devolton. Knowing they could not marry due to the social taboo between them, Jacob returned to sea with his men, leaving behind his love to fabricate a tale to explain her pregnancy to the Courts.

One month later, Jacob's ship was attacked by pirate vessels in the Indian Ocean near the coast of Africa. The ship was sunk without a survivor. Without Jacob to object, the young naive Lady Cherica was strong-armed by Lord Julian Cardone II to give up her love child to the Third Eye to avoid a forced termination of the pregnancy in the wake of the imminent scandal of a tainted lineage.

On the night that Malakai was born, he was cleaned and swathed and taken away without Cherica laying her eyes on him. Cherica refused to leave her chambers afterwards, haunted by the separation and betrayal of her only child that meant she had sent him to such a torturous black existence. Three months after Malakai's birth, asleep and alone in her chambers, the Lady Cherica passed away from grief. She was nineteen.

In the austere rigid structure of his governmental guardians, Malakai's intellect and endurance were finely tuned for his preordained role as assassin-spy. When he was barely out adolescence, Malakai had found himself surpassing his teachers and commanding officers in his skills and intelligence. Unable to control him any longer, he quickly evolved into what the Third Eye began to view as a dangerously radical element amongst their fleet of stable mindless drones. His abilities made him too valuable to simply discard without careful consideration, and so they tolerated him and his ruthless disregard for authority and, seemingly, life itself.

But, as time passed, Malakai began to take matters into his own hands, assigning himself missions and delivering such judgments as he saw fit. Society and the laws chiseled within its walls were abstract and meaningless to him in a world where he had known no light or laughter; the intricate construct of his mind was simply too advanced for such medieval political architecture. Where was the justification for fighting to maintain a constructed sense of *peace* and stability in a society that seemed bent on destroying what little remained of the "civilized", and all for a ruler he himself loathed? On his global excursions he began to travel further abroad, disappearing for months at a time as he delved deep into the subcultures of the fractured world, infiltrating the Phuree and other insurgent factions, not to gather information to take back to the Tyst, but to understand why the persecuted fought as they did against the Empire and the technology it coveted.

He had been entranced, much as I had been, by the power of their magic and their drive for freedom, his mechanically molded intellect struggling with the organic concepts of peace and passion. Malakai had found himself drawn to the Phuree; the Phuree not only held a profound understanding of ancient magical art, but they were also fierce warriors who held no fear of death. They were one part mystical enigma and one part pure tempered truth, a combination that appealed to an aspect of his soul he had never known existed.

It was not long before Malakai found himself ensnared in a tangled web of espionage and arms dealing with the Phuree. His alliance with Tiernan Eldrid strengthened as he began to deliver crucial instruments such as strategic charts, maps and ammunition. Before then, Tiernan and his people had had to fashion their weapons themselves from whatever scrap metal they could salvage in the dead of night.

When news of these excursions reached the Tyst, Lord Cardone III, who had for a decade called upon Malakai personally to take care of important political *details*, immediately declared Malakai a threat to the stability of his empire and his life. The Third Eye could no longer restrain him, the Tyst army could not subdue him; Malakai had become an invisible vigilante in an indiscriminate vague war upon the living world. Quickly and quietly, Cardone and his Council made the decision that Malakai be *removed* permanently, his life erased. Little did Cardone realize that Malakai had been listening, telepathically, while lying upon the terrace of the fortress rooftop, as they had flippantly dismissed his existence.

For a long while he lay on the ledge in the fine mist of icy rain listening to royal assembly carrying on with the remainder of their agenda without a second thought to the death warrant they had issued to him. He was numb, unwilling to cave to the temptation to slay the horrid men while they slept. In truth, he had known that this time would come and had often pondered what his next move would be. He knew there was only one future for him, sealed by his crystal red hatred for Cardone. Killing them would be too easy; the game would end too quickly. Malakai wanted to see them crumble slowly.

The vignette of Malakai's life flashed past my consciousness. I was astounded by the fury of the images I had grazed from his soul. What I had seen both moved and terrified me. A genius assassin existed within his dark sleek beauty, fearlessly existing beyond the borders of either encampment. A small part of me sympathized with his unfortunate upbringing and wanted to trust him, but the images of my brethren reduced to ashes and echoing screams haunted me.

I knew he was using the Phuree just as much as they used him, but the Phuree did not know as much as I did about his past or his personality. They trusted out of desperation, which made them weak, and Malakai knew this.

With the same feline grace with which he had risen, Malakai sank back into his cushion. Khanna turned to face her brother. The muscles of her neck and shoulders tensed and twitched as she tried to contain her anger. She placed her right hand upon Tiernan's upper arm and pulled him gently away from the table to a far corner of the tent. Their conversation may have been a mystery to mortal ears but to mine it was as if they sat beside me at the table.

"Is this what you call diplomacy?" Her voice was low and harsh. "Are you really and truly willing to throw away everything you've worked so hard to build because of your hatred for Malakai?"

"Khanna, I am sorry that you have given your heart so foolishly to such a dishonorable character, but I will not tolerate such insolence. Not from him; not from anyone." He struggled to control the volume of his voice as he became aware that everyone was listening.

Khanna reached up and took Tiernan's face firmly between both of her hands, forcing him to look down into her eyes. Quickly, she whispered, "Brother, please, let it go. Do you forget who is in the room with you? Please, do not disrespect them with this base show."

A flush of red traveled up his neck, though his face remained rigidly cold. He whispered, "We *will* speak of this later."

A note of fear flashed across her face. She nodded and released him, returning to her seat beside Malakai who sat smoking lazily as if nothing out of the ordinary had occurred.

Tiernan ran his fingers through his hair and took a small moment to collect himself before returning to his place at the head of the table. He knelt down as if lowering himself before an altar and placed his hands, palms down, on the stack of worn yellowed maps.

In silence, we watched and waited, a collective uncertainty building, vibrating dully beneath the thick stale scent of smoke stained leather and wood, threatening to break apart the thin fibers of congeniality that tenuously bound us together for the moment.

"My sincerest apologies." The muscles of Tiernan's jaw twitched slightly as his anger fought to claw its way back into the light. "But, if there is anyone who shares in Malakai's doubt, please feel free to take your leave now. I mean no disrespect, but I must have only those who I can trust with my own life fighting beside me in this war. And if there are none that I can trust with my life, I would rather die fighting alone."

He looked up and looked into Phelan's unwavering gaze. "Sir Daray, you and I have been allies for many years now. You have stood by me, battle after bloody battle and I have never once doubted your loyalty, as I hope you have never doubted mine."

That is because you do not know that loyalty means nothing to a creature such as he, I thought bitterly.

"Never." Phelan's voice was as soft and low as wooden wind chimes above the hiss and crackle of the fire. He reached out and laid a slender white hand upon Tiernan's bronze forearm. "I assure you my people and I are with you, heart and soul," he lied. "This is no longer your war, alone. It is ours as well." There was no room for argument in Phelan's carefully chosen words.

Why did I stay? How could I bear to digest the melancholy serpents inspired by such fragile humans and such arrogant vampires? I curled my hands into fists beneath the table, clenching them until my nails drew blood from my palms as my hatred for Phelan swelled once again. Far away, deep within the place that time could not touch with its reckless hand, I heard the low restless rumble of the dragons. I could all but feel the ground quake as the vision fought to gain substance in my mind. I squeezed my eyes shut and held my breath.

"Tynan? Are you alright?" Nahalo's voice was barely a whisper. The cold hard weight of his hand upon my wrist shattered my connection with the vision.

I uncurled my fists and looked down into my trembling upturned palms watching as the bloody half-moon slits quickly vanished, my skin thirstily reabsorbing my blood. The stale air around me, the closeness of others, the constant heat of the fire against my back, all of it was closing in on me making my head spin as it stole the breath from my lungs. Nahalo's cold fingers tightened on my wrist, grounding me for a fleeting moment from the dizziness buzzing within my head. Without looking up, I nodded. I could feel him pushing against the gates of my mind, searching for a way into the angry frightened mind that lay on the other side. His attempts were in vain, though; his own blood had made me too strong to be exposed and subjugated.

Silently, I reinforced the walls that incarcerated my soul. I needed the icy isolation of my silent secret void. Though Nahalo and I had shared a sacred moment, it was not enough for me to truly trust in him, nor was it enough to give him complete access to the vault where I hid my demons. I did not know how much he had already scoured from my soul, for he had been watching me as I fumbled and stumbled, unawares, through my nocturnal life. It did not matter, though, I knew now that he watched and those that watched would see only the shell.

At the far end of the table Tiernan had begun his diatribe about the war, oblivious to my weakening state. His voice was a muffled rolling wave of sound washing over my senses in a confused liquid blur. I could hear the strength building behind his words, as he pushed aside the bitter truth of his confrontation with Malakai and stepped back within his cocoon of denial. Slowly, I lifted my head to watch him. I realized, with a flinch of panic, that I had not been listening to Tiernan's words as he spoke to me.

He paused when I did not respond, his sun-bleached eyebrows drawing together in a deep knit. "Tynan?"

I squinted as if I were staring into the burning horizon until the sound from his lips congealed into dialect. In my silence, I became acutely aware of the intense attention of the other guests. I wanted to beat them away but I knew they would only circle again, slowly waiting for another weakened moment when they could take up roost.

"Y—yes?" My voice caught dryly in my throat. I wondered just how long he had been speaking of me, to me.

"Are you alright?" The sincerity of his concern touched me.

"Yes....I'm fine." I paused to draw a deep breath. *Do not let them see your weakness now. They prey on it.* "I was simply reflecting on what you said. I've heard your words. I've heard many words since I awoke to your world. In all honesty, I do not know who to believe."

I flicked my dying cigarette into the fire behind me. The silence was stifling. "I know you have placed great unquestioning faith in the visions that your seers have brought you, and I respect that. For some unexplainable reason, I feel a deep connection with your people and their plight and will try to fulfill your needs to the best of my abilities.

"But you must always remember, I am a vampire. The only reality I trust is the one I can taste. The only things I hold sacred are the sun and the moon and death. Life is meaningless to me now except for the ones I've taken. I have no fear of dying. In fact, I welcome it. So I will go with you willingly and without prejudice. It was your people, after all, who saved my life." I paused, feeling a sour resentment curdle in the back of my throat.

"But I must warn you, Tiernan Eldrid, if you lie to me, if your people lie to me...and I will know...I will vanish without a trace and you will be left with only your visions to guide you."

Tiernan's gaze held me steadily. I had unsettled the fine sand of lies that lay upon the dark tomb where the truth lay sleeping. The Phuree no longer owned me as their prophecies had predicted. The presence of true fear was beginning to make itself known to him, something he had denied himself his entire life. The subconscious uncertainty I had sensed in him earlier was finally bubbling to the surface.

Slowly, he spoke. "I assure you, Tynan. All I know I will share with you willingly. Always and at all costs."

To my right, Sea had begun to radiate a searing nervousness that shrieked upon the periphery of my senses. The discussion of truth was making him uneasy; beneath the table I sensed his hands nervously fidgeting, as they tended to do when he lost control of a situation. I felt the fine hairs on the back of my neck bristle.

Without asking, I reached across the table and grabbed Malakai's tobacco and papers, which he had left lying before him. He did not protest, but, in fact, leaned back away from the table, sensing the restless angry power surging within me, a roiling black sea. With slow deliberate movements I rolled a cigarette, lit it and drew a long deep breath of sweet smoke into my lungs.

I looked up into Tiernan's gaze and held it, unblinking, as I let the smoke drift from my nose like an old tired dragon. "Very well. What do you need me to do?"

* * *

A hundred years had not changed the ungraceful simplicity of human nature. Inside, I cringed at the cold delivery of my own ultimatum and the fear I inspired in one of such strength, but there was no other way. In a battle of wills, I would not be ruled by the dictations of others; if I remained and fought I would do so on my own terms, in my own right. I had had enough of lies and deception, and while I could not at once peel back the layers that still obscured the truth, I would not stand for equal deception from the humans who asked for my help.

Tiernan, sensing the ephemeral lifespan of this chance, quickly began to sift through the array of information before him. Phelan's deep green gaze remained anchored upon me, heavy and cold. He smiled, a delicate twitch of his lips that revealed nothing. I narrowed my eyes in suspicion and pressed my will against his mind.

"I think this is a good place to start." Tiernan's voice tore me away from my Maker's eyes. Startled and slightly disturbed, I stared at the sheaf of what appeared to be paper in Tiernan's outstretched right hand.

Pale gray and cold to the touch, the *paper* bent between my fingers as if constructed of a near weightless rubber as I retrieved it. After the sand and leather sensations of the Phuree base camp, the texture of such a highly refined synthetic sent chills spiraling up my spine. I placed it on the table before me, wanting to disconnect myself from the alien call of the grid in which it had been recently fabricated.

"What is this exactly?" For a moment I stared down at the face of the *paper*, scanning the small, neat type and images contained there.

"What you are looking at is a electronic device containing the compiled research and experiments conducted by the Tyst as it pertains to their resurrection of the Vicinus." Tiernan's heavy accent was flat and low as he pushed his emotions to the depths of his soul.

As he spoke, I ran a finger down the edge of the machine as I began to consume the information before me. The surface reminded me of the cold alien organics of shark's skin, somehow living in a realm detached from the physical. I stared at the file and touched the directional images at the bottom that allowed me to scroll through the countless pages.

Two columns divided the information; on the left was a highly detailed research of the lore of the Immortals and our god and Father, the Vicinus. It was an immaculately defined history of our species from ancient conception to the present.

I was stunned at the accuracy of the historical events and blood lineage that had been captured and recorded by the Tyst; indeed the information was so flawless it appeared they had been studying us for centuries and not simply the past few decades. I shuddered to think.

The right column was more obscure and would require closer examination, I realized. Alchemical symbols blended with long strings of code and scientific notations scrolling like hieroglyphs upon the faintly glowing screen. The information was both intriguing and perplexing as it seemed at the same time both completely alien and deeply familiar in its context. I had seen many of the symbols before, but where, I could not say. I focused on the left side for the time being.

"That one file holds everything from the initial conversations amongst Cardone's elite Council to the most recent progression of the Queen's pregnancy."

My eyes hovered on the end of a sentence. The concept of a physical pregnancy resulting from the Tyst's experimentations suddenly congealed into reality, a clock ticking at the end of a long dark corridor.

"How far along is she?" I kept my tone even and factual. I did not look up from the page, pretending to carry on with my studies.

"Four months, we believe, if the files are accurate. The data record you are looking at ends approximately three weeks ago, when Malakai was able to finish the download from the Chronous mainframe."

"Why three weeks? We are only days from the fortress, correct?" My head snapped up and turned abruptly to Malakai.

Malakai replied coolly. "Unfortunately, I was detained with other business to the north which could not be avoided."

"But you knew the importance of this information?" Once again, I found myself wanting to tear him apart and retrieve the secrets he kept coveted in his soul.

"There are many things of importance in this day and age, my vampire friend. Not all things are relative to one another." The sardonic bite that had laced his earlier quips had vanished, his voice lowering to a deadly edge that gleamed with poison.

"We have all we need in order to for you to proceed," Tiernan interjected hastily to ward off another interruption. "Please study them carefully."

"And you will also need this," Phelan lifted my journal from the table and offered it to me between the long white fingers of his left hand.

Without a moment's hesitation I snatched the leather bound book from his cold hand.

He paused, letting his hand linger empty in mid-air as he watched me, before slowly curling his fingers into his palm and returning it to the table. "We believe you will find a remarkable correlation between your writings and the hierarchy code of the information within the Tyst archives."

"Yes, you've mentioned that before." The ice in my voice chilled the air between us.

"Yes," he sat back from the table, drawing his shoulders up and his back straight, "that is why it was so important that you listen to us, why we needed you here."

I tucked the journal safely inside the waist of my pants beneath my shirt. "You have Malakai who was raised within the system and understands more about its code than any of us. Whatever I can learn, he must already know."

Malakai's eyes narrowed suspiciously at me as I disclosed some of the information I had stolen from his mind.

I shook my head in frustrated confusion. "Perhaps your Oracle was wrong. He is the one you need to carry out this execution."

"How much do you know about the Tyst fortress and the Chronous matrix?" Tiernan asked.

"Honestly?" I sighed. " I know nothing of the Tyst fortress. And as for the Chronous, despite what Phelan and Sea may have told you, I know only a few fundamentals."

Tiernan sighed, casting a sidelong glance at Phelan wonderingly.

"There was not time to brief him properly..." Phelan's voice was low and dark.

Tiernan did not push further and turned back to me. "The architecture of the fortress is constructed of three interconnecting rings. Within each of these rings are three layers of concentric circles. Each wing is devoted to a different aspect of the dictatorship. The code that makes up the defense structure guarding each ring is an organic biotechnological entity, constantly fluxing and rotating between each wing and layer of the compound. From one second to the next, the access codes are rewritten in random unconnected evolution patterns. The Chronous technology defines all parameters of the code architecture on its own with only mild supervision from a handful of Tetoni comply drones. In fact, the vast majority of those living within the fortress confines have absolutely no fundamental understanding of the Chronous technology at all. It exists completely independently of human interference."

Tiernan leaned forward on his elbows, his hands clasped thoughtfully in front of him on the stack of papers. "Tyst family and employees are implanted with a microchip tracking device which allows the Chronous matrix to monitor which person is in what quarter of the compound at all times. Each chip is programmed with clearance levels, which, according to our knowledge, cannot be altered unless removed from the body. The only person who has full clearance to all wings is Cardone himself. Even his top advisors are restricted in certain areas.

"The only people trained in the Chronous architecture are the members of the Third Eye, or ex-members as in Malakai's case, but their knowledge is limited to what they need in order to track the rogue hackers in the fringes of the cyber realm."

"Wait!" I interjected suddenly and turned to Malakai. "How far can the Chronous matrix track?" If he was ex-Tyst, he could still be under the watchful eye of the matrix.

Malakai smiled. "There is nowhere it cannot see, but don't worry. I removed the chip a long, long time ago."

I did not know if I truly bought his assurance, but I turned back to Tiernan.

Tiernan continued, "The living quarters of the Tyst elite are located towards the middle rings where they begin to overlap each other, with the Queen located at the direct center. Her clearance levels allow her access only to the most interior living quarters. Neither she, nor her handmaids, have ever seen the outside world their people have built. They are captives, in a sense. In previous decades the restriction levels were not so stringent and members of the Royal Elite were allowed to travel at will through the vast majority of the complex, but Cardone III's rule, at the suggestions of his advisors, has become increasingly more draconian."

"And what of the knowledge that Malakai has of the system code?" I bit back upon the sour frustration in my voice. I was weary, the Thirst building restlessly within me.

Malakai answered, "My training was only sufficient enough to understand the rudimentary structuring of the Chronous matrix, so I would know how to spot deviant cells of hackers if they jacked into the *flatlands*. There are those that I work with on the inside to help me with documents, and whatever else I need to obtain, I can easily scan for telepathically. The matrix still can't keep me out entirely."

"*Flatlands?*" I asked.

"Ah...hmmm. To put it in 21st century terms, cyberspace," Malakai smirked nonchalantly.

Tiernan reached for the pitcher in the center of the table. Quietly and quickly, he poured the dark wine into the mug closest to him. The thick pungent perfume of fermented grapes teased my senses with its heavy contradictory notes.

Tiernan continued with his history lesson. "For decades we have fought to surpass the Chronous matrix using energy workings such as astral projection. The idea was that a system so advanced and independently active, might be easily compromised by an outside energy force that it could not assimilate and synthesize. However, the deeper we plunged ourselves into the magic, the more convoluted and obscure the system code would become as it integrated the hieroglyphs and runes it stole from our minds while we worked within its field. The Chronous A.I. is far more advanced than anyone had suspected, perhaps more advanced than even the Tyst had predicted.

"It was my father who first bridged the gap between our tribe and the world of exiled Third Eye intelligence. Unlike the generations before him, he was not too proud to see we needed more information than our seers could scry for. It was my father who cemented the alliance between the Immortals and the Phuree—"

"I thought you said that the Immortals have been in alliance with your people for generations?" I interjected suddenly.

"Yes, that is true. The Elders of the Immortals have been lending their assistance since the beginning of the uprising, back before we knew exactly who they were. It wasn't until the past thirty years when the Tyst implemented the active genocide of your race in order to further their agenda of becoming the true immortal race.

"It was then that Phelan and others formed a solid pact with the Phuree. The balance of the world, of nature in and of itself, had become critically compromised. No one could deny that if it were not restored, the only result was the complete annihilation of both of our peoples and, possibly, the world." Tiernan took a long pull from the mug of wine and placed it carefully back upon the table.

For a moment he stared at me, gathering his thoughts, weighing the impact of his words on me. I silently held his gaze, unwavering.

He took a deep breath and continued, "When the vision of your essential role in our mission manifested to our seers, Phelan agreed to bring you to us for further discussion."

Laying the digital dociee upon the table, I drew the journal out from under my shirt. I ran my fingers over the worn brown leather cover, along its fire scorched edges and splitting spine. Slowly, I began to thumb though the pages. I knew now what they meant when they said that the key was within the pages. What had seemed to me to be the beginnings of an irreversible madness was code, a sophisticated blending of languages both ancient and as of yet unconceived; the ghostly resonating language of the Chronous matrix that danced in a cryptic continuous spiral to the core of the Tyst architecture.

At the center of the spiral were the Queen and the child she now carried, the reincarnation of the Vicinus that I must slay. At the periphery of my senses, the Phuree magic chattered in clipped hissed whispers like leaves rustling upon the wind. Beneath my feet, the ground tremored from the dull roar I refused to acknowledge. I knew the world was watching, waiting; my instinct told me that what I was being told was the truth, but it continued to slip from my grasp as I had not yet the true will to hold onto it. I felt as if my mind was beginning to unravel.

I paused at a page of solid rambling symbols. "This, this is what your seers saw?" I did not look up from the page, but waited in silence for Tiernan's response.

"Your notations are the only proof that there is someone in the world who possesses a complete *understanding* of the Chronous matrix. Your writings, if you compare them to the information found in the file I gave you, even reflect the metamorphosis of the code structure over the past year."

"But I don't possess an *understanding*. I don't know why I wrote this...hell, I don't even remember when I wrote this." I shook my head again, closing the journal with a snap.

Nahalo placed his hand upon my forearm, sending a cool and calming pulse of energy rippling up my arm into my chest, settling my senses into a crisp new focus. I could feel his eyes resting on me as he spoke. "You are fighting, but you have no just reasons as to why. Trust in your intuition. All that you need to help us is locked within you; only you have the power to release it. We have those who can open the portals to the understanding you possess, and I will be your mentor in the magic that calls your name now." The pressure of his hand became heavier. " You must only say 'yes'."

The weight of the Phuree settled once again upon my shoulders, its black wings beating in time to the sound of my resigning heart until settling itself silently never to leave again. I looked up into Nahalo's eyes knowing all too well that my resistance was futile and fumbling in the face of the Fates. More questions would only delay the inevitable.

I took a deep breath, covering Nahalo's hand with my own. "Then there can be no other answer, I suppose...Yes."

12

The few short hours remaining of the evening were spent hastily defining the next immediate strategic measures. With my final irreversible acceptance of their requests, I felt myself sink back to a far corner to watch the layers of my future unfold neatly around me, removed from my skin as if it were an anchor that could not be lifted. I fought to keep my Thirst at bay and focus upon the dictations dealt by Tiernan and Nahalo, but my attention span flitted uncontrollably from moment to moment as I weakened to its power. Nahalo assured me silently that he would feed me well before the night was through, but that time seemed eons away and circumstances made me wary. I did not want to partake of another dose from his veins fearful it would bind me even tighter to his being. If only I could maintain my balance until we reached the amagin, then I would be able to feed on my own, away from scrutinizing attentions.

My journey would begin the following night as I headed back northeast. There, with Malakai as my guide, I was to meet with two of the Phuree's most valued information experts, Loden and Josh. These underground Tyst exiles would guide me through my indoctrination to the Chronous technology matrix and attempt to help me connect the fractured lines between my subconscious ramblings and reality. From there, I would proceed onwards to a fortress far to the northeast, just outside what had once been the nation's capital, slip in undetected, ferret my way to its core and slay the queen. The plan seemed far too simple.

However, I kept my doubts to myself. I wanted to be done with the mission so that I could return to my tiny dark world of daft poetic musings and the forbidden creature comforts. My thoughts drifted to Jasmine and Dune and the barely constrained sadness that had brimmed in Jasmine's lovely eyes as I had turned and walked away. I missed them both terribly.

How weak I must be, I thought, *to be burdened by such attachments*, but I knew as soon as I reached the city limits, there would be nothing that could keep me from seeking them out one last time, against all better judgment.

I listened to the last details of my new assignment in silence as I watched Tiernan carefully roll up the electronic file he had given me inside a thin stack of maps and archaic blueprints, wrapping the bundle in a swath of tanned hide and securing it with a length of rough, handmade string.

"Josh and Loden will be expecting your arrival. They are a peculiar pair, as I'm sure you'll agree, but trust in them and their ways. If there is anyone who can guide you in unlocking the secrets of the Chronous, it is them." A wry smirk twitched briefly upon the corners of his lips.

"This should be all of the tactical information you will need once you're inside the compound. And, of course, there is the electronic dociee." He handed the roll of papers to me. "Please guard them carefully. It is our only copy of these records."

"Of course." I said solemnly, accepting the package. He did not release his grip as he hesitated one last time. I found my focus in his anticipation and whispered, "I will guard them with my life."

"Thank you." He let go of the roll and sank back into his seat.

He sighed deeply as if a burdensome weight had been lifted from his shoulders.

"Well, then," Tiernan spoke with a heavy exhale as he stood. In unison all that were gathered rose to their feet as if they remembered suddenly that they were indeed in the presence of a respected leader.

Tiernan forced a small weary smile and extended his hand to me. Holding his gaze steadily, I reached out and clasped forearms with him. The contact of his rough, blood-hot flesh against my cold shell sent a ripple of sharp, unrefined energy through me. In that instance, the material world I had always taken for granted vanished and it seemed as if I found myself standing on the edge of the cliff overlooking the hateful scorched crater where Nahalo had taken me the night before. In what could have only been a mere second or two, reality split before me, fracturing into past and future with the present barely holding the two together with a series of blue tendrils flickering in and out like unstable neon through a dirty window pane.

The cliff below me quaked with the ancient unspeakable wrath of betrayal and I fell to my knees, clutching terrified at the shelf of earth to keep from pitching headlong into the bottomless hell below. Instinctively, I knew something terrible and demonic waited for me there, coiled about the dragons that tortured my dreams, between the layers of time and space, between the residual smell of incense and candles of ritual, and the burning ozone of war. I looked up from the gorge at the fluxing fabric of existence before me. I was not ready to face them. Not yet.

An unearthly howling emanated from the obsidian shifting slits in its ethereal flesh. I tried to focus on the sound to stop the nauseating vibration of the planes, but it only grew worse till I feared the universe might shatter, atom by atom. The slices in the universe bled together forming one long black gash before me that pulsed putridly livid like an engorged leach. Something heavy and stale with death lingered upon the other side of the rift, watching warily me as I clung to the cliff's edge. The ragged icy breath in my lungs struggled to escape as my vision narrowed, tunneling into the dark gash as the remaining world began to ripple and fade into a fateless hollow oblivion.

From the depths of the void, a voice drifted to me, cool and sharp as a sacrificial blade.

"*What you do, dear Child of the Eons, is unnatural. You and your brethren are meant to walk as gods amongst your earthly plane. Instead, you assist your subjects in your own demise. Tsk! Tsk! I pity you, truly, my son.*"

"I am no son of yours," I hissed through fear-clenched teeth.

"*Ah, but you are. You, all of the* vampires, *as you call yourselves, are my children.*" The voice slithered across the ether seamlessly, curdling my blood with its lack of conscience.

The roar of a wind I could not feel had begun to rise up out of the cavern, deafening in its blind chaos.

"Who are you?" I yelled over the disorienting storm, my throat dry and cracked from the painful Thirst, my chest now filled with the grit of the eroding cliff. I knew the answer, but feared to speak the name aloud as if it might fully open whatever unearthly portal the being called to me from.

"Tell me your name?" My lips moved as air was forced from my lungs, but my broken voice was lost upon the roar of chaos and lost souls.

There was a second of hesitation where the wind died in a suffocating and damned silence and I thought, perhaps, that the demon had vanished, but then the wind returned with a vengeance, and out of the pulsing black gash before me, a blood red hand tipped with slick, black talons burst. Before I could scream, the hand had wrapped about me.

"*You know my name...*"

Beneath the sickening crack of my bones collapsing within the Vicinus' grip, the last gasp of air escaped me in a desperate scream that was lost as it echoed off the scorched walls of the gorge below...

Reality compressed and snapped back into solidity. I stood before Tiernan, clasping forearms with the Phuree chieftain as I had been what seemed like an eternity before. Nothing had changed; I stared into Tiernan's blue-grey eyes searching for answers to where I had just been, and why no one in the room seemed to have noticed, but all that reflected back was the weariness and resolution I had seen in the moment before the strange vision.

Am I going mad? I thought to myself fearfully, but I knew the answer and the answer inspired more terror in me than the alternative: it was the Vicinus that had held me in its claws. I tried desperately to retain my composure. *These people have no idea what we are up against and now I truly do. Phelan and Tiernan think they are safe until the Queen gives birth, but they are wrong. Oh, dear gods, help me.*

"Thank you." Tiernan said. "Until we meet again?" There was a secret, barely disguised doubt in his voice.

I nodded and released his arm as my hand had begun to tremble slightly. Beneath my clothes, a fine film of blood-sweat had begun to form, chilling me in the thick close heat of the fire-warmed tent.

I took a step back.

Nahalo came up beside me and placed a firm fatherly hand upon my shoulder. His fingers tightened slightly letting me know that he had sensed something amiss. "Tomorrow night at dusk you and Malakai will leave for the amagin. For what remains of tonight rest and reflect. The journey is just beginning. Come." He gestured to the tent's entrance.

His words were not comforting as they spoke only of hardship and bloodshed to me. Without acknowledging another soul within the room, I allowed Nahalo to lead me out, past the scrutinizing gazes of Phelan and Sea, past the terrified guards barely containing their instinct to flee, and into the crisp cold night, now grown more subdued as the Phuree had, for the most part, retired to their beds.

We walked for some time through the maze of animal skin tents in silence until we came to the edge of the encampment. I stared out across the rolling prairie landscape at the night sky now blooming to a dark purple as dawn sleepily announced its arrival to the world.

"You saw something tonight, when you clasped arms with Tiernan. You faltered. I sensed it." Nahalo's gaze was steady on the lightening horizon. "What did you see?"

The Sleep had crept up from deep within the earth, wrapping its sinewy tendrils about my limbs, pulling me slowly into the quicksand. I resisted, afraid of what waited for me on the other side in my dreams.

My throat was parched. "The Vicinus, he spoke to me." The words seemed incorporeal, slipping from parted lips I could not feel move. "He told me that we were his children and what we were doing was wrong, against nature. He warned me…" The caustic wet pop of my bones deafened me again above the gentle breath of the awakening land. I shivered.

"Do you believe him?"

I couldn't answer. Whether from fear of the truth or from

210

absence of much desired wisdom, I did not know. For a long while we watched the warming horizon in uncomfortable restrained silence as the last sleepy stirrings of the Phuree encampment grew silent behind us. I wondered if I could possibly muster the courage to wander out into the desert and allow the cleansing rays of the morning sun to wipe away my sins. My fear of sunlight was suddenly eclipsed by the dread that clutched frantically at my spine. My limbs felt heavy as if filled with cold gray lead.

I turned my gaze to Nahalo who continued to watch the impending dawn with a strange sad wistfulness.

"Please send Malakai to my quarters when he is awake. I wish to speak to him in private before we head out tomorrow night." I had barely energy enough left to speak.

Nahalo turned slowly to face me, his eyes narrowing slightly in deep thought. He placed his right hand on my shoulder. A warm golden energy flowed from his palm into my body, filling my being with a profound and comforting strength.

He lifted his left wrist in offering for me. "You are weakening, your system has not yet adapted to your new powers. Please, drink."

I honestly did not want to tie myself further to the Ancient and I stared at the lines of blue veins that ran beneath the tan glow of his pseudo human complexion. Nahalo was correct though. At my core I could feel my nerves fizzing and snapping as if I had been electrocuted. Without a word, I took his wrist and brought it to my mouth, my fangs quickly puncturing the flesh and then filling my mouth with the same pungent current of Immortal blood I had experienced the night before. I closed my eyes and pulled hard on the draught, light spiraling behind my closed lids, reflecting images of a beautiful foreign existence beyond my Immortal youth. Again, the primal energy of the universe grappled with my own DNA, fusing it instantly with that of the Ancient from which I drank. I felt as if he was absorbing me, as if I was absorbing him; fear gripped me as I felt myself washing away with the archaic song of his soul. With a sharp gasp, I pulled away from his arm, dropping it as if I had been shocked.

211

Nahalo watched me silently as I regained my balance. I could hear my cells chattering, frenzied in a healing restructuring dance I could not control. The wound in his wrist smoothed over and vanished as if it had never been there at all.

"Though young yet, you are a very strong. Stay true to what is in your heart and all else will follow." He paused, letting his hand fall away from my shoulder slowly. In ghostly silence, he turned and began to walk back down the sandy path towards the center of the encampment. "I will have Malakai come to you as you requested."

13

I woke with a start the following evening as if I had been shaken awake by unseen hands. The fire in the center ring of the tent had not yet been lit and I was unsure if the sun had set completely behind the horizon outside.

I was not alone.

In the far corner opposite of where I lay, Malakai sat cross-legged on the ground. He watched me silently, back straight and strong, head tilted slightly to one side in predatory consideration, lit cigarette loosely held between the fingers of his right hand. Smoke lazily spiraled up from the glowing orange tip, drifting ghostly in front of his face. I could feel the fine hairs on my neck and forearms bristle, the muscles of my back readying with caution.

He straightened his head, his steady unblinking gaze filled with a dangerous mystery that raked against my spine, cold as frozen barbed wire. He lifted the cigarette to his lips. His fingers poised before his parted lips, he spoke, "Sleep well?"

"How long have you been sitting there?"

"There are many things I know about your kind, but your sleep patterns always intrigued me the most. You are such powerful creatures, but you are controlled by something so simple as sleep. You do not control your bodies, you are controlled by them."

"Will Nahalo be visiting us before we leave?" I ignored his patronizing insight, lifting myself into a sitting position as I spoke. I looked back through the shadows at Malakai.

He took another long drag on the cigarette and lowered his hand back to his knee. He said nothing for a long while and then slowly shook his head. "No. He will not."

Malakai leaned forward and snuffed out the dying butt in the sand inside the cold fire ring. "We are on our own now, my soldier friend, until we get back to the amagin." He flashed a dazzling white smile that cut through the darkness.

My eyes locked with his wild blue stare. "Malakai, I will be honest with you; I want this job over and done with so that I can go back to my simple quiet life. I want to make myself very clear. If you have ulterior motives, which I suspect you do, I would strongly advise you not to get in my way."

"Ooh. A threat!" Malakai chuckled under his breath. "I'm trembling."

He stood, grabbing the dusty army green canvas satchel on the ground next to him as he rose. He threw the worn wide strap across his chest and tightened the buckle on the outside with a quick tug. "Whether you trust me or not is your dictation, not mine. I trust no one. I was hired to be a part of this tangled mess. It's just another job." He drew another carefully prepared cigarette from the tin of tobacco he carried, shoving the container into a side pocket of his bag with one hand. As he lit the cigarette, he began to walk towards the entrance of the tent.

"Where do you think you're going?" I rose quickly, blocking his path.

He stopped and looked up. Casually, he exhaled the thin white smoke into my face. "I'm sorry, I thought you were a mind-reader?"

Something inside me snapped and the dangerously thin glass vial that held my patience shattered as my hand flew from my side towards him. In that brief instant, he moved with a speed unlike any human I had ever witnessed, his right hand a blur as he reached for a throwing knife beneath his shirt. Leaping backward like a cat, the blade flew from his fingers, slicing the air between us with a sharp hiss, aimed for my face. Easily, I sidestepped the knife just before impact, lunging towards Malakai with a feral growl. His agility may have served him well against lesser Immortals, but with my heightened powers, his speed and strength was simply no match for me.

Catching him as he tried to duck past me out of the entrance, I whirled him around, closing my right hand around his throat. My left fist struck his arm as he plunged another knife towards my chest. The impact knocked the blade from his hand, sending it hurtling to the far side of the tent. I could feel the muscles and tendons of his throat creak as I lifted him from the ground. A small, terrified gasp slipped from his parted lips, fear of the impossible flashing across his gaze as he stared down at me. His free hand clawed at my iron grip in desperation, his feet thrashing and kicking at me as he tried to gain leverage on my waist to kick backwards out of my hold. I could see in his eyes that he desperately did not want to admit he had finally met his match.

Pain shot through my left shoulder suddenly, just above the collarbone. Suppressing a howl, I glanced down to see long narrow spike of metal deeply embedded through me. So focused I had been on my own grip around his neck, I had not noticed as one of his hands disappeared in a flash behind him to retrieve the weapon. The frantic heavy pulse of his heart beneath my fingers maddened the Hunger inside me. Keeping my gaze locked with his, I reached up with my left hand and slowly pulled the spike free. As I did so, forcing my face into a mask of deathly calm despite the pain, Malakai's struggles slowly ebbed. I could tell he was fighting to breathe in my vice grip and, perhaps, he had run out of weapons.

The desire I had felt before to break him apart and drink his secrets crashed upon me in a tsunami wave. I could feel my own heartbeat throbbing through the thin flesh of my lips, the delicate capillaries in my canines as they elongated ever so slightly in the wake of a fresh kill. But reason, wickedly strong reason, stilled my hand. I knew I could not kill him, not yet anyhow.

The bloody spike gripped in my fist, I lowered him to the ground slowly, until he could support his weight on his toes, and brought him face to face with me. I could feel my shoulder already knitting itself back together, the skin sealing over and reabsorbing the blood that had been spilt. Malakai's boots scraped the ground as he struggled to find his footing. I knew he could sense the Hunger in me as he trembled uncontrollably beneath my fingers, a man humbled by his own arrogance and the realization that death was close at hand.

I took a deep breath and lowered him even further to the ground, though I did not release my grasp entirely, keeping him so close I could see my demented reflection in his irises. I felt him swallow hard, drawing air deeply into his starved lungs, his mind frozen with the revelation of what had just occurred.

My cold harsh breath was broken as I spoke. "Now you are trembling. You will remember this moment."

His eyes widened, calmed ever so slightly with the knowledge that he would live to see the sun rise one more day. His heart continued to race beneath my grip as I lowered him completely to his feet. Slowly, I unwound my fingers from his neck revealing dark bruises beneath.

I drew a deep breath. "Do not ever question me again." I tossed the spike aside.

Malakai remained motionless in stunned silence.

"I will be taking to the skies rather than accompanying you across land," I said with a heavy sigh, forcing the last of my anger to leave me.

"May I ask why we will traveling separately?" There was a new resonance to his voice, flat and respectful, a soldier's voice.

"I have some *business* I must attend to. A personal matter." He did not need to know details.

"Yes. Of course." He paused as if waiting for direction. When I did not respond, lost in my own rambling thoughts and the fight with my Hunger, he spoke again, "I have something I must tend to as well. I will locate you when it is time to move on to Josh and Loden's location?"

"Exactly." I stepped away from him as another wave of Hunger hit me, making my head spin nauseatingly.

Like a dark wraith of wind and shadow, he quickly left the tent without another word.

I ran my fingers through my hair, pulling the tangled mess back from my forehead with a strangled exhale. I felt disoriented as the Hunger pulled at the center of my being with a will of its own. I glanced down at my shoulder and the circular bloodstain on the ripped fabric. With irritation I searched the tent for another shirt and quickly changed.

"Focus, focus, focus..." I muttered to myself as I retrieved the maps, files, and book from where I had hidden it beneath a pile of blankets behind the sleeping pallet. Once safely in

Jasmine's apartment, I would be able to examine them more closely.

Outside the tent I could sense the anxious energies of the posted guards. Though not as frantic in their fear as the previous evening, their incessant subconscious hand wringing grated against my frayed nerves. There was no need to disturb them with my departure and I slipped out beneath the rear edge of the tent again. I would have to wait till I reached the city to feed; I could not live with the idea of taking a Phuree innocent's blood.

So swift that even the wind did not take heed, I raced to the edge of the encampment. There, without a moment's hesitation I threw myself into the sky, hell-bent on pushing my new powers to their extremes. I flew upwards against the stark black canvas of night. The tents, the neighing horses, the fragile mortals, all fell away from me in flash of blurred textures and sounds. The world became an abstract of lost dimension, bleeding into the horizon. Around me, stars danced a dizzying defiance in their fading legacies, some already millennia old in their deaths. The air became thin and ice began to form on my lashes as I reached above the clouds to the higher altitudes. There, as the chill sank to the very marrow of my bones, reason took hold of me and I stopped suddenly, my heart thundering uncontrollably with the thrill of my journey upwards.

I stared out across the rolling blue-gray clouds that separated the hidden turmoil of the earth below from the serenity that lay in the heavens above. I had never before risen so high, never seen so far or clearly as my newly defined sight outlined every detail of the universe around me. I understood suddenly why Galileo had burned out his eyes staring at the sun.

The moon was full and pregnant, dominating the sky. Through the thin clear air every haunting gray crater seemed to echo with ancient mysteries, ghost stories of a simpler time when the elements controlled the universe and not the warped demons of the human race. She, too, stood eternal vigilance over the earth, just as I had for so many centuries. In silence with only the wind whistling quietly in my ears, I bowed my head and prayed for protection one last time.

When I opened my eyes again, the weight of the rolled files I clutched to my chest seemed disjointed and surreal, as if the material had lost some of its substance in the moment of prayer.

* * *

I reached the center of the amagin quickly, touching down quietly near the riverbank amongst the overgrown reeds and sand. The night had turned bitterly cold, the wind rippling the surface of the water and distorting the glow of the city's street market just beyond its far banks. The dank reek of dirty river water and mud pulled at me, heavy as the currents that moaned just below its silvery surface. I dared not linger there too long lest the lure of my last victim's ghost drag me down with it.

Above me the stark, dingy, gray bridge loomed, the heavy rank scent of bat guano lacing the air as the wind moved through the colonies that lived within the arcing ledges of cement and steel. I knew I must be careful now not to loosen my guard for one moment. I crouched down and, with one powerful leap, sprung upwards to the bridge railing above. My muscles hummed as I moved, filled with the new power, Nahalo's Dark Gift to me.

Perched there upon the narrow steel bar, I quickly scanned the street in both directions for signs of life. South of the river, the world was a ghost town of dark derelict businesses and abandoned homes. Faintly, I sensed the auras of a few lost souls far off in the distant darkness, but none of them contained enough strength or maliciousness to warrant my concern. For the most part, no one ventured to the southern districts of the city, hovering close to the Tyst facilities for protection from the dangerous wandering gangs that often took up roost in the haunted old buildings, and causing small bloody wars of their own out of greed and boredom. On a regular basis, the Tyst would clear the area, rounding up the criminal youths to be executed. However, despite their efforts, the area would once again become populated with new vicious characters, time and time again.

Satisfied that I would not be followed, I leapt down from the railing to the cracked concrete of the street sidewalk and began to walk swiftly towards the wavering golden glow of the marketplace that burned a molten river between the towering black skeletons of the skyscrapers. As I reached the other side of the river, the acrid perfume of the bazaar overwhelmed my newly refined senses, sending me reeling as it had done on my first night back in the world. The pungent heavy weight of survival in the amagin wrapped itself about my chest, squeezing the air from my lungs. I wasn't ready yet, I decided, to plunge myself into the midst of such chaos.

Besides, I knew Jasmine would not be there. She sold her lovingly crafted clay wares during daylight hours. Jasmine would be safely tucked away within her apartment by now, oblivious to my desperate desire for her mortal warmth and affection. I needed the reassurance that there was still good in the world, that innocent souls devoid of conspiracy or lies thrived in the face of those that plotted about them in secret. I worried for her safety. If I revealed all of my new knowledge to her, it would bring her directly into the tangled web of mayhem and magic I was about to weave. Yet, the selfish beast within me could not deny myself one last night of comfort before heading off to face the unknown.

I could not see her though. Not just yet. The Hunger still slithered through my insides, a pit of agitated rattlesnakes. I could not trust that I would not take more than warmth from her in such a state, and I could not bear that thought. I closed my eyes and, pulling the nauseating air into my lungs, I sank deep within myself in search of my center. For a long moment, I stood masked by the shadows of an abandoned riverside hotel, overgrown with ivy and four o'clock vines, till I fastened hard to my core.

When I opened my eyes, my vision had sharpened turning the once ambiguous angles and planes of familiar buildings into a harsh yet surreal landscape that seemed too brutal for mortals to transverse. I shook my head and watched as my vision settled somewhat. It would take time to become completely used to the way the world appeared through my new eyes.

The night was not growing any younger and my hunger for Jasmine's presence far outweighed the plight of my dark nature and thus, I knew I must act quickly. It would be a simple thing to catch a wandering soul on the perimeter of the market. I had done it on so many occasions that it was ritual to me. At the edge of the bazaar I waited in the shadows between booths, surveying the crowd for a wayward soul that few would miss. It was not long before such a being fell into my line of sight.

Drunk and aimless in his wandering, the man, of some forty mortal years, weaved in and out of the ceaseless flow of pedestrians till he reached the edge of the market where I lingered. He hummed to himself quietly, a random symphony of notes only he and I could hear over the oblivious background cadence. I read the details of his soul quickly, for there was little to gather; a widower without children whose only friend was the wine merchant from whom he nightly bartered his drink. Sad and alone, in a world that made him resentful and fearful, he only found pleasure wandering through the bazaar at night to lose himself amidst the soiled flood. It was as if he begged the world to take him, tempting fate each night as he stumbled home through dark alleyways to his cold silent apartment.

I beckoned to his subconscious, tugging at it gently so that he found something of interest in the booths between which I waited. He paused before the first booth, his drunken stare wandering aimlessly over the bolts of colorful textiles and vats of glass and clay beads. He thought to himself that he had never noticed the booth before, or how beautiful the work of the artisan who owned it was. He thought of how his wife would have loved the purple silk fabric and how well it would have complimented her pale freckled skin and red hair.

I pulled at his curiosity further, luring him back between the booths to the darkness behind them. He had no fear of the unknown; the alcohol he had consumed numbed life's natural anxieties with its distilled anesthetic. His eyes widened as he saw me, a porcelain statue hidden amongst the cold wind-tossed shadows. He wondered if he had drunk too much and if I were a dream. He wondered if I were the angel that took his wife from him. I let him dream what he may and wrapped myself in the sad longing of his imagination to sooth his pain.

His lips parted as he made to speak to me aloud.

I raised a single white finger to my lips and his mouth closed. Still clutching the leather bound maps in my right hand, I reached forward with my left hand to take his. He did not flinch at the chill of my skin, his eyes still stunned with unblinking awe, as I led him back to the darkest cave of shadows I could find. No one who ventured so far from the protective warmth of the bazaar torches would look too closely at us. And if they did, all they would see was what they wanted and nothing more. The human aptitude for denial was at times a sweet reprieve.

Safely tucked away in the folds of darkness, I wasted no time unleashing the starved Hunger I had contained and falling upon him like a wolf on a rabbit. The man did not struggle, accepting the initial pain of my deep bite in silence, a just and priestly judgment. His blood was a river of sweet honey wine, hot copper and bittersweet sorrow as it rushed through my lips and down my throat, filling my starved body with a gale force. As his heart began to slow into its last fading beats, I let him slip to the cold cracked concrete at our feet. His upturned face was serene, though ghostly pale. I knew in his last thoughts, he was finally with his love once again.

With a silent *thank you* I left.

I turned down a moonlit side street towards what had once been known as the Warehouse District, swiftly skirting the remaining few blocks to where the building where I had once dwelled still stood with its soot mired façade of brown brick and quietly eroding granite. I walked up the front stairs I had thought I would never climb again, past the huddled form of a shivering drunken derelict, to the dimly lit hall of flickering lights and stained cracked concrete flooring.

I paused before Jasmine's door, my fist hovering mid-air as I gave myself one last chance to leave her to her peace. Recharged with the new life force within my veins, I could smell her perfume already through the door, the blend of her sweet natural musk with clay and cloves; I could hear her soft footsteps as she padded barefoot across the floor. She would be wearing the robe I last saw her in, as she did every evening. She would have been drinking from the flagon of wine she had bartered from her friends in the market.

I felt my knuckles hit the metal door before me. The sound reverberated through the empty corridor, hollow and strange. It traveled up my arm to my heart, stopping it for a brief moment before time began again with the careful click of deadbolts being withdrawn from their casings. With a squeal and a sigh, the door opened slowly.

Jasmine stood before me just as I had imagined, her hair tumbling about her shoulders in unkempt and unorchestrated loveliness. Her lips parted to form my name, but her voice failed her in her confusion, as joyous tears slid down her clean tan cheeks.

There was no need for words: words would only complicate and disrupt and cause pain. Without a moment's hesitation, I stepped forward and wrapped my arms about her, burying my face in her hair and letting go for a moment in a great sigh of exhaustion.

I heard her muffled wondering voice at my shoulder. "I thought for certain that I would never see you again."

With closed eyes, I hushed her indirect inquiry with a soft shush of breath, holding her tightly against me as if her small slender body could keep the bad dreams outside away. After a time, I bent down to cover her trembling mouth with my own. Her body rose, pressing against mine, her arms moving from my waist to wrap tightly about my neck. I wondered fleetingly whether she could taste my victim's blood on my lips, and then I was lost in the strong currents of desire. If she could, she obviously did not care to question it.

Through the thin materials that kept us apart, I could feel how every supple curve of her body had become electrified by the sudden surge of infallible need. Every question that may have arisen in her mind, every doubt and fear within mine, was drowned beneath the sweet warm sensation of being entangled with one another. We moved through the threshold, closing the door quietly behind us. She pulled away for a moment to fasten the four deadbolts back into their housings. I remembered suddenly the weight of the files in my hand and suddenly felt ill at ease about their presence in her loft. I stared down at them, resentment threatening the perfect passion of the moment.

She turned back to me from the door and followed my gaze. "Where did you go? What are those?" Her voice was riddled with concern.

I only shook my head slowly, unable to take my eyes away from the materials. "Do you have a safe place where I can put these for tonight?" I knew I should spend the evening pouring over the information, analyzing every bit of data I could, but I suddenly wanted to burn them instead.

I should not have brought them or myself to Jasmine, I thought bitterly.

She hesitated, not knowing whether she should foster something that, obviously, caused me such dread. But her blind love for me distilled her concerns and she answered with a nod of her head. Jasmine quietly led me to her bedroom, her bare feet padding softly upon the soft hand-woven rugs. Kneeling beside the bed, she withdrew a small, scarred metal trunk from underneath. Inside, she had hidden several large and neatly bound stacks of paper currency, two ledger books and an antique handgun from the early 21st century. It struck me as odd that I had never known about the trunk, though I had spent many a night in her bed. Of course, it had never been such things that I had been looking for on the nights I had requested her company.

I dropped the bundle, along with the journal, into the trunk and she closed the lid, locking it and sliding it back under the bed with a hiss of metal on concrete. I sat down on the edge of the bed, my limbs feeling heavy and weary for a moment, my mind suddenly, uncontrollably preoccupied with the future. Sharp clean light from the full moon poured through the windows behind me casting my shadow long across the room. Jasmine remained kneeling beside me on the floor, her patient worried face watching me carefully with wide eyes.

"Is Danny home?" I asked quietly as I stood.

"No," she replied, her voice barely more than a whisper. "He is staying at a friend's tonight."

I nodded, drawing a deep breath. "Good," I replied. It was not that I did not enjoy her young brother's enthusiastic energy, but that night I needed the peace only Jasmine could bring me.

In another time, in another place, I knew she would not have remained so silent and would have demanded the truth despite my will. However, now it was different, and the grave distinction cut through to the very marrow of her bones.

A flash of black in the bedroom doorway caught my attention: Dune. He had sensed my entrance and had finally come to greet me. Purring loudly in his innocent delight, he leapt up onto the bed beside me. I pulled him into my lap, cradling him like a baby in my arms as I scratched the fur about his neck and ears. His large golden eyes stared up at me, glowing gold lanterns in a pitch forest. He, like Jasmine, intuited my stay was to be brief. I could sense this as his purring quieted to a low tremor. Gently, I returned him to the floor. Dune wandered to the windowsill and leapt up to perch there, staring out across the dark cityscape.

I turned back to Jasmine, who still waited patiently. I reached out and stroked the side of her face with the back of my fingers. Her skin was satin smooth, her human warmth radiating a seductive invitation of its own. As close as we had grown, I had never once considered giving her the Dark Blood for I could not bear the thought of her skin growing cold and hard like mine. Taking her by her upper arms, I pulled her onto the bed beside me.

"You're not staying, are you?" she whispered.

I ran my fingers down her neck and across her collarbone, slipping the fabric from one lovely shoulder as I studied the fine lines of her body through the moonlit blue silk. I said nothing; I did not want to impress my powers upon her mind to take the comfort I needed and prayed she would cease her questioning. She shivered at the caress and took my hand in her own to still me.

"This is part of the war, isn't it? We are in danger, aren't we?" Though she composed herself bravely, her voice depicted a childlike fear I had not seen in her before. She had always been so strong and willful. "Those are Phuree garments you're wearing..."

I shook my head, "Please. I beg of you. Do not ask me questions now." I cupped her face in my hands and stared deep into her eyes. "I need you. I need tonight... I don't want to think about last night or tomorrow."

Without another word she melted into my touch, willing herself to forget her concerns and tend only to the desire we shared for each other's company, as if it were the last candle of light upon the earth. I gathered her tight against me and kissed her hard and deep so that I could almost taste the very essence of her soul, the sweet strong song only a mortal woman could possess. I lost myself within her song and prayed I would not break her in my need. As her mouth moved against mine, she began slowly to undress me.

My right hand upon the nape of her neck, curious fingers threading between the velvety locks of her hair, my left hand deftly untied her robe, moving beneath the fabric to her warm naked breasts. I could feel her heartbeat through them, fast and strong, her chest rising and falling with deep sighs of breath. She pressed her chest against mine, flinching not at all at the sharp cold of my skin. My body drank in her heat and for a moment I, too, felt truly warm and alive.

My hand slipped from her breasts down over the small sensual curve of her belly to the place where every woman's truth lay hidden. I moved my fingers between her legs over the hot wet divide, driving them deep within her to the secret place she could not escape. She gasped, her fingernails digging into the flesh between my shoulder blades, and bit down hard upon my shoulder as I unleashed something primal deep within her.

She pulled me down to the bed on top of her, her strong thighs wrapping about my waist, her hands tangling in my hair, caressing my back, touching my face. I took her slowly, deeply, savoring every shudder, every cry, every taste, as if the night would go on forever. And, indeed, the world around us did seem to vanish completely somewhere between the curves of her body and the soft linen sheets that smelled faintly of her musk and smoke of extinguished candles.

Selflessly, she gave me the perfect oblivion I craved so desperately and, in my heart, I knew there would be no proper way to ever repay her. I lay awake beside her as she slept, watching her naked chest rise and fall in a perfect sated rhythm. The moon had transversed the sky as the night waned, its sacred glow dimming to a soft dark amethyst that threatened to be consumed by the fathomless shadows that congregated in an expectant hush about the room. Jasmine's face was a perfect painting of otherworldly serenity, her long tangled hair fanned out upon the pillow like seaweed. Tomorrow would come and she would still have no answers to calm her mortal fears, just as I would have no one to bless away my sins to be. I leant forward and kissed her forehead.

I rose from the bed and drew the heavy, velvet curtains against the sleeping city below.

14

I awoke the following evening just as twilight had begun to descend upon the earth. The deep musk of Jasmine's handmade perfume lingered, a ghostly sensual essence of lilac and amber, embedded within the waves of soft linen blankets on her bed where she had lain with me for a while in silence, her strong tan arms wrapped tightly about my weary frame, until the Sleep had overcome me. The unspoken trust and love that existed between us was beyond the sanctity of the sacred, it was simply a miracle.

The room was empty again, with the exception of Dune who had nestled himself into a humming ball of black fur in the crook of my left arm. I listened carefully to the creaks and groans of the old apartment building, letting my senses lazily snake through the dimly lit halls in search of Jasmine's presence. I knew she would be returning from the market where she sold earthenware pots and cooking utensils during the daylight hours. She shared the booth with a friend and sometime lover of hers named Miles who I knew secretly wished to be her only lover. As the sun began to set, he would take her place in the booth of wood and clay and batiked curtains and watch her leave with a heart full and lonely, as he did every evening. I had thought of telling her once, but was too selfish, wanting her attention as much as he did. I needed my saint, my goddess to heal that which was broken within me, though I knew such things were far beyond mending.

The heavy green curtains in her bedroom were still drawn tightly to ward off the lethal rays of the sun that had scorched the sky while I slept. Tiny shafts of dying orange light still attempted to break in near the floor and ceiling. I did not fear them; in fact I marveled in the warm molasses of their beauty, the light made thick by particles of dust, swirling and dancing to the lure of a phantom violin. In my heart, I thanked the gods for allowing me to wake soon enough to witness the fiery ghost of what I would never embrace again. Death was close that evening; I knew what lay ahead might mean my last nights on the Earth. Death sat at the end of the bed, a gaunt and weary being of shadow, silently watching the dusty patches of gold with the same simple awe as I; it too could not embrace the power of life, lest it wither to ashes beneath its touch.

As if it sensed my attention the illusion of Death turned its face towards me. Liquid eyes, large and lightless, staring back at me, black holes in the fabric of the universe, holding me without judgment from within a face of bones so fine the wind could carry them away. The light outside was quickly fading into the tranquil violet hue of irises, the chill of night creeping in to greedily consume the warmth from the living world. We were old friends, Death and I, equals in our power to destroy what was fleeting and fragile, but that night we both sensed the necessary balance between dark and light become unstable. The sensation was slight, imperceptible except to beings such as we. The imbalance brought with it no malice or resentment or fear; it simply was as all things are with creatures of the eons.

A small smile stretched upon Death's thin colorless lips.

Outside, I sensed Jasmine's presence at the front of the building; I closed my eyes for a moment to gather her essence close to me as if I could not wait for her to hurry to her flat where I waited, naked and cold, in her bed. When I opened my eyes again, Death had gone, leaving me to my visions of my little goddess. Ancient water pipes creaked in the ceiling above me as a gust of wind howled past the darkened window. Slowly I rose, careful to disturb Dune as little as possible, and walked to the drawn curtains. Without the warmth of the blankets, the chill of the room quickly ravished my bare flesh, sending an electric shiver through me. With my right hand I pulled back one of the curtains to expose the city below.

Behind the flawless white statue of my reflection sprawled the ghostly remnants of what was once a thriving metropolis. The streets were a black grid etched into the concrete and brick like dormant electrical wires. Occasionally, a human form scurried along the edge of the street, hunched and plagued with fear of who or what might be lurking in the shadows, desperately trying to reach the false sense of safety within whatever shelter they called home.

Behind my vision the metallic syrup of the Chronous matrix texturized the underpinnings of reality with its alchemical strands of hieroglyphs. As alluring as the raw ancient magic of the Phuree, the code beckoned to me, a siren from within the walls of the Tyst compound. The hum of the pseudo-organic thought patterns, each busily redefining the physical world in its own specialized way, wove together in a deep collective voice, so subtly human, yet alien. Just as with the Phuree magic, it would take every ounce of my will to maintain a separation from the network as I tapped into the currents of information in my quest to gain entry to the Tyst fortress. Once inside, if I made it that far, I would be so close to the ultimate source of its energy that it would remain a constant pressure upon my psyche.

I honestly did not know if I possessed the strength to resist its call.

Metal keys jangled outside the front door; one by one the multiple locks were released and slid back into their housings. Jasmine entered, her leather sandals light as a deer's footsteps upon the scarred floors, her silken gypsy skirts hissing with each subtle shift of her hips. I continued to gaze through my ghostly reflection and out across the amagin nightscape.

The door to the bedroom opened slowly upon quietly creaking metal hinges. Thick amber light poured into the room from a lamp behind her; I sensed her pause as she entered and studied me with a tormented mixture of love and lust that struck me like warm rain. In her mind, she played over the few words we had exchanged the night before, steeling herself for the unexpected pain my hastened departure would bring to her, once again. I did not want to leave. She knew this all too well, but there had not been time to completely divulge the reasons why. I had been too swept up in the smell of her hair, the taste of her lips to tear myself away from her for long enough to tell her of all that had transpired since she and I had last parted ways. And perhaps it was for the best. I had come for my little goddess and had taken from her all that I could.

She walked to me in the shaft of dusty dark gold light, her movement fluid, her only sound a soft acquisition of breath. She pressed her body against my back, wrapping her lean tan arms lovingly about my chest, her skin still warm from the kiss of the afternoon sun and smelling of amber oil and clay. Silently, I took her hand in my own, kissing her palm as if it were a saint's.

"You leave tonight?" Her voice resonated with strength and understanding, for all its quiet whisper.

I paused, not wanting to answer, and stared out across my ominous future. "Unfortunately, yes."

Her arms tightened slightly about my torso and she sighed, burying her face between my shoulder blades. The warmth of her breath upon my bare skin sent shivers through my limbs, breaking my concentration on the skyline. The curves of her body through her linen and silk garments seemed to obliterate the warrior's path I had dedicated myself to; how easy it seemed in that instance to simply turn my back on it all and take her back to bed with me, to lose myself in her naked form once again as I had the night before. So tempted was I to forsake my resolve to be the messiah the Phuree so craved, but I knew the restlessness of the dragons in my soul would never let me free of that path, no matter how badly I craved another.

The thought that I should not have visited Jasmine at all wrung my soul. I should have remained a ghost so that her soul would one day forget me. It was not fair that I played with her as a god might, and then vanish just as easily. She was mortal, her soul tender and uncalloused. I had left her once without explanation; a second time seemed an insult to her kindness. But, how else could it be? To reveal my secrets, my newfound knowledge of myself and of the world, to her, as I longed to do, would only draw her fatally into the web in which I was already ensnared. That would not be an insult, but betrayal.

I tried not to listen, but I could still hear the jumble of sad words within her that caused the breath to catch in her throat as if it were lined with thorns. The dark mystery that cloaked my existence gnawed relentlessly at her soul but still she withheld all of her questions, violently torn between a childish demand for the truth and her desperate desire to protect her heart. I knew the truth she longed for would only destroy her.

"I will be here, if you return," she whispered into my skin.

Her words gripped my heart painfully. I turned away from the window to face her. Wrapping her in my arms, I stared down into her wide chestnut eyes. I did not have words to console her. I reached up with my right hand and touched the side of her face, running my fingers lightly over the contours of her cheekbones down to her jaw-line. I thought of the young poet who loved her more than life itself now sitting quietly amongst the clay wares of his marketplace booth, watching the filth of the city dance about him as he scribbled his confessions in a small hand sewn journal. That man deserved the adoration in her eyes, not I, not the alabaster statue she so willingly bent to.

As if I could draw her turmoil into myself through tenderness, I bent and covered her mouth with my own. I felt her tremble quietly with her passion, pulling her body closer to my own. Her kiss held me with a power unto itself and I found myself removing her garments with quick nimble fingers. The silk and linen slipped to the floor with a hiss that was all but lost beneath the roar of Jasmine's heartbeat in my ears. Effortlessly I lifted her, her slender legs wrapping around my waist, her arms about my neck, and stepped to the bed from which I had just risen.

Our lovemaking that night was delicate in its passion, deeply engrained with the unspoken love we shared and the tragedy of my inevitable departure. We spoke no more, of the past or the future, of our hearts or our paths, but allowed the subtly of our movements to sate our desire to find words. Afterwards, in the eerie crossbeams of lamplight and moonlight, I lay beside her until I was certain she was deep within the labyrinth of her dreams. Kissing her forehead, I whispered a final *thank you* and slipped from the bed. I knew better than to linger too long for such comforts were merely an illusion. Retrieving the materials from beneath the bed, I dressed quickly, grabbing an empty messenger bag from behind the door as I left. I refused to say goodbye again, to Jasmine or Dune. Best to leave them both with what little peace I could offer.

I fled the warmth and solace of Jasmine's simple mortal world down the steps into the empty street, desperate in my determination to deny the aching deep within my chest. At the end of the darkened city block, I paused and, drawing a deep long breath of crisp cold night air, turned my face to the sky. Wind whistled down the alleyway to my left, eagerly tugging at my clothes and hair as if it had something important to tell me. I closed my eyes and listened.

For the first time since my youth, I truly heard the wind.

OTHER IMMANION PRESS TITLES

Student of Kyme
A Wraeththu Mythos Novella
Storm Constantine
9781904853411
£10.99 trade paperback
IP0016 A sequel to The Hienama. The young Wraeththu har, Gesaril, has been shamed and cast out of Jesith, after an inappropriate affair with his hienama, Ysobi. Ysobi's reputation was at stake, so Gesaril was made the scapegoat. Taken in by Huriel Har Kyme, a codexia of the famed Alba Sulh academy, Gesaril vows to begin his life anew in the Wraeththu city of learning. He is determined to put the past and its ghosts behind him, to restore his name and prove to hara he is not what Ysobi painted him to be. But sometimes the past will not lie quietly in its grave, and Gesaril soon learns he must confront the restless ghosts and fight them. Ysobi is not done with him, but no har will believe him. If he is to retain his sanity and his hard won new life, Gesaril must win this bitter war alone, with magic dark and light.

This is a powerful story of obsession, betrayal and doomed love, sure to be a hit with Wraeththu fans and followers of the dark and Gothic alike.

The Wraeththu Chronicles
Omnibus edition of The Enchantments of Flesh and Spirit; The Bewitchments of Love and Hate and The Fulfilments of Fate and Desire
Storm Constantine
1904853293
£16.99 trade paperback
IP0012 The expanded versions of Storm Constantine's ground-breaking trilogy, which first appeared in 1986 and has remained in print ever since. In 2003, Storm re-edited the books, inserting new scenes and reinstating material that was originally cut. These are the author's preferred editions.

Wraeththu have inherited the world from the dying race of humanity. Androgynous, exotic and psychically powerful, they struggle to avoid the mistakes that led to humanity's downfall. But Wraeththu initially derived from humans and carry within them the traits they claim to despise. The trilogy follows the story of the human boy Pellaz who is led to become Wraeththu by the charismatic and enigmatic Cal. Pellaz eventually becomes a figurehead of his people, whereas the doomed Cal trails destruction wherever he wanders. The story of their tragic and fated love has enthralled readers for over twenty years and continues to do so.

The Fourth Cleansing
Book 3 of A Dream and Lie
Fiona McGavin
9781904853435
£13.99 Trade Paperback, first edition
IP0074 In the ancient city of Gel-Terridar, the enteri Nightshade, has been planning for centuries for the events that will lead up to the Fourth Cleansing. Now, with Alix's arrival in the city, it seems that nothing can stop his plans from reaching fruition. But Alix is determined not to do as Nightshade wishes, and together with a few loyal friends, he strives to fight the destiny Nightshade has planned for him.

But in Gel-Terridar everyone has their own agenda and Alix must find his way through a maze of plots and intrigues and false friends to find out if he is strong enough to resist Nightshade.

The third book in Fiona McGavin's acclaimed fantasy trilogy, **A Dream and Lie**. The story of Alix Reste and the mysterious Enteri comes to a stunning conclusion.

A Blackbird in Silver Darkness
Omnibus: A Blackbird in Silver; A Blackbird in Darkness
Freda Warrington
9781904853503
£15.99 3rd edition paperback
IP0080 In another universe there drifts a strange Earth, encircled by three Planes – three mysterious dimensions that

help sustain the world in its vigorous life and beauty. But the Earth is doomed, overwhelmed by the evil of the great Serpent M'gulfn that dwells in the snows of the far north.

At the House of Rede, last refuge of the wise, Ashurek, Estarinel and Medrian gather to launch a desperate Quest against the Serpent. Ashurek, to right the wrongs he has perpetrated as Prince of the terrible empire of Gorethria. Estarinel, to save the gentle land of Forluin that has been ravaged by the Worm. And Medrian... silent and sinister, she can tell no one her reasons. Together they must travel through realms of wild beauty and utter horror to make the ultimate, impossible sacrifice.

Three warriors. An epic Quest. They are the world's last hope...

First published in the 1980s and rarely out of print, the classic, weirdly atmospheric fantasies **A Blackbird in Silver** and **A Blackbird in Darkness** are united for the first time in one volume telling the complete story.

Curse of the Coral Bride
Brian Stableford
9781904853510
£12.99 trade paperback
IP0081 *The Curse of the Coral Bride* is a far-futuristic fantasy in the tradition of Clark Ashton Smith's tales of Zothique and Jack Vance's accounts of the Dying Earth. Billions of years in the future, the Earth has been repositioned around the red giant that the sun has become; earlier races having emigrated to the stars, its last inhabitants are physically similar to the humans who first achieved self-consciousness and primitive civilization, but the heavens and other aspects of their experience have been rearranged in order to make certain kinds of divination possible—to the extent that any divination is logically possible. Alas, that divination has revealed that the world is now no more than a generation away from its ultimate end, and the instrumentality of its demise is already manifest in such devastations as the Silver Death.

Fleeing the Silver Death, the diviner Giriaizal ends up in a tiny island kingdom in which a young fisherman has been abruptly propelled to the throne for political reasons. Girzaizal becomes the young king's vizier and wise adviser—but the king has already been entranced by the sinister coral from which he forges an artificial bride after his human bride-to-be is slain by magic, and from that moment on, the patient hand of fate manoeuvres both of them, and all their companions, towards a suitably ironic doom...which is, after all, what the hand of fate is bound to do, in a world designed to die in an aesthetically appropriate manner.

LaVergne, TN USA
07 July 2010
188654LV00003B/56/P